Memories

Memories

Deanna Lynn Sletten

Prologue

Today

Danielle Westerly-DeCara stood stoically, clutching the folded American flag to her chest as the minister said his final words over the casket. She neither saw the minister nor heard his words. Her mind only registered the fact that she had to get through this painful day, one moment at a time. The sun in the autumn sky belied the bleakness she felt inside. She was burying the man she loved, and no amount of sympathy or prayer would comfort her today.

Dani lifted her eyes and glanced at the group of people surrounding the gravesite. Her dearest friend, Catherine, stood only a few feet away, next to her husband, Richard. Dani knew Cathy was trying to be strong but tears welled in her eyes. Kevin Lindstrom, a dear family friend and Michael's closest friend, stood with the other veterans from the Veterans of Foreign Wars in his dress uniform looking serious and sad. Other veteran friends of Michael's, as well as employees, neighbors, and business associates, huddled around the gravesite, all dressed in black with somber faces.

"Oh, Grandmom." Dani's twenty-one year old grand-daughter, Michelle, came up beside her and slipped her arm around Dani's waist. Dani did the same, and the two women who loved Michael DeCara the most held onto each other as the last prayers were said.

Ashes to ashes, dust to dust. Amen. Dani heard the words being repeated by the group of family and friends but did not repeat them herself. She and Michelle held each other tighter as the coffin was slowly lowered into the ground. As it was lowered inch by inch, Dani's heart sank with it.

The minister nodded to Dani and Michelle and the two women stepped forward. Dani bent and picked up a handful of fresh dirt and let it slowly fall through her fingers onto the coffin now resting deep within the earth. Michelle kissed the single red rose she was holding and dropped it into the open space. It landed softly on the center of the coffin. So, this is what it all comes down to after eighteen years of happiness, Dani thought. A prayer, a handful of dirt, and a single rose. One lone tear trickled down her cheek as she reached out to embrace Michelle, and then the two women slowly made their way back to the small crowd of people.

The minister handed Dani a snowy-white handkerchief to wipe the dirt from her hands, then hugged her gently as she thanked him for the lovely service. In turn, she thanked the veteran members from the VFW for participating in the military funeral. She knew that the playing of Taps and the twenty-one gun salute would have made Michael very proud. She hugged Kevin, thanking him for arranging the military funeral for Michael. Cathy came up to Dani and hugged her friend close, the flag pressed between them. A quiet invitation to come back to the house for lunch circulated around the group as Dani held out her hand to Michelle and they walked slowly back to the limousine with Michelle's boyfriend, Alex, following close behind.

All Dani wanted to do was go home, draw the shades, and crawl into the bed she and Michael shared for the past eighteen years, but she knew that wouldn't be possible for several more hours. There was lunch to be served, people to commiserate with, and sympathetic nods and words to endure. It was all well-meaning, but draining nonetheless, but she steeled herself to make it through the rest of this heartbreaking day.

As the limousine made its way through the curving roads of the cemetery, Dani took one last look at the now deserted gravesite on top of the hill. She wouldn't remember Michael this way, nor the way he looked just before cancer took his last breath. Her memories would always be of him exactly as he was the first time she loved him and the second time they found each other again. She reached for Michelle's hand and looked into her green eyes, so much like her mother's, and it brought all those memories flooding back to her.

Eighteen Years Earlier

Chapter One

Danielle Westerly cruised along the Wisconsin Interstate in her royal-blue Grand Am as the radio played softly from the back speakers. The midday sun felt glorious on her arm perched outside the window as the spring breeze whipped at her golden-blonde hair. She had chosen to take the extra time to drive instead of fly to Chicago, and as she viewed the lush scenery around her, she was pleased with her decision. Although she had already been driving eight hours, and still had several more to go, she felt happy and carefree sailing along the highway on this beautiful May afternoon.

Dani's boss had thought her crazy when she said she was going to drive. "That's too far to go alone," he'd told her. Dani had shrugged off his protests. At thirty-seven, she was used to doing everything alone, and a drive from Minneapolis to Chicago didn't seem far to her.

She also appreciated the time away from work, even though the trip was work related. As the sportswear buyer for Chance's Department Store, one of Minneapolis' largest department stores, she worked long hours keeping on top of the latest trends, marketing the purchases, consulting with the department managers and salesclerks, setting prices, and everything else her position entailed, that she rarely took time off. And now, since jewelry had been added to her buying activities, she was busier than ever. But she loved her work and all the travel that went with it. After all, it was her entire life.

Seeing that the highway she wanted to continue taking veered off to the left, Dani checked her rearview mirror and moved into the left lane. She noted a van as it passed her on the right and saw a small face look out at her, then a little hand wave as the van took the road to the right.

Dani smiled at the young child's face until he disappeared from view. Children. She had once wanted children, two, maybe three. But all that was decided for her when she'd made the mistake of falling in love with the wrong man. Because of one bad decision made in her youth, she would never have children of her own. And even though she had accepted that fact many years ago, it still came back to haunt her, especially lately, ever since her friend and coworker, Janette, became pregnant with her first child. Throughout the months, Dani had watched Janette grow large and heard nothing but talk about babies. Janette complained about being fat and clumsy but Dani knew that deep down she was enjoying every precious moment, every kick and wiggle inside her.

Dani was happy for her friend but found herself thinking more and more of what she would never experience, and the thought depressed her. However, Janette had done everything right. She'd finished college, married, built up her career as the coat buyer for Chance's and now, when everything was perfect, was having a baby. It wasn't Janette's fault that Dani had made a fateful decision that changed her future. It was only Dani's fault. His fault, too.

Dani turned up the volume on the radio in an attempt to keep her mind in the present and on the road ahead and not on the past. "Hotel California" by The Eagles began playing across the airwaves and Dani had to force herself not to snap the radio off. Another reminder of her past. She had once loved this song and The Eagles like she had loved him. Now the music only reminded her of the past and the man that she wished she could forget. After all, what had happened was another lifetime, back when she still lived with her parents in northern California. After leaving home to attend college at the University of Minnesota, then landing the position at Chance's upon graduation, Dani had decided never to go back. And now that her parents were retired and living in a small resort town in northern Minnesota, she no longer had any reason to go back to California. That was fine with her since it meant no chance of ever seeing him again, not even by accident.

Once again, Dani tried turning her thoughts to the trip at hand. As she drove along, reaching the Illinois border, she thought of Catherine, the friend she was going to see tomorrow in Chicago. It had been two years since she'd last seen her former roommate, so Dani was happy the buyers meetings in Chicago had come up. It gave her an excuse to see Cathy and to finally meet Cathy's new man, Michael, who Dani had heard about through Cathy's letters. Dani laughed to herself over Cathy's excited banter on paper. She had always been energetic and cheerful and even her letters could not contain her vivaciousness. In college, Catherine had been the light side to Dani's serious nature. Whenever Dani became depressed or discouraged, Cathy was there to keep her smiling and laughing. Without Cathy's upbeat personality, Dani might never have made it through the rigors of college life. The two helped each other through economic courses, impossible professors, and over-eager males. Even now, when things got tense, all Dani needed to do was talk to Cathy and she felt much better.

Since they were both in the retail business, they could relate to each other's work problems. Cathy was the assistant to the owner of Regal Coats, a premier coat manufacturing company, and it was her boss she'd raved about over the past year. She was in love, thought he might actually be 'the one', and couldn't wait for Dani to meet him.

Night fell as Dani entered the city and found her hotel. It was late by the time she slipped between the bed's crisp sheets. She had to rise early for an eight o'clock morning meeting and then head over to Cathy's apartment for lunch. As Dani drifted off to sleep, exhausted from her long drive, Chicago's lights sparkled below her hotel room window.

* * *

Miguel DeCara lay crouched beneath the jungle bushes and vines, not quite sure where he was or what direction to go next. He knew for certain that the enemy was up ahead but he had no idea how close or how far—or how many. His comrades were beside him and behind him, but the jungle's dense brush hid everyone from view.

The smell of smoke and gunpowder assailed his senses as he clutched his M-16 tightly, listening for any movement, any sign. Without warning, all hell broke loose and gunfire flailed around him. He heard the soldier on his right yell out as the bullets hit him and the sound of another body falling in the brush to his left. Screaming and yelling surrounded him as he stood from his hiding place in time to see a Viet Cong come straight at him. Without hesitation, Miguel fired his weapon, killing his enemy. And for only a second, he looked at the dead man before him, thinking how different it would have been had they met somewhere sane like New York or L.A. or even Chicago. Hell, they might have even been friends. But instead, here, they were enemies.

"Fall back!" the commanding officer yelled from behind, and Miguel instantly doubled back in the direction he had come. Shots snapped over his head. To his left a hand grenade went off, making him veer off to the right when suddenly his left foot stepped onto a hidden mine and all he heard was 'click'.

Michael sat straight up in bed and instinctively reached down to feel his left leg. Yes, it was still there, not completely perfect, or the same as it had once been, but there. Wiping the sweat from his face with the back of his hand, he looked around the dark room for several minutes before assuring himself he was not in Nam, it was not 1970. He was safe in his own apartment high above the Chicago lights.

Michael checked the clock on his nightstand. 3:30 a.m. He slid out of bed and walked through the dark apartment, opened the refrigerator door, and drank deeply from a carton of orange juice. In the light of the refrigerator, he smiled to himself, thinking of his daughter, Vanessa, and how she used to say "Gross Dad!" every time he did this. But his daughter was no longer living with him, she was grown-up and married and had a daughter of her own now, and she ran the New York division of Regal Coats.

Michael had raised her by himself after his wife decided she could no longer handle being his wife or a mother. He'd only been home from Vietnam for eight months, trying his best to cope with civilian life and get back to being the husband and father he had been before shipping out. But Diane couldn't take the nightly screams of anguish he suffered or his constant tenseness or times of distraction. All she knew was he wasn't the same man she'd married and she didn't want to get to know this new man, so she left him and Vanessa to fend for themselves and joined a commune in Oregon to 'find herself'.

Michael juggled the next few years raising Vanessa alone while going through an endless procession of jobs and women, unable to commit to either. He felt so dirty, so unworthy of enjoying life after all the death he'd seen and been a part of in Nam that he was unable to maintain a relationship with any one woman for a long period of time. He knew it was wrong to jump from woman to woman, and he was careful that Vanessa never caught on to his exploits, but he couldn't stop himself. Like the pot he'd become addicted to in Nam, so was he addicted to women. He'd meet a woman and feel good for the moment, the hour, or the day, then he'd plunge back down and need another and another.

He remembered few faces and names, and the women all reacted much like his wife had to his constant nightmares. It scared them, or baffled them, except for one young woman. When he'd screamed out in fear or pain from a nightmare, she'd held him and rocked him in her arms until he'd calmed down. She'd whisper over and over to him that he was all right, he was home, and she was with him, until he would slowly come out of his nightmare state and back to his senses. She had also been the only one to suggest he go for counseling to help him through his pain. "If not for you," she'd said gently, "then for Vanessa." Sweet little six-year-old Vanessa who she had grown to love in the few months she'd known them. But he'd balked at the idea that he needed help. He could handle everything on his own. He didn't need an eighteen-year-old girl to tell him what he should do.

She had been one of the longest relationships he'd had, and she had been the last of the string of women. After her, his life changed overnight, without warning or preparation. He was forced to change his ways and clean up his act as responsibility was dropped into his lap.

Michael placed the half-empty carton back into the refrigerator, walked to his bedroom, and slipped between the sheets. He had an eight o'clock meeting in the morning and he had promised Catherine he'd be at her place by eleven o'clock for lunch. She was expecting an old college roommate of hers to visit and she wanted Michael to meet her.

He smiled to himself at the thought of Catherine. At forty-four, he was seven years her senior, but he looked much younger than his age. His build was strong from regular workouts, and even though his dark hair and full beard showed a few strands of silver, it only added to his rugged good looks. His deep gray eyes and golden brown skin could not deny his Portuguese heritage, although he had given up his true first name of Miguel for the American version. Women were attracted to him easily, but he'd been out of the market for a long time while he worked hard at the business and raised Vanessa. Only with Vanessa married and gone did he begin to allow himself the pleasure of women in his life again, and along came Catherine, beautiful, softly rounded, energetic yet easy-going. He enjoyed her company, especially in bed, and they had a few interests in common, like racquetball and tennis, along with working in the coat industry. Unfortunately, he wasn't interested in much more from her than just fun and companionship and lately he'd sensed from her an eagerness to commit. He wasn't ready for that now, and maybe he never would be.

This time when Michael finally fell to sleep his dreams were not filled with smoke and heat and death, but instead with the face of a young, blonde, blue-eyed woman telling him he was okay, everything was going to be fine.

Chapter Two

Dani spent the morning looking over jewelry samples and listening to sales presentations until her head ached. When finally she escaped the dealers with her purchases completed and walked out of the stuffy showroom into the bright morning sunlight, she felt as if she could breathe again.

It was only ten o'clock, and although she wasn't expected at Cathy's until eleven, she hurried in the direction of the city train in the hope of arriving early so they could chat. Dani hated driving the busy streets in downtown Chicago, so she had left her car in the hotel parking garage and used the trains instead. While waiting in the crowd to board, a load of people alighted the train and passed through, and a man in a tan trench coat, with briefcase in hand, elbowed into Dani, stopping only long enough to turn and say a quick "excuse me" before hurrying on his way. For a moment, Dani thought she recognized him, but then shook her head. He wouldn't be here, in a trench coat, on his way to the garment district. There was simply no way. But, as Dani rode along in the crowded train car toward the suburbs of Chicago, she couldn't help but see that man's face over and over in her mind.

Catherine Jamison squealed with delight when she saw her old friend.

"Oh Dani, it's been so long!" she exclaimed as the two hugged in the doorway. Dani took off her light coat and hung it in the hall closet while Cathy talked a blue streak. "How was your drive? Isn't the weather gorgeous? Oh, I wish you had stayed with me instead of at a hotel. There's so much to talk about."

Dani laughed at her friend's barrage of questions and comments with no chance for her to reply. Cathy looked refined in her red silk blouse and cream trousers, her three-inch heels giving her five-foot, three-inch frame added height. But her bubbly nature defied her appearance, changing her into the college girl Dani remembered so well. Finally, Cathy steered Dani to the plush cream sofa, sat down, and simply asked, "How have you been?"

Dani answered her friend's questions one by one as the two visited easily in Cathy's comfortable living room. "I would have loved staying here with you," Dani told her. "But with my meeting schedule, I thought it best to be at a hotel."

Cathy nodded. "I understand how buying trips are," she said. "More meetings and paperwork than there is time."

"Speaking of which," Dani raised her eyebrows at Cathy. "Tell me about this new love in your life. All I know is his name is Michael, he owns Regal Coats, and he's your boss."

For the first time since Dani arrived, Cathy was quiet, her eyes pensive. Pushing back a strand of her thick, auburn hair, she said, "Michael is, well, different. Not in a bad or strange way, he's just his own kind of person. He's a great boss to work for and a much respected businessman, and he's very kind and attentive..." Cathy's voice trailed off.

"But?" Dani asked.

"Well, sometimes he seems so far away, distant, hard to get close to. And then his mood breaks and he's warm and loving again."

"Do you think he's *the one*?"

"I don't know," Cathy answered. "For a while, I thought we were becoming that close but lately things have been different. Like something is missing. I wonder sometimes if he just doesn't want to commit to anyone, now or ever." Cathy sighed. "Guess I can't blame him though. He's already been married once and has a grown daughter. He's even a grandfather." Cathy made a face and both women laughed, their mood brightening again.

"Not that it matters," Cathy continued. "I don't know if I would want to start a family now, at this stage of the game. Children are so much responsibility, and I'm not sure I'd have the patience to raise any now..." Cathy stopped mid-sentence. "Oh Dani, I'm so sorry. Here I am blabbering on about children. I mean of all people, I should know better."

Dani placed her hand on Cathy's arm. "It's okay," she assured her friend. Cathy was the only person, besides Dani's parents, who knew about her inability to have children. Dani had confided in her late one night in the dorm room they shared in college after their conversation turned to the future and having children. Cathy understood how much it pained Dani not to be able to have a child of her own, and that's why she stumbled over her words now.

Dani changed the subject back to Michael. "I'm sure he's just hesitant about the relationship," she consoled her friend. "Most men are, you know. I'm sure he'll change his tune in time."

Cathy smiled hopefully. "You're probably right." Looking at her wristwatch, she gasped. "Oh, oh, it's getting late. I'd better finish making lunch." Cathy hurried toward the kitchen with Dani at her heels.

"I couldn't decide whether to have lunch or brunch. It drove me crazy just thinking about it." Cathy rolled her eyes, making Dani laugh out loud. "But I decided lunch sounded better. Michael will be here any minute. Will you set the table, Dani? Everything you need is sitting on the sideboard."

"Of course." Dani began setting out the place mats and silverware on the oval glass-topped table as Cathy banged and clattered in the kitchen beyond. A centerpiece of fresh flowers rested on the glass, its colors matching the cream and blue tones of the china. As she completed her chore, the door chime rang and she saw Cathy hurry to answer it.

Cathy's apartment was small, but stylish. Her decorating style was as elegant as the way she dressed. The dining room opened up into the living room and the entryway was beyond that. Dani stole a glance in the gilt-framed mirror above the sideboard, checking her makeup and smoothing her hair. Beyond her, the mirror reflected a man with a trench coat and brief case in hand, leaning over to place a kiss on Cathy's cheek.

"Dani, Michael's here. Come meet him," Cathy called out.

Dani turned and walked across the living room toward the couple. She stopped short as Michael's face turned in her direction. *My God...it can't be.* Her heart pounded in her chest. The room swirled around her in that one instant Dani recognized him. *No, this isn't happening. It's not him.*

Michael walked up to Dani, his hand extended in greeting. "It's so nice to finally meet you," he said, unaware of the turmoil brewing inside her. "Cathy has told me so much about you that I feel like..." Michael stopped mid-sentence when he was only inches away from Dani. "Well, I'll be," he exclaimed so softly that only Dani heard him.

It was him! Dani's mind raced between past and present, as her eyes traveled slowly over the man before her. His silk suit was impeccable, his dark hair was groomed and neatly trimmed, as was his beard. A complete opposite from the shaggy-haired man in blue jeans, sneakers, and T-shirt she once knew. But it was the same man. From his wavy black hair to the tips of his polished leather shoes he was every bit the businessman. But to Dani, he was the past come alive. "Miguel," she whispered, and only Michael heard and understood.

"Yes," he said, his steel-gray eyes searching her blue ones

intensely. "Danielle, I never thought I'd see you again." He smiled softly at her, that warm, caring smile she remembered so well, as he reached out to hug her.

Instinctively, she drew back, away from his touch. Slowly, the shock of seeing him again after all these years registered within her. She stood there, eyes narrowed, daring him yet denying him with her eyes to move one step closer. Michael stopped short, a confused expression on his face.

Cathy watched the scene before her, dumbfounded. "Dani, are you all right? What's wrong?" Looking from Dani to Michael, she asked, "Do you two know each other?"

The concern in Cathy's voice broke Dani from her reverie. This was no longer her Miguel. This was Cathy's Michael, the man who had made her friend so happy. What had happened to Dani in the past had nothing to do with Cathy's life today. With great effort, she forced herself to calm down, a curtain closing off the hatred in her eyes and softening her expression.

"I'm sorry, Cathy," Dani said, choosing her words carefully. "I was just shocked to see someone I knew from so long ago. Miguel, I mean Michael and I met a long time ago when I still lived in California."

"Oh." Cathy gave Michael a puzzled look. "You never mentioned California before."

"That was another lifetime," Michael told her. "One I rarely think about anymore."

Dani glared at Michael. The emotions in the room were strong, and the tension between the two did not go unnoticed by Cathy.

"Well," Cathy said, glancing from Michael to Dani. "We can talk over lunch. Everything is ready. Michael, please sit down while Dani and I bring the food in from the kitchen." Cathy quickly headed to the kitchen's swinging door with Dani close behind. Dani took the farthest path possible around Michael.

"Dani," Cathy whispered once they were alone. "Are you okay? I mean, really?"

"I'm sorry, Cathy," Dani said, doing her best to control her emotions. "I didn't mean to worry you. It was such a shock to see someone from those days, that's all." She smiled at her friend. "I'm okay." Cathy didn't look convinced, but dropped the subject.

Cathy served a delicious shrimp cocktail followed by a Chef Salad and French bread still warm out of the oven. The food tasted wonderful but Dani hardly noticed. She was too busy trying to ignore her lunch companion, yet at the same time acting pleasant for Cathy's sake.

Dani listened to the conversation between Michael and Cathy while picking at her food, hardly tasting a bite, trying to ignore the memories that threatened to surface. A faint scent of cologne drifted past her, opening a doorway to the past. He had always worn the same cologne, one that smelled spicy and masculine. It didn't matter if they were spending a day on the beach, at the playground with Vanessa, or eating burgers at the coffee shop where she waitressed, he wore that masculine, enticing scent. She rarely detected it on any other man but sometimes she'd catch a scent of it in the air on the street or in an elevator and she instinctively looked for him. And now he sat in the same room as she, that same cologne she knew so well drifting toward her.

Dani grew angrier by the minute as the past replayed in her mind. How could she sit here, quietly eating lunch only inches away from the man she'd despised for the past eighteen years? Every fiber of her being wanted to stand up and scream. She wanted to tell him how he'd ruined her life, but he just sat there, smiling, making pleasant conversation in his most eloquent manner, oblivious to Dani and the rage growing inside her.

"So tell me, Dani, since Michael won't. How did you two meet?"

Cathy's question brought Dani back to the conversation at hand. Dani sent a frigid look in Michael's direction before answering her friend.

"I waitressed at a small coffee shop the summer after I graduated high school," Dani explained without expression. "Michael used to be a regular customer there." He came there to meet women and ruin their lives, she wanted to say. Instead, she finished in a sharp tone. "Except he used to go by the name, Miguel." Dani stared hard at Miguel. Let him explain everything, she thought. Her eyes dared him to.

"Yes, Miguel is the name my parents gave me," he answered calmly. "But when I took over the family business, it was easier to use Michael."

Michael turned and smiled at Dani. It was a warm smile that made his gray eyes sparkle, but Dani only glared back at him.

Michael ignored her glare. "I remember those days like they were yesterday," Michael said, warmly. Dani? Do you remember crazy Karen? The waitress who used to get her orders all mixed up and then yell at the customers for confusing her. We never could understand how she kept her job there. I wonder what ever happened to her."

Dani didn't reply. She only stared at him.

Cathy took a deep breath, her eyes gliding from one friend to the other. Hurriedly, she stood and interjected, "Who's ready for dessert?"

Dani seized the opportunity to get away and declined, insisting she had to leave.

"I have another meeting at two o'clock," she explained as she stood up. It was already one o'clock and she was surprised she'd lasted this long. "I really should go if I want to make it back to the merchandise district on time."

Dani thanked her friend for the delicious meal as she headed for her coat and the door. If she was lucky, she could get out without having to say so much as a goodbye to Miguel. To her horror, he followed.

"I should head back to the office, too," he told Cathy. "I also have a meeting at two. Everything was wonderful, Cathy. I'll take a raincheck on that dessert tonight, okay?"

"Do you want me to come, too?" Cathy asked Michael. "For the meeting, I mean."

"No, there's no need. Just enjoy the rest of your day off. I'll be back at six to pick you up for dinner."

Michael turned to Dani. "If you'll wait, I'll go with you to the train. We're both heading in the same direction."

No, Dani thought. I don't want to wait. I want to get as far away from you as possible. Once again a look of contempt shadowed Dani's face, but Michael seemed not to notice as he slipped on his overcoat and picked up his briefcase. The look did not go unnoticed by Cathy either, and neither did the tension that still embraced the room.

Dani stood politely by as Michael kissed Cathy goodbye on the cheek. Then, once again, Dani thanked her friend for the lovely meal, promised to keep in touch, and was finally out the door.

* * *

Cathy watched as Dani practically ran ahead of Michael to the elevator before closing her apartment door. It was quite obvious that Dani did not want to be in Michael's presence, but the looks that had passed between Dani and Michael had also been very obvious to Cathy. Even with the hatred, the underlying electricity was palpable. Michael's eyes sparkled when he first recognized Dani. They had been more than just friends, she was sure of it.

Cathy had been questioning her own relationship with Michael for some time. She'd wondered if there was a past person who still held his heart, and if that was why he was unwilling to commit. A thought struck her. What if that person was Dani? She decided she would ask him tonight about his past relationship with Dani and about where their relationship was heading. As much as she cared about him, she knew it was time they came to some sort of understanding. It was time she made him face the future head on

Chapter Three

"I don't need your company back to the train," Dani insisted to Miguel in the elevator on the way down to the lobby. "I'm very capable, thank you." Before he could reply, the doors opened and she stepped out and hurried through the lobby and into the May sunshine.

Michael did his best to catch up with her, practically breaking into a full run. "Dani," he called softly when he caught up behind her on the street. "Dani. Can we just talk a minute?" He reached out and touched her on the shoulder. She turned with a violent jerk.

"Don't touch me!" she hissed, making Michael stop short.

"I'm sorry. I just wanted to talk a minute." Michael searched Dani's burning eyes. "There's something I'd like to explain to you," he said, gently.

But Dani's stance was unbending, her eyes unyielding. "There's nothing I want to hear from you. Just stay away from me." Her voice cracked and she broke into full flight from Michael. She kept running until she was at the first train she saw and stepped aboard without looking back. As she sat, trying to catch her breath, she calmed herself with the thought that she would never have to see Miguel DeCara again.

* * *

In the end, Dani was late for her meeting. In her haste to flee

Miguel, she had boarded the wrong train and ended up on the opposite side of town before she realized her mistake. She fumed at herself all the way back to the merchandise district and barely paid attention to the presentation delivered by the jewelry distributor.

How stupid I must have looked to him, she thought, when she finally escaped the meeting. No better than the girl that fell blindly in love with him years ago. Dani took the train to the station nearest her hotel and walked the last few blocks, easing her anger with each brisk step. She hated him for being so calm and controlled while she was agitated and emotional. Stopping at a deli on the corner, she picked up a sandwich and headed straight to the safety of her hotel room where she drowned herself in paperwork over anticipated purchases. She'd already decided to finish up business first thing in the morning and leave the city. There was no way she wanted to run into Miguel again. Her emotions were running high, and she knew she'd be unable to control herself if they met again.

* * *

Michael sat quietly at his desk, looking over various accounts on the computer monitor before him. The Grandfather clock in the corner chimed six times. The clock had once belonged to his grandfather, who brought it from his homeland of Portugal almost sixty years ago. It was the only piece of furniture Michael had brought with him from New York when he'd left Vanessa in charge there so he could build up the division in Chicago. As a boy, the chimes of the carved, maple clock had annoyed him, but with age, he'd come to appreciate the clock and the time it represented.

Michael swiveled his chair around to survey the view from his twenty-first floor office. An expanse of city bustled with activity below him as his mind struggled to understand what past occurrence had caused such pain today. He tried to conjure up anything that may have inflamed Dani's hatred of him, but the only memories he had of her were happy ones.

As she'd glared at him over lunch, he'd studied her face. Even with her unpleasant expression, she was still beautiful. Her golden hair had been tied back in a smooth ponytail at the nape of her neck, giving definition to her square jaw line and prominent cheekbones. Her face had become sculpted with age, making her more beautiful than ever. One feature that hadn't changed was her small 'ski-nose', which he used to teasingly call it. Movie stars paid a fortune to have a nose like that, yet she was born with it. In that brief moment he'd studied her, he thought about the donut fights at the restaurant, the way her hair always smelled of honeysuckle, and Sundays on the beach holding hands, sitting in the wet sand while watching Vanessa jump the waves at the water's edge. God, those were such wonderful times.

He knew he hadn't been a saint in those days, but he'd never done anything deliberately to hurt her. In fact, he had been very much in love with her. But she'd been so much younger than he, and his life was such a mess then, that he hadn't allowed himself to give in to that love.

Dani had brought calmness to his and Vanessa's life back then. She was always there when he needed her, her presence quiet and reassuring. He knew her love for Vanessa had been genuine. Unlike so many other women he'd known who'd only tolerated his daughter's presence, Dani truly enjoyed being with both him and Vanessa. Yet, when his father died suddenly, he'd left Dani behind without a word because he thought that was best for her. She had been so young and had so much life ahead of her. He hadn't wanted to get in the way of her having a full life.

As evening settled over the city, Michael was surprised by the flood of memories that enveloped him. Memories he hadn't thought of in years. All were warm and strong and he wondered how he had ever let them escape from his thoughts. The first time they'd been alone on an 'official' date without Vanessa. The time the three of them rode the roller coaster at the wharf and her silky hair blew in the wind, tickling his face. The very first time he'd made love to her. Now, she wouldn't even speak to him. Why?

Michael finally gave up trying to understand Dani's anger with him. It was past six, and he was already late picking Catherine up for dinner. For a quick moment, he contemplated canceling his evening with Catherine and seeking out Dani to talk to her, but then he brushed aside that thought as quickly as it came. It was obvious she wanted nothing to do with him. He was better off leaving her alone.

As he left the office, he wondered if Cathy might know why Dani felt such resentment toward him. Yes, he'd ask her. He relaxed a bit for the first time since lunch, thinking how nice it was going to be to spend the evening with Catherine.

* * *

It was six-thirty by the time Michael made it over to Cathy's place. He had driven his car so they could go out to dinner, but when he arrived, Cathy suggested ordering something in and staying home for the evening.

Later, snuggling on Cathy's cushy sofa, full from the egg foo yung, sweet and sour pork, and egg rolls they had consumed, the couple sat in semi-darkness watching *Casablanca*, a favorite movie of Cathy's. Michael's arm lay across Cathy's shoulders, his hand caressing her arm. He burrowed deeper in the plush sofa, snuggling her neck with his face. He loved the closeness they shared, the comfortable silences, and their nights together.

As he continued to nuzzle her neck, Cathy also sank deeper in the sofa beside him. For a while, they sat there, warm, close, comfortable, until Cathy broke the silence in a quiet voice.

"Michael?"

"Mmmm?"

"Just how close were you and Dani years ago?"

Michael lifted his head and stared at Cathy, surprised by her question. "What do you mean?"

"Well, I could tell by the way you both acted that you were more than just acquaintances. I was just curious as to how close you both were." Her voice remained soft, not angry or accusing.

Michael assessed her a moment then answered honestly. "Very close. At one time we cared very much about each other."

"Were you lovers?"

"Yes."

Cathy turned to face Michael. "Are you still in love with her?"

Once again, she had caught him off guard. He backed up a bit on the couch, taking his arm from around her and stared at her, surprise displayed on his face. "What kind of question is that?"

Cathy maintained her calm, her voice still warm. "I could feel the electricity between you two, and the hostility. I was only wondering if you still had feelings for her."

"The hostility was on her side. As for the current between us, well, I don't know. We were once very close, very in tune with each other. Maybe, in a way, you never lose that. There have been too many years between us for me to say we're still in love." He answered as honestly as he could. He couldn't tell from Cathy's calm expression how she was taking all this.

Another moment of silence passed. On the television, Ilsa recounted to Rick why she had left him in Paris years before. As the two lovers on screen rekindled their love, Cathy felt her own relationship was cooling down.

"Why is Dani so angry with you?"

Michael had neither been watching nor listening to the movie, but had been studying Cathy's face the entire time. "I was hoping you might be able to tell me. I'm not sure why Dani feels the way she does. You're her closest friend. Has she ever told you?"

Cathy shook her head and smiled. "Dani is a very private person. We share a lot together, but there are some things she'd never tell even me."

The two sat back in thoughtful silence, eyes on the television screen. Michael slipped his arm around Cathy once again and she snuggled closer. But once again Cathy broke the silence with her questions.

"Michael?"

His eyes looked at her warily. "Yes."

"What do you want out of our relationship?"

Michael sighed. So this is what she was working up to. He chose his words carefully before answering her question. "I enjoy our relationship just as it is."

"So do I," Cathy said, reaching up to hold the hand he had circled around her shoulder. She faced him. "But we can't stay like this forever. We either have to move on to the next step, or…" her voice trailed off.

"What step is that?"

"I'd like to be married someday, Michael. Maybe even have children."

"And you should," Michael said warmly. "You're still young. You deserve to have those things."

Still caressing his hand, Cathy asked softly. "Are those things you want, too?"

The time had come, Michael understood that now. No

relationship could stand suspended forever. Choices had to be made, decisions held to. He'd always been honest with Cathy from the very beginning, and he was now. "I really care about you, Cathy. I enjoy spending time with you, I enjoy working with you, and I have a great amount of respect for you. But I can't see myself settling down to marriage and children again. Not at this stage in my life, maybe never."

Cathy continued holding his hand, nodding her head in understanding. Deep in her heart, she'd known this would be his answer, but she had never been brave enough to ask before. She really loved Michael, but there was so much more she wanted out of life yet.

Michael continued to hold her. He couldn't tell what was going through her mind, but he could see the tell-tale moistness in her eyes. She was making a decision, he knew, but what it was he couldn't say. "Cathy," he said, his voice tender. "No matter what happens, I still want to be your friend. I still want to work with you. I really do care about you. I'm sorry I can't give any more than that."

The couple sat, holding each other on the couch as the two lovers on screen replayed their historic goodbye. In her heart, Cathy knew that this was also goodbye for her and Michael. The decision was up to her, and although it was going to be difficult, she knew what choice she had to make.

Chapter Four

Dani stood on a table in the small office lunchroom hanging a pink crepe paper umbrella from the light overhead. Today was Janette's last day before she began maternity leave and the office staff was giving her a baby shower. Even though her baby wasn't yet born, she was due any day, Janette already knew it was going to be a girl and was thrilled at the prospect of buying lacy pink dresses and Mary Jane's.

It was June, almost a month since Dani's disastrous trip to Chicago, yet she still couldn't keep from thinking about Miguel. The drive home had been a long one, filled with memories and tears. Dani had wished she hadn't driven after all because it gave her too much time to think. But no matter how much she replayed the past in her mind, she always came up with the same conclusion. She hated him. She hated him for what he had done to her, for taking away her youth, and for leaving her. She would always hate him.

Two weeks after Dani returned home, Cathy had called. After a few minutes of small talk, Cathy casually mentioned she had ended her relationship with Michael.

Dani was stunned. "What happened?" she'd asked her friend. Dani had wondered if Miguel had said something about their past relationship. She hoped that she wasn't the cause of their breakup.

"It wasn't anything dramatic," Cathy assured her. "It was just something I finally realized I had to do. He understood, and everything is okay. We can still work together without a problem. We're good friends."

When she'd hung up, Dani thought about what Cathy had said. She probably caught him cheating on her, she thought. I certainly wouldn't put it past him.

As Dani twirled and hung the last of the pink and white streamers, Traycee Caverns came into the lunchroom.

"Looks great," she said, smiling up at Dani. Traycee was a new employee at Chance's, but already had a good rapport with Dani. She'd interned in the buyer's office from the merchandising school she'd attended and upon graduation was hired as an assistant in the office. The twenty-three year old was thrilled at the opportunity to work for one of the largest department stores in the area. With the exception of Traycee's overly exuberant nature, she reminded Dani a little of herself at that age.

"Mr. Trindell wants to see you in his office," Traycee announced. "I think it's important," she added in a whisper.

Dani chuckled quietly at the serious tone in Traycee's voice. To Traycee, everything Carl Trindell said was 'important'. He was the Executive Merchandising Manager, a hefty title that just meant he was the boss. But Dani had worked too many years with Carl to be in awe of his title. He was more a friend and co-worker to her than a boss.

"I'm coming," Dani told Traycee as she taped up the last streamer. She stepped down off the table and walked through the office, past the buyers' desks separated by partitions and toward Carl's office. Traycee followed close behind. "He asked me to come, too," she explained as they walked.

"Well," Dani said, looking slyly over her shoulder at Traycee before reaching the office door. "Then it must be important." Dani held back a smile, knocked twice, and entered the office with Traycee.

Carl Trindell rose from his seat as the two women entered.

He was a sturdy built man in his early fifties, his once dark hair almost completely gray. His smile was pleasant, when he chose to use it, but his stern eyes could be frightening to someone who didn't know him as well as Dani did.

"Come in Dani, you too, Traycee. Have a seat. I was just talking with Janette."

Dani and Traycee sat in chairs opposite Trindell, next to Janette.

"We've been discussing a replacement to fill in for Janette while she's on maternity leave," Trindell said.

Dani raised an eyebrow. Surely, they wouldn't consider Traycee for the position. She was much too inexperienced to take over coat buying, even if it was only going to be for three months. But Trindell wasn't looking at Traycee. He was speaking directly to Dani. "We've both agreed you would be perfect to fill in for her while she's gone."

Dani's eyes widened. This was the last thing she'd expected.

"Of course, I've anticipated you'll need help if you take over Janette's responsibilities," Trindell continued. "So, I'd like for Traycee to be your assistant with sportswear and jewelry while you concentrate on coats."

Traycee nearly squealed with delight. She'd only been at Chance's four months and she'd already become an official buyer's assistant.

Dani, on the other hand, was far from delighted. "Even with Traycee's help, I don't know how I'll be able to juggle all three departments," she protested. "Coats take a tremendous amount of time and the buying season is just beginning." Dani knew how much time Janette spent on her job and she just couldn't picture herself doing both, not even for three months.

"I know it will be difficult," Trindell agreed. "But that's why I chose you, Dani. I'm confident you can handle all three departments."

Dani was about to protest again when Janette touched her arm. "Please, Dani. I wouldn't trust anyone else but you at my desk. You're the most organized person here, and I trust your judgment. Please say you'll do it. I'll feel so much better about leaving if you do."

Dani looked at her friend's pleading eyes and sighed.

Trindell took that as a yes. "Good," he said. "It's all settled. Janette can fill you in on the details before your first trip." Trindell looked intensely at Dani. "I know you'll do a fine job," he said with certainty.

Later, at Janette's party, everything except the event at hand was plaguing Dani's thoughts. Janette had gone over a few of the details Dani needed to know and the list of places she'd be visiting on her first coat buying trip to New York City in July. It wasn't the extra work or trips that bothered Dani, she knew she could handle those. It was one of the names that appeared on the list that worried her. Regal Coats was Chance's leading coat distributor, and that meant there was a chance of Dani and Miguel crossing paths again.

The only thing that helped to ease Dani's mind was that Janette had mentioned she'd be meeting with Vanessa DeCara-Chandler instead of Mr. DeCara because Vanessa had taken over the New York division. Dani wondered what it would be like to see Vanessa again, all grown up and married. She'd always adored her as a child. And, although Miguel had many faults, there was one thing she could never fault him with, his love for Vanessa.

While Janette cooed over petite pink dresses and booties, and Traycee still beamed over her recent promotion, Dani could only wonder what was in store for her in the weeks ahead.

Chapter Five

June's cool temperatures slowly gave way to the sultry days of July as Dani prepared for her first coat buying trip to New York. Janette had her baby two days into her maternity leave. Both were doing fine, and they had named her Darci Marie, which Dani thought suited the little seven pound, twelve ounce wonder when she visited. She couldn't help but feel a tug at her heart as she held the round, rosy baby and the beaming pride on Janette's and her husband's faces only added to its intensity.

But the feeling passed and the days went by and soon it was July first and Dani and Traycee were on their way to New York City for a week. Traycee was accompanying Dani on a two-fold mission, to assist with the few sportswear meetings they were to attend and to help with any paperwork involved with the coat buying.

Dani spent countless hours going over details with Janette on the phone and studying the style sheets and order forms sent out in advance from the coat manufacturers. She understood why Chance's preferred dealing with Regal Coats above all others. Their styles were classic, materials well made, and their prices were unbeatable. They certainly put out a fine product despite her opinion of the owner.

As their plane departed from Minneapolis, Traycee could hardly contain her excitement over her first official buying trip. Although Dani had made several trips to New York City and other large cities, Traycee's enthusiasm was contagious and she found herself chatting and giggling with her younger companion and looking forward to arriving in the Big Apple.

Their plane landed without mishap at LaGuardia and a shuttle bus was waiting to take them to their hotel. Traycee marveled at the sights, having never been to New York City. "I've never seen so many people and buildings," she whispered to Dani.

Dani only smiled at her as she also took in the bustling view. There was something contagious about New York City, an excitement that began to well up inside you until you wanted to become immersed in it all. She looked forward to walking Seventh Avenue again where the garment district was alive and bustling with activity like no other place she knew. Sometimes, she secretly wished she lived and worked here among all the great stores and designers. But that was only a dream.

By the time they settled in their Manhattan hotel suite, it was late afternoon. Traycee was mesmerized by their view of Central Park South.

"Chance's does allow the best accommodations," Dani commented. Traycee readily agreed.

Dani suggested a walk in the park before dinner, and the two did just that. After they dined on seafood in the hotel restaurant, the two women headed back to their room for a good night's sleep.

The next morning, after a quick breakfast delivered by room service to their room, the two women set off to their first meeting of the day. They attended a showing of sportswear along with fifty other retailers, marking down possible purchases and quantities as they watched each model pass. Dani was pleased, and a bit surprised, by Traycee's good judgment and input. Traycee had an eye for what would sell in their store, and Dani was impressed by her natural ability.

After the sportswear showing, they caught a quick lunch

from a sidewalk vendor and took a taxi to their next meeting at Regal Coats. Dani was silent during the ride, not knowing what to expect or who she might see. She knew that seeing Vanessa would bring back memories and she wasn't quite sure how she was going to react to those feelings.

Traycee misinterpreted Dani's silence as nervousness. "Are you worried about your first coat purchases?" she asked.

"Maybe just a little bit," Dani told her, not wanting to reveal the true reason for her nervousness. "But if I do as well with coats as you did this morning with sportswear, then I'll be just fine."

Traycee beamed at the compliment.

Regal's Corporate Office Building was located in the heart of Seventh Avenue. Upon arriving, Dani and Traycee were informed by the receptionist to go up to the 14th floor and someone would meet them there. As promised, when the elevator doors opened, there stood a young woman with a small group of retail buyers waiting for them.

"Hello," she greeted the two women. "You must be Miss Westerly and Miss Caverns." Dani nodded. "Mrs. Chandler is waiting in the conference room," the woman continued. "Please follow me."

She led the way down a richly carpeted hallway to a large set of walnut, double doors. Dani couldn't help being impressed by Regal's extravagance. She hadn't been aware that Miguel's family was so wealthy. He'd lived such an ordinary life in California, basically living paycheck to paycheck. Yet, all along his family back East was very well-to-do. It was a lot for her take in at once.

The double doors opened, exposing an enormous room containing a long, dark, walnut table and rows of padded chairs on each side. The walls and chairs were done in hunter green, giving the room a warm, friendly feeling. At the head of the table where sunlight spilled through a wall of plate glass windows stood a woman with auburn hair, dressed impeccably in a hunter green suit that complimented the decor. Dani's heart skipped a beat as she gazed upon a very grown up Vanessa.

"Hello," Vanessa greeted, walking up to the group. "I'm happy you could all make it." Vanessa smiled, her green eyes sparkling. "Please have a seat and we can begin."

Vanessa made her way back to the head of the table but continued to stand while everyone chose chairs and were seated. Dani chose a spot some distance from Vanessa. She was still trying to maintain her composure from seeing her and didn't trust herself being too close.

"Karla will pass out a folder to each of you," Vanessa announced, indicating the woman who had escorted them into the conference room. "Inside, you will find information sheets about our upcoming winter line and order forms that you will find useful for Monday's fashion show."

Dani listened as Vanessa continued explaining some of the new styles and fabrics, passed out fabric samples, and answered questions from a few of the other buyers. Vanessa was so composed and seemed to fit perfectly in this element. So different from the shy little girl she had been. Yet, at times, Dani caught the twinkle in her eye, the one she knew too well, and memories flooded over her. Pictures of the days at the park and the beach, or watching her ride her bike up and down the sidewalk, swirled in Dani's mind. Dani had spent most of her free time with Vanessa, babysitting her while Miguel worked. It was her excuse to her parents for spending so much time there. And she remembered other times, too, with Miguel, as the three of them went to dinner, the wharf, the mall, or just hung out around Miguel's apartment together. It was just like being a family. Those times felt like they'd last forever, yet ended so quickly.

As Dani tried to concentrate on what was being said, she

couldn't help but compare the Vanessa of yesterday to this one before her. Yet, with her composure and easy manner, it was easy to believe Vanessa had been born for this.

Vanessa closed the meeting with a reminder of the fashion show, and also a personal note. "There's an invitation in your folders to join us this Sunday at the house for our annual Fourth of July celebration. I hope that all of you will come. Directions are also included as to which trains you need to take and the times the limousines will be waiting at the station to shuttle guests to and from the house."

A few of the other buyers began talking animatedly among themselves about the good time they'd had at last year's party. One by one, they left as Vanessa stood at the door shaking each person's hand and saying goodbye. As Dani and Traycee approached, Vanessa extended her hand.

"Miss Westerly, I'm happy to meet you. I heard that Janette had her baby. How is she?"

"She's doing fine," Dani replied, shifting a bit under Vanessa's searching eyes. "She's taking a three-month leave, but should be back in time for the spring buying season. This is Traycee Caverns, my assistant," Dani said, trying to shift the attention away from herself. "She's helping me while I take over Janette's responsibilities."

Vanessa smiled and nodded a hello to Traycee, but her eyes returned to Dani. "I'm sorry for staring," she finally said. "You seem so familiar to me."

Dani's heart pounded in her chest. Part of her wanted Vanessa to remember her, but the other part kept hoping she wouldn't. There was no need in bringing up the past. Dani was relieved when Vanessa finally changed the subject.

"I hope you both will join us at the house this Sunday. We always have a good time. There will be close to two hundred people there. It's sort of a mixture of business and pleasure."

Dani said that they would try to come, all the time knowing she didn't mean it, and quickly made her exit with Traycee close behind her into the safety of the corridor.

* * *

All that evening and the next day, Traycee spoke of nothing else but attending the party on Sunday. "The buyer from Macy's said the house is on a long stretch of beachfront and they put on a food spread you wouldn't believe. I've never been to the ocean before. It would be so much fun."

Dani tried to discourage her by insisting they had plenty of paperwork to catch up on and suggesting that the Fourth's celebration in the city might be just as exciting. But Traycee could not be swayed.

"It's so hot here in the city," she complained. "And the party is in Southampton where it is sure to be cooler. It sounds like such a good time. Please say you want to go, Dani."

Dani finally gave in Saturday night after they had finished the paperwork from that day's meetings. As she drifted off to sleep that night, she assured herself that she wouldn't be running into Miguel since he was in Chicago. As long as Vanessa didn't remember her from the past, she might have a good time after all.

Chapter Six

The morning of the Fourth broke with a stifling heat, reinforcing Traycee's complaint about the weather. Dani dressed in cotton khaki pants and a pink silk tee, pulling her hair back in a neat French braid which made her look younger than she was. Traycee anticipated the heat by dressing comfortably in walking shorts, a cotton shirt, and sandals.

The two walked to Penn Station, taking the train indicated on Vanessa's instructions. After a brief switch at Jamaica Station, they were on their way through Long Island, finally reaching the station in Southampton where several limousines waited to take guests the rest of the way to the house.

It was past noon by the time the two women were seated in a limousine. Vanessa's notes had indicated there would be limousines arriving and departing from the station every hour from noon until the last train of the evening departed.

They shared their limousine with six other people. Traycee began talking animatedly with the young man beside her who introduced himself as an advertising executive from Regal.

Dani kept her eyes focused out the window hearing very little talk, but enjoying the view. She was pondering a million "what ifs"? What if Miguel was there? What if Vanessa recognized her? What would she say? Finally, she decided to stop worrying and take each encounter as it happened.

The "house", as Vanessa had described it, turned out to be an estate that boasted a mansion and extensive waterfront property. Dani's eyes widened as she surveyed the place before her. The driveway curved through white gates and circled in front of the main house, which boasted three stories and four white columns holding up the second floor balconies. Paned, white-trimmed windows broke up the brick that covered the exterior. Obviously, this mansion was large enough for several families to live in. Once again, the fear that Miguel might be here crept up in Dani.

The party of people stepped out from the limousine and entered through open double doors where Vanessa stood, greeting the guests. She looked young yet elegant in a white cotton halter dress and flats, her mass of red hair tied up with a satin ribbon. A large emerald solitaire hung from her neck, reflecting the sparkle in her eyes.

Upon entering the house, Dani stood spellbound. The entryway boasted a vaulted ceiling from which hung a chandelier that sparkled brilliantly upon the white marble floor. A grand staircase curved up countless steps to the second floor with a hallway to the left of that. At the far left was an enormous living room with several sets of French doors leading out onto the veranda facing the ocean. Already, there were a hundred people milling around both inside and out.

Traycee whistled softly and exclaimed Dani's own thoughts. "Quite a house."

After greeting her other guests, Vanessa walked hurriedly up to Dani and Traycee, a smile playing on her full lips.

"Dani," she exclaimed, reaching for her hand and squeezing it. "I'm so happy you came." She smiled a hello to Traycee before returning her attention to Dani. "You should have told me yesterday who you are," she continued, pouting a little like the child she had once been. "I knew you looked familiar, and last night when I mentioned your name to Daddy, he told me. I'm just so thrilled to see you again." Vanessa continued squeezing

Dani's hand as Traycee shot Dani a puzzled glance.

It took a moment for the news to settle on Dani. The word 'Daddy' had thrown her the most.

"Your father is here?" Dani asked.

"Oh, yes, of course. He's the one who has been putting on these parties for years. He's around here somewhere. Do you want me to find him?"

That was the last thing Dani wanted. "No, no, don't bother," she answered quickly. "I'm sorry I didn't tell you myself. I didn't know if you'd remember me."

"Remember you?" Vanessa looked shocked. "How could I forget you? We had so much fun together back then. I can hardly wait to spend some time with you, catching up." She looked over Dani's shoulder at the approaching guests and sighed. "As soon as I've done all my corporate duties, I'll search you out. And I can't wait for you to meet my husband, Matthew, and our daughter, Michelle. She's upstairs taking a nap now. As soon as she wakes up, I'll bring her down."

"I'd love to see her," Dani said smiling back at Vanessa. "I bet she's as beautiful as her mother."

Vanessa reached out and hugged Dani. "I'm so happy you're here."

"Me, too," Dani told her. And she truly meant it.

* * *

Traycee and Dani wandered through the party awhile before Traycee spotted her advertising friend and went down to the beach. Left alone on the veranda, Dani was thankful that Traycee didn't prod her with questions over Vanessa's sudden familiarity. Traycee was proving to be more mature than Dani had originally given her credit for.

The party was unlike any Dani had ever attended. On the

beach were several carts, like street vendors, offering free hot dogs, pretzels, and tacos, along with soft drinks and beer. On the veranda, which surrounded the entire back of the house, sat a large table with an endless supply of food, and two bars were open for anyone wanting stronger refreshment.

The aroma of the food was too tempting for Dani to pass up, so she filled a plate with several different hors d'oeuvres, steaming butterfly shrimp, and a piece of French bread that was still warm from the oven. Aware she could run into Miguel at any moment, she assessed the crowd before choosing to sit at one of the tables on the veranda. At least she was prepared with the knowledge that Miguel was here. It wouldn't be as much of a shock as it had been at Cathy's apartment. But she did wonder how she'd react when she saw him again.

"Vanessa told me you were here, but I could hardly believe it." A voice came from behind Dani and she turned to see her old friend standing there.

"Cathy! What are you doing here?"

"I could ask you the same question," Cathy said, laughing at her friend's surprised look. "But I already know the answer." Cathy sat opposite Dani in a brown wicker chair covered with a plump pastel cushion. Her apricot silk blouse made her skin glow. "Why didn't you tell me you were buying coats this season? I had to find that out from Vanessa, too."

"I guess I've been too busy to keep in touch," Dani replied. "Coat buying fell into my lap at the last minute. But what about you? Why aren't you in Chicago?"

"Michael invited me to come. He said he could use extra help supervising the party." Cathy smiled, putting both hands palms up in the air. "How could I refuse such a tempting offer?" she asked, laughing.

A worried frown spread over Dani's face. "I thought you and Michael split up."

"Oh, we have, but we're still good friends. Actually, I think we were better as friends than as a couple anyway." Cathy's eyes sparkled as she continued. "As a matter of fact, I've been seeing one of the men in the Accounting Department at Regal back home." She laughed again. "Imagine me, with an accountant. But we have a great time together."

Dani couldn't help but laugh along with her and the two settled in to catch up with each other's lives since they'd last talked. Between the warm summer air cooled by the salty ocean breeze and Cathy's company, Dani began to relax and enjoy herself.

Vanessa's husband Matthew came along while the two women were visiting and introduced himself to Dani. He seemed very pleasant and easy-going, and Dani liked him immediately. He also liked to joke about his position at Regal.

"I'm only the head of the Advertising Department," he told her with a twinkle in his brown eyes. "So I work for the 'big boss' like everyone else."

"The big boss?" Dani questioned, assuming he meant his father-in-law.

"Vanessa, of course," he said. "And what a tyrant she can be."

Dani laughed at the picture of Vanessa as a difficult boss and the other two joined in with her laughter.

The time passed swiftly and soon Matthew excused himself to make the rounds. Cathy also needed to go check on the preparations in the kitchen. Dani followed her toward the kitchen and asked where the nearest bathroom was where she could freshen up.

"Down the hall by the staircase, first door on the left," Cathy instructed her.

Dani followed her directions down the oak paneled hallway and opened the first door she came to on the left. As she entered the room, she realized she had not found the bathroom but an office instead, and began backing out when something caught her eye, drawing her back inside.

The room was paneled in oak like the hallway and finished in the same hunter green as the conference room at Regal's. Over the gleaming oak desk hung a full length portrait of Vanessa. She wore a velvet, emerald green, off-the-shoulder gown, which made her eyes of the same color shine brilliantly. Her mane of auburn hair tumbled over her bare shoulders. The intensity of the portrait's colors were so stunning and lifelike that Dani could only stare, mesmerized. It was obvious it had been done recently because it looked exactly as she looked now.

Taking her eyes away from the portrait, Dani slowly assessed the room around her. The desk, under the portrait, was strewn with papers as though someone had recently been working there. The wall to the left was floor-to-ceiling bookcases, filled completely, and to the right were heavy drapes drawn closed against the summer sunshine. On the table behind the desk sat several smaller photographs of Vanessa as a child, her wedding day, and another of a baby girl who Dani guessed to be Michelle. In another glass-encased frame were military medals, a Purple Heart and various lapel pins. Upon seeing these, Dani realized that this was Miguel's room, his home office.

She turned to leave, fearing she might run into him, when once again something caught her eye. The closet door to the right of the desk was slightly ajar, revealing a poster hanging on it. She stepped up and opened the door wider, seeing what she had suspected was there. On the poster-sized picture stood a very young Miguel in camouflage clothing, flanked on both sides by two Army buddies. All three men were holding their weapons in front of them with the dense Vietnam jungle in the background.

Dani remembered the poster from Miguel's small apartment, where it also hung on the inside of a closet door. The photo had been taken by a fellow soldier the last day of his tour, before he was shipped home. One week later, Billy, one of the men standing beside Miguel, had been killed. The other man became missing in action several weeks later. When Miguel returned home to the states, the man who had taken the picture sent him this poster-sized version of it.

Dani's heart ached as she remembered the Miguel from the past. How his eyes turned sad as he spoke of Billy's death in Vietnam. The nightmares that he awoke from screaming. The pain of almost losing his leg when he'd stepped on a land mine. Those things, along with his tenderness toward Vanessa, were what had drawn Dani to Miguel. He'd been so human, so warm, and caring.

Lost in time, unaware of her surroundings, Dani's hand instinctively reached up to touch the photograph of the man she had once loved so dearly.

"Some things are hard to let go of."

A deep voice drew Dani out of her trance with a start. She knew before looking who was in the room with her. Turning, she faced Miguel, who was standing only inches behind her.

Startled and embarrassed to be found in his private room, Dani said the first words that came to her. "I didn't mean to intrude. I was looking for the bathroom and accidentally came in here." Dani hesitated a moment. "When I saw Vanessa's portrait, I couldn't help but come in for a closer look."

Michael only smiled at her and then turned toward the portrait. "It's beautiful, isn't it? I had it done right before Vanessa married. I guess I wanted to capture her youth and innocence forever."

Dani studied Miguel as he stood admiring the portrait. Dressed casually in jeans and a red polo shirt, he looked much like the Miguel she had met years ago. His face had that tender look, the one he always wore when speaking of his daughter, and

Dani couldn't help but soften towards him. He glanced over at her and she was once again embarrassed to be caught staring at him. Quickly, she changed the subject by turning back to the poster.

"I see you still have this." He was so near, she caught the scent of his cologne. She had to force herself to ignore its enticing scent and focus on what Miguel was saying.

"Yes," he answered, softly. "I've thought about putting it away from time to time, but I never have the heart to."

"It's a part of your past," she told him, still staring at the poster, not trusting herself to look into his eyes. "An important part. I don't think anyone expects you to give it up entirely." She wanted to ask him if he still had nightmares and if his leg still ached at times, but then she reminded herself that it wasn't her business anymore. She wasn't supposed to care, she admonished herself harshly.

"You always did understand about that part of my life," he said, tenderly. "More than anyone I've ever known."

Dani turned and faced him. He was too close. His eyes showed the tenderness that his voice conveyed. She walked across the room to the windows to escape his nearness. How dare he make me care about him again? Even for a moment, she thought. He still had the power with only a look to reach her soul.

Tartly she said, "Obviously, I didn't know as much as I'd thought." She spread her arms wide. "All this comes as quite a surprise."

Michael walked over to the drapes, standing close to her again. He pushed aside one heavy drape and the room filled with sunshine. The view of the beach and the ocean beyond was spectacular.

"I tried running away from all this," he told her. "My grandfather started the business when he came over from

Portugal, and my father continued in his footsteps. I was being groomed to take over when I went out to Berkeley for college. But once I'd escaped to California, and away from the family, I didn't want to come back." He sighed and Dani watched him as his eyes searched the ocean beyond.

"So you left it all behind?"

"For a few years. I married Diane while in college and we had Vanessa right away. Two years into college, I was drafted for Vietnam, which really pissed my father off. He wanted to try and get me out of serving, but I insisted on going. When I came back and Diane left me, I still couldn't bear coming back here. So I stayed in California all those years and, well, you know the rest."

But Dani didn't know the rest. She had only been a part of his life for a few months. And although she had thought then that she knew him well, she now realized that she hadn't really known him at all.

"But you are back here now," she told him.

"I had to grow up finally." Michael gazed at Dani as if memorizing her every feature. "I'm happy you're here," he said.

Dani looked up into Miguel's gray eyes and suddenly felt as if she were drowning in memories. He was too close. She had to get away. She hurriedly walked past him to the door. "I should get back to the party," she said, although she knew it was a feeble excuse. After all, no one was going to miss her.

"Have you met Michelle yet?" Michael asked.

Dani stopped reluctantly and turned to face him again. "No. She was napping earlier. Vanessa said she'd bring her down later."

"Let's see if she's awake. I love showing her off."

Before Dani could say anything, Miguel grabbed her hand and led her out the door, across the hall, and up the back stairway.

"You really don't have to do this," she protested. But her

words fell on deaf ears as he led her up the stairs, then down the hallway that led to the family wing. Everything here was done in light colors, a complete contrast to the rooms downstairs. The walls were waist-high cream wainscoting, and the top half of the walls had cream wallpaper with delicate peach and rose flowers. The carpet was a soft cream color. At intervals, there were small oak tables holding flower vases, figurines, or baskets of dried flowers.

Turning a corner, they practically ran into an elderly woman carrying a little girl in her arms. From the red, curly hair and emerald green eyes, Dani knew instantly that this was Vanessa's daughter.

"Oh, Mr. DeCara," the older woman said, looking startled by his sudden appearance. "I was just bringing Michelle down to her mother."

"That's fine, Mrs. Carols. I'll be happy to take her." At that, the woman handed Michelle to Michael and turned back down the hall.

Dani studied the child in Miguel's arms, warmed by her resemblance to Vanessa. Miguel's eyes beamed with pride.

"Michelle," he said, in mock introduction. "This is Miss Westerly. Miss Westerly, I'd like you to meet my granddaughter, Michelle."

Playing along, Dani reached out her hand to touch Michelle's petite one. "Happy to meet you, Miss Chandler," she said. Michelle cocked her head and giggled in reply.

"She's beautiful," Dani told Michael, who nodded his agreement.

"And shy, too, as you can see. She takes after her grandfather," he teased.

Dani rolled her eyes at him and looked once again at the lovely little girl. Seeing Miguel there, holding his granddaughter, the love so obvious in his eyes, reminded her of his warmth with

Vanessa and how much that had once touched her heart. It brought back the side of him she had loved so much. The side of him she had forgotten in the years she told herself she hated him.

For a moment, it seemed they were transported back in time. Back to the Miguel and Dani they had once been. By sharing this special moment with him, Dani almost forgot she had ever hated him, or why.

"Doesn't she make you wish you had a little girl of your own?" Michael asked.

It was an innocent question, but it felt like cold water had been splashed in Dani's face. She forgot the warm feelings she had experienced only seconds before and the bitterness of the past returned. Suddenly, she was seeing Michelle in a new light. This should have been their child they were admiring, their little girl they were fussing over. But that didn't happen. It was an experience she had been cheated out of. All the anger of the past welled up inside Dani and she knew she had to get away from Miguel.

Michael instantly saw the change in Dani's expression. "What's the matter?" he asked, confusion creasing his brow.

"I have to go," she said, turning and running down the hall the way they had come. With Michelle in his arms, Michael was unable to pursue her. All he could do was watch her disappear around the corner and wonder why.

Chapter Seven

Once downstairs, it took Dani a full half-hour to locate Traycee in order to tell her she wanted to leave. By then she had regained some composure, although she was still shaken on the inside. She had to get away from this house and Miguel as quickly as possible. She had known it was a mistake coming here in the first place, and was angry at herself for letting her guard down and giving in to coming. She'd spent years forcing the painful memories of Miguel from her mind, now only to have him reopen those wounds by appearing in her life again. She was confused by the feelings he had revived in her and angry he had brought them to the surface. She just had to get away.

She found Traycee sitting on the beach with the advertising executive she'd met in the limousine. Traycee was disappointed to hear that Dani wanted to leave so soon.

"Don't you want to stay for the fireworks?"

"No. I really want to go back now."

Cathy had spotted Dani and approached the group. She saw the strain in Dani's face. "Is everything okay here?" she asked her friend.

"I was just telling Traycee I'd like to leave now," Dani said. Her voice sounded calm but the pain in her eyes told a different story. Trying to control her emotions, Dani turned to Traycee. "I don't want to spoil your fun, but I wouldn't feel comfortable leaving you here to take that long train ride back alone."

The man beside Traycee spoke up. "That's not a problem. I

have to ride back into Manhattan, too. I'll be happy to escort Traycee back to her hotel."

Traycee nodded agreement to this, but Dani looked skeptical. Being the older of the two, Dani felt an unwritten obligation for Traycee's safety. A moment passed as she struggled with his offer to bring Traycee back to the hotel against her desire to leave this house.

"That's a great idea," Cathy said, making the decision for Dani. "Jeff will see her back to the city." She turned to Dani. "Don't worry, I can vouch for him. He's very dependable."

Dani didn't have the strength to argue and, after all, Traycee was a grown woman. She said her goodbyes and she and Cathy walked across the warm sand to the house together.

As they approached the limousine, Cathy said, "I don't think I'll be needed here for a while. I'll ride to the station with you."

Once seated in the comfort of the limousine, Cathy directed the driver to take off with only the two of them riding. The silver car glided around the curve of the driveway and headed out the gates of the estate.

Dani sat quiet, looking out the window, yet seeing nothing.

"If you're still worried about Traycee, you needn't be," Cathy offered. "Jeff is a nice guy. He'll watch over her."

Dani only nodded.

"Tell me what's bothering you," Cathy said, gently. "It's Michael, isn't it?"

Dani turned to her, surprise registered on her face.

"I saw you two together earlier," Cathy confessed.

Dani looked out the window again. The sun was tilted to the west as early evening approached. They passed an 18th century inn, its white clapboard siding shining brightly, and the surrounding garden lush in colors of red, blue, and deep pink, with the lawn lying lush green between colors. She thought how peaceful the setting looked in comparison to the turmoil she felt inside.

"I ran into him by accident," Dani finally said. "I should have left the minute I saw him, but I didn't." Seeing him there among his personal things, the poster from the past, the portrait of Vanessa, all those things had softened her feelings toward him enough to make her question her resolve about hating him. How could she explain the perplexity of her feelings to Cathy when she still didn't understand them herself?

But Cathy knew more than Dani realized.

"Michael is the one who hurt you all those years ago. Isn't he?" She spoke the words softly.

"Yes," Dani admitted, looking directly at Cathy. "He is. That's why it was such a shock when I saw him at your apartment."

Cathy nodded. "I thought so. I've thought about you and Michael a lot since that day, and then I sort of pieced it all together." After a moment's silence, Cathy asked, "Does Michael know what happened to you after he left? From what I can tell, he has no idea why you hate him."

"No. He never knew," Dani replied. "He disappeared before I could tell him."

"Maybe you should tell him now."

Dani laughed tightly. "As if he would care. He didn't care then, and it makes no difference now."

"He might care more than you realize," Cathy said, softly.

Dani stared at Cathy a moment. Maybe Miguel had confided in her. "Did he tell you that?"

"No," Cathy answered. "But I know he feels something for you. It really bothered him that you were so angry toward him."

Dani shook her head, but Cathy ignored her and continued. "Even if I'm wrong, it wouldn't hurt to tell him. Maybe you could shed that hatred you've been carrying around all these years. The past could finally be put to rest."

"No," Dani said. "Miguel's never felt anything for anyone,

except Vanessa. I'm sorry, Cathy. I just don't see him in the same light as you do. And it won't matter one way or another if he ever knows. My feelings for him will never change." She touched her friend's arm as they reached the station. "Promise me you won't say anything to him either."

"I think you're making a mistake," Cathy told her honestly.

"Promise," Dani insisted.

"I won't say anything."

The two slipped out of the car and hugged goodbye. "Keep in touch. Okay?" Cathy said.

Dani nodded and forced a smile, then turned and boarded the train that would take her back to the city.

Throughout the two-and-a-half hour ride back to Penn Station, Dani's thoughts wandered between past and present. The short time she'd spent with Miguel had completely unnerved her. Not what he'd said or done as much as how her feelings had been altered from one minute to the next. For a brief period, she had actually enjoyed spending time with him. The man she had once believed him to be, warm, caring, compassionate, had resurfaced, and she'd found herself drawn to him as she had eighteen years ago. But then the sight of him with Michelle had been a slap in the face, reminding her why she no longer trusted him, and hated him.

Her thoughts flooded with all her reasons for not trusting him. The anguish she'd felt when she'd found him gone. The hurt and humiliation of finding out that other girls from the coffee shop had been involved with him at one time or another and had also been dumped at the drop of a hat. The pain in her parents' eyes when the deception of her relationship with Miguel had been found out. How could she possibly forget, for even a moment, all the pain he had caused her, the pain still real in her heart? It would not happen again, she told herself. She may have to be civil to him at times, but she certainly wouldn't let him make a fool of her again. Once in a lifetime was enough.

Night had completely shrouded the city by the time Dani arrived at her hotel. She stood for a long time on the balcony, overlooking Central Park. Fireworks shot up into the darkness and exploded into brilliant suns of color over the park as the crowd below marveled over their magnificence.

Dani's resolve to thrust the day's events from her mind faded like the fireworks and tears threatened to fill her eyes. She couldn't push the image of Miguel with Michelle cuddled up against him from her mind. Would their little girl have looked like Michelle? Would she have been a fiery redhead from the combination of his dark hair and her blonde hair? The guilt and pain of what she'd done never went away. It only deepened with the years.

Her hatred for Miguel now equaled, if not exceeded, the love she'd once felt for him. Could she ever let that hate go as Cathy had suggested? How could she when she had to live with the pain of her actions for the rest of her life? The actions caused only because of her association with him.

Finally, the fireworks ended and the streets below flooded with people as the crowd dispersed. Dani gave up her thoughts and readied herself for bed. She knew it would be some time before Traycee came in, due to her long ride back on the train. As she turned out the bedside lamp, she tried not to think of Miguel, and prayed he wouldn't be at the showing tomorrow.

Chapter Eight

The fashion show displaying the Regal Coat winter line was an elaborate event and was attended by over seven hundred buyers from across the country. Round tables covered with crisp, hunter green tablecloths and white rose centerpieces in crystal flute vases lined the room with the stage and runway down the middle where the models would display Regal's finest.

Dani and Traycee arrived early and were escorted to their appointed table by a young woman in a suit of hunter green. Dani decided that hunter green must be Regal's trademark color for it was used frequently in the décor. She pushed all other thoughts aside as she turned to the business at hand and lay out her folder of order forms in preparation for the show.

Although Traycee was tired from her late night at the DeCara's party, she became animated at the sight of such a prominent event. This was her first major buying event, and she seemed to want to soak up every detail. Her pent-up enthusiasm made Dani smile. It was times like this that Dani envied her inexperience and youth.

Dani kept an eye on the crowd as the room filled, keeping a lookout for Miguel in the event he should appear. She hoped he wouldn't, but that seemed unlikely under the circumstances. She didn't want to be caught unaware. She wanted to be prepared by seeing him first.

Finally the tables were filled and the lights dimmed and the noisy room fell into a quiet hush. Vanessa appeared on the tshaped stage that filled the center of the room. Her eyes searched the crowd a moment before resting on Dani, and then she gave one of her fabulous smiles, her green eyes twinkling. Dani knew the smile was just for her, and once again her heart warmed.

At Vanessa's introduction, the show began, and lithe models glided down the runway to music displaying coats of all styles and colors. Classic cuts in navy, black, and gray, pea coats that were just coming back into style, and modern block-colored styles displaying brilliant greens, yellows, hot pinks, and reds. Dani and Traycee became immersed in the business of buying, marking down notes of quantities and colors of each style that caught their eye. Once again Dani was pleasantly surprised by Traycee's buying abilities. She noticed important details, and was a great help in selecting styles.

At last the show concluded with applause for the models and fashions they had displayed, and as the chandeliers above illuminated the room, Vanessa invited the buyers to stay and enjoy the luncheon buffet set out on the side wall. She explained that there would be advisors available for anyone having questions on the new line or about the order forms. Having thanked the buyers again for attending, she made her way off the stage and headed straight over to Dani's table. Watching her, with her smooth movements and graceful walk, Dani couldn't help thinking that Vanessa could easily be taken as one of the models.

"Dani," she said, her voice warm as she sat across from her. "I'm so happy I saw you here. You left so quickly yesterday that I didn't get a chance to visit with you."

"I know. I'm sorry, Vanessa," Dani said, searching for an explanation. "Something just came up and I had to leave." She knew it was a flimsy excuse, but couldn't come up with anything else to say. How could she tell Vanessa that her father was the reason for the sudden departure? No, she could never do that.

Vanessa seemed satisfied with her excuse. "Daddy said he had the honor of showing off Michelle to you." She pretended to pout, making Dani want to laugh at the child-like gesture. How many times had she seen that look years ago? And Vanessa always did get her way in the end. "I really wanted to be the one to show her off," she continued.

"I'm happy I was able to see her before I left," Dani told her honestly. "She's so beautiful. You're very lucky to have her."

Vanessa smiled at Dani's approval of her daughter as if it was important to her. Once again, Dani's heart cried out on the inside and tears threatened to spill from her eyes. She had missed so much of Vanessa's life, a life she would have enjoyed sharing. Just one more reason to blame Miguel for ruining her life.

"Well, I know Traycee stayed until the end," Vanessa turned her attention to the assistant. "Did you enjoy the party?"

Traycee beamed. "Oh yes, we, I mean I, had a great time." Traycee blushed a little at her stumble over the word *we*. Dani figured she meant her and Jeff.

"I'm happy you enjoyed yourself," Vanessa told her. She sighed then. "I'd better get back to business. If you two need anything, let me know." Standing to leave she turned again to Dani. "I hope I see you again soon. Maybe we can have a real visit next time."

"I'd like that," Dani said, and instinctively stood and hugged the young woman. "I'd like that very much." Then Vanessa was gone, playing hostess to the other buyers, and Dani and Traycee once again immersed themselves in the process of order forms and coat details.

Just as the two were wrapping things up, Traycee announced she was starving. "Do you mind if I get a bite to eat?"

"Of course not." Dani had been so engrossed with the orders that she'd forgotten all about lunch. "Go ahead. I'll finish these and get something in a minute."

Traycee left the table as Dani sorted and placed the order forms in their respective folders. She was concentrating so hard on her work that she didn't notice the person who had sat down beside her until he spoke.

"Hello Dani."

Dani jumped in her seat, then recognizing Miguel, let out a sigh. "You scared me!" she said sharply. "I didn't hear you sit down."

Michael gave her one of his smiles, the one that used to melt her heart but now only irritated her. It made her feel he was laughing at her. "I'm sorry," he said. "I didn't mean to scare you. I only thought it better to catch you first before you saw me. Otherwise you might run away again."

Dani didn't say a word. She continued filing the papers in order and finally closed the Regal Coat folder on them. Her hands were visibly shaking and she hoped he wouldn't notice.

Michael placed his hand lightly on her arm. "I'd like to talk with you, privately. Are you free tonight?"

Looking straight at him she pulled her arm from his touch. "I'm busy tonight with another meeting."

"Tomorrow, then. Afternoon, night, it doesn't matter. You name the time."

"No. I'm busy tomorrow, too. And we're leaving the next day."

Michael's eyes bore into hers. "Dani, please, we have to talk."

"There's nothing to talk about," Dani told him. She tried to keep her composure, aware of the people surrounding them. But the more he stared at her, the harder she found it not to burst out in anger at him.

"I think we have a lot to talk about," Michael persisted. "I want to know why you're so angry with me. When we met at Cathy's apartment, it was so blatant. Then, yesterday at the party, you seemed so much like the old Dani I remember that I thought everything was okay. Until you ran off. Now your eyes are burning at me again. Dani," his voice broke in obvious frustration. "Please. I need to talk with you. Maybe we can clear up whatever the problem is."

"Why?" Dani hissed. Her eyes were burning as he had said and her face flushed with anger. "Why, after all this time, do you care how I feel?"

Michael straightened a bit, assessing Dani's behavior. His voice remained soft. "I've always cared. I'd like for us to be friends."

His words made Dani even angrier. Friends. How dare he even suggest such a thing? When she spoke, her voice was steady, but dripping with hatred. "It's too late for us to be friends. If you remember, we were past being friends years ago. There's nothing you can do or say now to change my feelings. Just leave me alone. That's all I want."

Michael opened his mouth to reply but Traycee appeared at the table with her plate of food. She looked from Dani's flushed face to Michael's shocked one and hesitated to sit down. But Michael slid smoothly back into the part of host and stood to help Traycee with her chair.

"I'm happy to see you are indulging in our buffet," he told her, his face returning to its usual composure. "I hope you will help yourself, too, Dani. If you both will excuse me, I'd better get back to business."

He turned to Dani, "I'm sorry we couldn't resolve our differences," he said. And with a nonchalant nod he was lost in the crowd of buyers.

"Is everything okay?" Traycee asked Dani cautiously. "Things seemed a bit tense between you and Mr. DeCara.

Dani closed her eyes a moment and forced herself to be calm. Then she looked into Traycee's concerned face. "I'm okay," she assured her. "We just had a difference of opinion."

Traycee nodded, but didn't look completely convinced. She began eating her food as Dani sat, staring off across the room.

"Aren't you going to eat?" Traycee asked after a few moments of silence.

Dani shook her head. "I'm not hungry after all," she said. All Dani wanted to do was get out of there and go home. She wanted to put as many miles as possible between herself and Miguel DeCara.

Chapter Nine

Dani sat at the patio table on the outdoor deck of Janette's suburban home as her friend brought out a tray with a pitcher of iced tea and chilled glasses. It was late August and a very hot day, but the breeze was refreshing as they sat in the shade of the overhead awning.

"You really have a nice back yard," Dani commented as she gazed over the colorful flower gardens and trees that outlined their acre lot. "I didn't know you were such a gardener."

"Thanks," Janette said as she poured the tea. "Since I've been home with Darci this summer, I've had a little time to really work on it. Actually," she looked a bit sheepish to be admitting such a thing, "I've really enjoyed it."

Dani looked over at her friend who not so long ago was intensely involved with her career yet now seemed to have slipped so easily into motherhood. She marveled at the transformation, and wondered if it was that easy or if Janette just made it look that way.

Dani took a sip of her iced tea. "I know I'll be happy to have you back at the office next month."

"Has it been that much trouble?"

"Not really," Dani replied honestly. "With Traycee's help it has gone smoothly. She really surprised me with how capable she is. I'd never have thought it when she first started working there."

"I guess people aren't always as they first appear," Janette suggested.

Dani shrugged. "I guess not. All the same, I'm looking forward to your return."

Janette shifted a bit in her seat and Dani instantly became alert.

"You are coming back?" Dani asked, staring hard at her friend.

"Actually, that's part of the reason I asked you out here," Janette said. "I've already talked with Trindell and he's okay with everything. But I wanted to be the one to tell you."

Dani continued looking steadily at Janette. "Tell me what?"

"I'm extending my leave until the first of the year."

Dani was dumbfounded. Janette had already taken off three months and now she wanted four more. "Why?" she asked in amazement.

Janette shook her head. "It's so hard to explain. I don't even understand it myself. The whole time I was pregnant, I kept telling myself that after the baby came nothing would change. I'd go back to work and everything would go on as before. But now that Darci is here…" Janette paused a moment and took a breath. She looked close to tears. "I just can't stand the thought of leaving her with someone else. My job has always come first, but now nothing else seems as important as Darci."

Janette stopped again and stared out at the trees as if looking for an answer. Finally, she looked back at Dani. "I thought if I took a little more time off, I could make a more rational decision. The trouble is you're the one who'll be stuck with my job until I do decide, and I feel awful about doing that to you."

"You mean you might not come back at all?" Dani was too stunned to believe she had heard right.

"It's possible," Janette told her. "I just need some more time to decide."

Dani sat in silence for a long while staring at the droplets of water making trails down the outside of her tea glass. Never coming back? Janette had always been so dedicated to her work. And now she's made a complete turnaround.

Janette broke the silence. "I'm sorry to drop this all on you, Dani. But I hope you understand. This is something I need to do."

Dani looked up at her friend. "I can't say I do understand," she told her. "But then, I've never been a mother, so I guess I wouldn't." She smiled then, making the worried frown on Janette's face disappear. "You take the time you need and don't worry. I'll take care of things until you do decide."

Janette sighed with relief. "Thanks, Dani. Thanks for being such a good friend."

Dani only smiled, even though she didn't feel like smiling on the inside.

* * *

Later, after leaving Janette's home, Dani decided to take a drive through the winding roads between Chaska and Apple Valley before returning to her own apartment. The drive past the river and through the small hills helped ease the tension she was feeling and let her mind wander.

She still couldn't believe Janette was considering staying home permanently. It was just so unexpected. But then, when Janette's husband had come out on the deck with Darci, and Janette's eyes lit up, Dani could see the bond between mother and child. Perhaps Janette was right in wanting to stay home. She just didn't know.

Dani did know that by continuing in Janette's position as coat buyer, she'd have to work on the spring line, and that meant once again working with Miguel. The thought upset her terribly. She'd been so successful at dodging his calls over the past month and a half and she was sure he'd finally given up trying.

She'd talked to Cathy several times, too, and had found out Miguel had been inquiring about her. But Dani had made it clear to Cathy, she was not interested in his concern. Now, just when she thought she might be home free from having to ever see Miguel again, she was going to have to continue with coats.

As Dani turned her car north toward her St. Louis Park apartment, she tried for the thousandth time to figure Miguel out. After all these years his sudden interest in her didn't seem real. After all, he'd been the one who left. Yet, ever since she'd been to New York, he'd tried several times to call and talk with her. She never returned his calls. She couldn't see any point in doing so. Dani figured he was just playing his old games again, trying to see how many women he could add to his list of conquests. And maybe adding her twice might be a new game for him.

What scared her most was that for a few minutes at the party in Southampton, she'd seen the side of him that she'd once loved so much. And she was still drawn to him. But she'd just brushed it off as a pang of nostalgia, trying to recreate that old feeling because in reality, she knew he was incapable of feeling love for her. He didn't take that kind of love seriously.

The sun was just fading into evening as Dani pulled her car into her apartment's garage. She hadn't resolved anything. She'd only rehashed the same old thoughts she'd been fighting with for years. Fortunately, the spring buying season was still a couple of months away so there was still a chance she might get out of going on the actual buying trip. She clung to that thought as she took the elevator up to her apartment.

There were two calls waiting for her on her answering machine and she listened to them as she changed into comfortable sweats. The first was her mother calling to say hello and telling her how happy they were that she was coming up for a visit Labor Day weekend. Dani had sent them a note last week telling of her plans to come. She hadn't had time to visit all summer, and wanted to make it up there before the warm weather completely disappeared. They lived only four-and-a-half hours away on a quiet lake outside of Walker. She was looking forward to a peaceful weekend of sun, fishing, and tranquility.

The second message was from Cathy. She only wanted to say hi and said to call her if she had a chance. So Dani did.

"Hi, Cathy. I got your message. What's up?"

On the other end of the line, Dani could hear music playing. As Cathy answered, she told someone to turn the stereo down. For a moment, Dani wondered if it might be Miguel.

"Hi, Dani. I'm glad you called. How have you been?"

"Fine," Dani replied. "The same. Working too much, playing too little." She hesitated. "Did I interrupt something? It sounds like you have company."

"It's only Gary," Cathy told her. "You remember, my accountant friend."

Dani laughed. "That's right. You two must be hitting it off well, huh?"

"Not too bad. So, tell me, what did you do all day?"

Dani told Cathy about her visit with Janette. "She's changed so much I can hardly believe it. I always thought she'd make her career an important part of her life. It's such a surprise."

"People change as life changes," Cathy said matter-of-factly. "Speaking of change, Michael was asking about you again the other day."

Dani groaned. "I wouldn't use the words Michael and change in the same sentence. What did he want this time?"

"Oh, he was just wondering if you were still in charge of coats at Chance's. I told him I didn't know." Cathy hesitated a moment. "You know, Dani, he still wants a chance to talk with you."

Dani sighed. "Why doesn't he just give up? I've told him as

plain as I can. I'm not interested."

"You really should give him a chance to explain," Cathy told her softly. "You know, people do change."

"So everyone keeps telling me," Dani said with a sigh.

Chapter Ten

Dani sat at her desk going over price cuts on various sportswear items. The office was quiet today, many of the buyers were down in their various departments preparing for the upcoming Labor Day weekend sale. Traycee sat at Janette's desk going over coat prices Dani had given her to reduce. She'd taken over the desk for the time being until Janette made her decision. Dani was proud of the way Traycee handled her work. She really was a fast learner and competent assistant.

As Dani studied the figures in front of her, Carl Trindell walked up to her desk.

"Dani. Could I see you privately a moment?"

"Sure." She followed Trindell into his office and sat in a chair in front of his desk. Trindell closed the door and than sat, placing his elbows on the desk in front of him, touching his fingertips together thoughtfully.

"I received a phone call today from Michael DeCara of Regal Coats," he said. He studied Dani's face a moment as if gauging her reaction. "He'd like to come this weekend for a tour of our store, especially the coat department. He says he's interested in seeing how we display our merchandise, and thinks he might be able to offer some helpful advice."

Dani held her composure. "That shouldn't be a problem," she told him. "We could ask Traycee to give him the tour and introduce him to the department manager. Traycee's quite knowledgeable with the coat department, and I don't think she has any plans this weekend." Dani knew this because of an earlier conversation with Traycee. She was confident Traycee would be more than willing to take on the assignment.

"He asked specifically for you," Trindell said steadily.

This threw Dani off-balance. "Oh. I see. Well…"

"Now Dani," Trindell interrupted. "If there is any reason you don't want to do this, I'll understand completely. Don't feel you have to just because he asked for you." He emphasized the word 'he' coldly, like a father protecting his daughter from some unseemly character.

Dani couldn't help but smile at his protective behavior in spite of the anger she felt over the spot Miguel was putting her in. To push himself on her in his own territory was one thing, but to do so in her office was another.

For a moment, she thought of saying no. After all, she had plans that she didn't want to cancel. But then, she knew that if she didn't go along with it this time, he'd only keep trying. Finally, she decided she had to put a stop to him once and for all and the only way was a face-to-face confrontation. Once she made it clear to him she was no longer interested then they could get on with their lives.

Trindell misinterpreted Dani's long silence. "I'll just tell him you can't make it," he offered. "After all, it was too late of notice for a holiday weekend anyway."

Dani shook her head. "No, Carl, it's okay. I'll meet with him if that's what he wants."

Trindell studied her a moment. "Are you sure? He seems a bit…" it was Trindell's turn to hesitate. "Pushy," he finished.

Dani laughed, making Trindell's creased frown turn into a smile. "He is pushy. And arrogant. And over-confident, and a few other choice words I'd rather not say. But it's okay, Carl. I've know him a long time, and I know how to handle him." She stood to leave, and Trindell walked her to the door.

"All right," he said. "But I think I'll be around that day, just in case."

"Thanks, Carl." As Dani opened the door to leave, she had a thought. "Do you think we could arrange an early morning meeting? Maybe I could still get out of here by noon and make it up to my parents for the weekend."

"Sure. I don't see why not. And Dani, thanks."

Dani smiled at him and headed back to her desk. As she sat there, she began to think that maybe this meeting was for the best. She could get Miguel out of her life once and for all. The more she thought about it, the better she felt.

* * *

Saturday morning, Dani arrived early at the store for her meeting with Miguel. Since it was a holiday weekend, and expected to be very busy, she'd arranged for the coat department staff to be there an hour before opening to meet with him. She figured she could give him a tour of the rest of the store afterward and, hopefully, be out of there by noon.

Dani had called her mother earlier in the week to let her know about the delay. Her mother understood, knowing how seriously Dani took her job, and was pleased to hear she still planned to come. This morning, though, her mother had called her again to warn her about the storm reports.

"They're predicting thunderstorms and hail for this afternoon and evening," Dani's mom, Joan, said with concern in her voice. "Check the weather report before leaving, dear. I don't want you getting caught in a storm."

Dani promised she would and was annoyed to see it begin to rain, the wind blowing fiercely, as she drove into Minneapolis. Minnesota weather was so unpredictable at times, especially summer and fall.

She brushed aside her annoyance at the weather as she examined the coat department. Everything looked in fine order. Coats were tagged for the Fall Sale and the displays looked wonderful. Who did Miguel think he was, suggesting that a prestigious store like Chance's might need his advice on coat displays? That just showed the gall and conceit he had.

Kelly Suther, the Coat Department Manager, came over and talked with Dani about the Regal Coat line. She was young, but very competent in her position, yet she admitted to feeling some anxiety over Mr. DeCara's visit.

"Do you know what he's like?" she questioned Dani. "Mr. Trindell made him out to be some corporate tyrant who wants to control everything."

Dani laughed at the picture Carl had painted. From only one phone call he'd decided he didn't like Michael DeCara, and she suspected it was because of DeCara's insistence on seeing her. She should have felt offended by Carl's protective attitude toward her, but instead she felt lucky to have a boss who was looking out for her.

"He's not quite the tyrant Trindell made him out to be," she assured Kelly. By then the other sales assistants had joined them, curious about the mysterious visitor. "As a matter of fact," Dani continued, a bit sarcastically, "he will more than likely be very charming to you all."

"Why, thank you, Miss Westerly. I couldn't have asked for a more pleasant introduction."

Dani recognized the voice behind her instantly and her back stiffened with outrage. She turned to find Miguel directly behind her, his ever-present smile upon his lips.

"Good morning, ladies," Michael DeCara approached the group, looking fresh and crisp in his navy silk suit, his damp overcoat slung over his arm. "I didn't mean to eavesdrop. The janitor was kind enough to let me in early and direct me to the coat department." He smiled warmly at the other women before turning his gaze to Dani. Standing directly beside her, he winked at her familiarly, bringing an angry rush of blood to her face.

"Mr. DeCara," Dani said crisply. "I'd like to introduce you to our Coat Department Manager, Kelly Suther, and her two full-time assistants, Cris Eastman and Jamie Carlson. I'm sure they can answer any questions you have about the department."

Michael gave Dani a sideways glance, laid his coat over the counter and approached the group of women, his hand extended. "First of all, please call me Michael. I'm not so old that I'd want you lovely ladies to refer to me as Mr." He smiled as he shook each woman's hand in turn, holding each hand longer than necessary, and giving a warm personal comment to each.

"I'm pleased to meet all of you," he continued. "I enjoy knowing the people who sell our merchandise. It's nice to be able to put a face to the names I hear over the phone."

The group of women beamed like schoolgirls, obviously entranced by Michael's good looks and manners. Dani rolled her eyes at his overbearing charm. It took more than a silk suit and polished shoes to impress her. She knew what he was like on the inside.

For more than an hour, Michael discussed the winter line with the women, going over details they might have missed, which would help them in their sales presentations. He discussed fabrics, washing instructions, snap-off collars, and linings. He complimented their displays, suggested different ideas for merchandising, and joked about ways to sell to the hard-to-sell customer as the three women hung on his every word. Dani had to admit he knew his product well, but was continually annoyed at how hard he was working to impress the other women.

The store had opened by then and Dani tried unsuccessfully several times to end the meeting. Just as her irritation began to peak, Michael pulled a long, red wool coat from the rack to show the women. "This coat definitely looks better on a person than on a hanger," he told them. "Dani dear, would you come model this for us?" He turned back to Kelly, Cris, and Jamie. "You know, she'd make a perfect model. Personally, I think she should be modeling these clothes instead of hiding behind the scenes buying them."

Dani was outraged. How dare he belittle her job when, thanks to him, it was all she had. Or ever would have. She wanted to scream her anger at him, but with the women watching her, and customers wandering between the racks, she had no choice but to comply with his request.

Michael slowly slipped the coat over her shoulders and stood close behind her longer than necessary. Dani stepped away from him and buttoned up the coat. Michael only smiled and began showing off its detailing to the saleswomen and a few customers who had gathered around them as Dani seethed with anger.

"Remind me to send you this coat," Michael whispered in Dani's ear. "It looks stunning on you."

Dani had had enough. "It's time we let these women get back to work," she said, taking off the coat and flinging it at Miguel. She walked quickly out of the coat department and down the aisle and could faintly hear Miguel thank the women for their time and say goodbye. Dani was at the housewares department by the time Michael caught up with her.

"Hey, wait up. What was that all about?"

She stopped abruptly and faced him. "How could you?" she blurted out. "It's bad enough you conned your way in here with this tour crap, but then you purposely embarrassed me in front of the people I work with. I've worked hard to earn the respect of my co-workers and you blew it all away by suggesting I should be some air-headed model."

Michael looked stunned. "I thought it was a compliment."

"Well, it wasn't," Dani kept her voice low, conscious of the customers and salesclerks around them. Venom spilled from her tone. "I take my job seriously. I work hard, and I expect to be treated as a professional. And I expect the same treatment from you."

She spun on her heel and walked away toward the elevators. Michael followed her.

"I'll take you up to the offices," Dani said, coldly, as they reached the elevators. "I think Mr. Trindell plans to meet with you up there."

The ride in the elevator was a silent, tense one. Michael was afraid to say a word in the chance he'd make her angry again. Dani was too upset to say anything.

The doors opened to the large room crowded with desks and partitions. Dani snapped on the lights, perturbed by the fact that Carl wasn't already there. She had hoped to deposit Miguel on him and leave. It was already close to eleven and she wanted to be on her way to her parents' house by noon.

"Is this where your office is?" Michael asked, interrupting her thoughts.

Dani laughed. "I don't have an actual office," she told him. "This is where my desk is." She waved her hand to the row of desks separated by partitions.

"Show me your desk," Michael said.

Dani stared at him. "Why?"

"Because, I'd like to see it. You can tell a lot about a person by their desk." Michael smiled at Dani's frown. "Besides, you got to see mine at home. It's only fair."

Dani shook her head at his childishness. "It's over there," she pointed. "The second one down from Mr. Trindell's office."

Michael walked over and studied her neat, well-organized desk. Everything had a place, but something was missing. He tipped his head a bit and scratched his beard, a gesture that was so familiar to Dani that it tugged her into the past for a brief moment.

"Interesting," he commented.

"What's interesting?"

"Your desk is neat and organized. It shows you're a very good worker."

"So."

"It's missing something. How long have you worked here?"

Dani couldn't figure out where he was heading with all this, but she answered him out of curiosity. "Fifteen years."

"Fifteen years," Michael's voice trailed off a moment. "That's a long time. Yet, there's nothing here that says 'Dani's desk'. No pictures, no mementos, not even a coffee mug with your name on it. Seems strange for having been here so long."

Dani looked closely at her desk and then slowly studied those of her co-workers. He was right. They all had pictures of family on their pin-up boards or in frames on their desks. Plants, flowers, and even stickers with funny sayings were strewn around other work areas. Little things that made their work stations personal. Even Traycee had already begun personalizing her own area and she'd hardly been there six months. Yet, Dani's desk looked sterile, like anyone could have worked there. The thought depressed her, and she was irritated by the fact that Miguel was the one to point it out. But before she could make a smart comeback, Miguel changed the subject.

"Do you want to see my latest picture of Michelle?"

Dani's face softened. "You know I do," she told him.

Michael pulled out his wallet and sat on the corner of her desk, flipping through the photos. "Here it is." He handed her the wallet.

Staring up at Dani was a curly-headed little girl with a big, wide smile. The emerald dress she wore only added to the brilliant green of her eyes. "She's adorable," Dani said. "So much like Vanessa."

Michael beamed. "I knew you'd appreciate it."

"You always did know where my soft spot was." Dani said the words without thinking. She began flipping through the other pictures. There were others of Michelle at different ages, Vanessa's senior picture, another of Miguel and Vanessa walking down the aisle at her wedding. Dani smiled softly at the pictures as Michael watched her transform back to the girl she'd been.

"I'm sorry I embarrassed you downstairs," he told her. "I really did mean it as a compliment."

Dani closed the wallet and handed it back to him. "It's okay. I guess I am a little sensitive about my job."

Michael reached for the wallet, but instead clasped Dani's hand in his. He looked deeply into her eyes. Yes, the warmth was still there. If only he could penetrate it.

Suddenly uncomfortable by their closeness, Dani pulled away and looked at her watch. "I wonder where Trindell is?" she said aloud. "It's almost eleven thirty."

"Oh yes, Carl Trindell," he said. "I spoke with him on the phone. He seems very protective of you."

Dani didn't like the implication of his tone and immediately became defensive. "Carl Trindell has been my supervisor for many years," she said coolly. "He's also a very good friend."

"I'm sure he is," Michael said with a smirk.

Dani wanted to slap the smile right off his face. "Not everyone thinks, or acts like you," she told him, anger once again seething inside her.

"Oh? And just how do I act?" Michael asked, still looking amused.

Like an egotistical, manipulative jerk, Dani wanted to shout out, but she never had the chance. The elevator doors opened and out stepped Carl Trindell.

"I'm sorry I'm late," he said, his attention directed more

toward Dani than to the both of them. "The rain was much heavier than I'd realized. It took me longer than usual to make the drive in." He looked at Dani with questioning eyes as if to ask, *Are you alright?*

Dani smiled at Carl. "That's okay. We were just looking over the offices."

Dani turned to Miguel. "Michael DeCara, this is Carl Trindell, our Executive Merchandising Manager."

The two men shook hands and exchanged greetings, both a little wary of the other. Although Trindell really wasn't much older than Michael, he had a fatherly look about him. Michael could have kicked himself for making his offhanded accusation to Dani about her relationship with Trindell.

"Well," Dani announced. "I will leave you two to talk. I'll see you Tuesday, Carl."

Trindell walked her to the elevator with Michael tagging behind.

"Be careful driving," Trindell warned Dani. "There's a heavy downpour and strong winds. They've had severe storm warnings all morning."

Dani smiled affectionately at Carl. "I'll be careful," she promised him.

Michael extended his hand to Dani. "It has been a pleasure, as usual," he said, smugly.

Ignoring his outstretched hand, Dani stepped into the elevator. "As usual," she replied, and the doors closed in Michael's face. The iciness in Dani's words did not escape Michael.

Chapter Eleven

It took Dani much longer to reach her apartment than it had to get to the store that morning because of the heavy downpour. From time to time, the cars on the freeway were almost at a standstill until the rain would let up a little and everyone could continue. The trees along the highway swayed furiously from side to side, and the wind made it almost impossible at times to stay in one lane. Dani cursed Miguel several times during the drive, and once more when the garage door opener for the apartment's underground parking didn't work and she had to park outside and run through the rain to her building. She was soaked to the skin in the few seconds it took her to get inside, which only added to her annoyance.

When she got inside her apartment, she was relieved to see that the electricity was still working, and she quickly turned on the television to catch the weather report. Her hope was that the storm was only local so she could still drive up north to her parents' place, but she was disappointed to see the weather was bad throughout most of the state. "Damn you, Miguel," she swore for the hundredth time.

Joan was relieved to hear her daughter on the phone. "I'm glad you didn't try coming," she told Dani. "I was afraid you'd get stuck in this storm."

Dani told her she was disappointed. "This is the last weekend I can come up until the holidays," she complained.

"I know, dear. We wanted you here, too. But I feel better

knowing you're safe."

Dani spoke to her mother awhile longer until the static over the lines became so loud that they had to give up and say goodbye.

Still seething at Miguel for ruining her weekend, she decided that exercise was the only way she could relieve her anger. She quickly changed into sweats and popped her favorite movie into the VCR, then began furiously pumping the stair-stepper machine she had located behind the couch, in front of the glass patio door.

As the rain pounded against her patio, Dani mindlessly pounded her feet, hardly noticing the movie playing on the screen. Her mind was still absorbed with Miguel and the events of the day. Why did he keep bothering her? She'd been clear in her feelings toward him, yet he continued pursuing her. She just couldn't figure him out. He could be so nice one minute and then the next minute say some mean-spirited remark like his insinuation about her and Trindell today. The very idea! Just because he saw every woman as a conquest didn't mean all men thought that way.

Hot and sweating, Dani was surprised to see she'd been exercising longer than her usual twenty-minute workout when she looked up at the clock. She made herself stop, pulled the movie tape out, and turned the volume down low, then headed for the shower.

Later, wrapped in a white cotton robe, her hair toweled dry and hanging loosely, Dani curled up in front of the television with a plate of food. She felt much calmer after her workout and shower. Her anger with Miguel had subsided, and she tried not to think about it as she ate and watched an old Bogie and Bacall movie.

The storm was still full-blown throughout the state, and tornado and severe storm warnings flashed across the bottom of the screen for several counties. Dani heard the rain pounding outside one minute, and then softly falling the next against her patio window as occasional thunder and lightning ripped through the sky. Everything in the city was closing up, and even the airport had shut down until the weather cleared.

Worn out from her hectic day and the workout and shower, Dani stretched out on the sofa and fell into a deep sleep. She hadn't even realized she'd been sleeping until she was awakened by the buzzing of her doorbell. The piercing sound startled her, and it took her a moment to register where it had come from. Looking at the clock, she was surprised to see it was already 8:00 p.m. Had she really slept that long?

Again the doorbell buzzed. "Who could that be?" Dani grumbled, walking to the door and looking out the peephole. When she recognized the face staring back at her, she was disgusted. "I can't believe it!" she practically screamed, and forgetting her appearance, she quickly unbolted and opened the door. "What are you doing here?"

"So nice to see you, too." Michael DeCara said, grinning. "May I come in?"

"No, you may not."

Michael's expression turned from a smile to a frown. "Come on Dani, only for a few minutes. I have to talk to you."

"How many times do I have to tell you there is nothing to talk about? Don't you get it? There is nothing to talk about."

"Just five more minutes of your life and I won't ever bother you again. I promise."

Dani narrowed her eyes. "Five minutes," she said, stepping aside to let him pass into her apartment.

Michael surveyed his surroundings. "Nice place," he commented, turning back to Dani. She had closed the door but her hand still grasped the knob. "Nice outfit, too," he teased.

Looking down at her robe, she was suddenly aware of how

she must look. But she didn't care. "I wasn't expecting company," she replied, crisply.

"I know. I'm sorry. Do you mind if I take off my coat? I'm dripping wet."

Staring at his trench coat, Dani saw the puddle that was beginning to form on the floor. She only nodded her assent and he hung it up on the coat rack by the door.

The silence was unbearable for both sides. As Dani continued standing by the door, Michael turned and walked over to the patio doors. Thunder rolled across the sky and lightning zapped in the distance. "That's some storm you're having here," he commented.

"You didn't come here to talk about the weather. Did you?"

"No." Michael faced Dani. "I came to talk about us."

"Us?" Dani screeched, padding across the carpet and stopping only inches from Miguel. "What do you mean by 'us'? There is no us."

"I mean the us we used to be. The friends we could still be if you'd only let me."

Dani crossed her arms. "Why?"

"Because I remember the girl you once were. The girl I cared very much about. And I still believe that under all that hostility, I'd like the woman you've become." Michael's eyes softened as he looked into Dani's, but hers only glared back at him.

"The girl you knew is gone forever," she told him icily. "Thanks to you. And there's nothing left of her to revive. So just let it go."

"What do you mean 'thanks to you'? What did I do to make you hate me so much? All I ever did was love you."

Dani's head flew back and she laughed haughtily. "Yeah. Me and every other girl who worked at the diner and God knows how many others. Did you think I was so stupid I didn't know?"

Michael studied Dani's face. "Is that why you hate me?"

"That, among other reasons."

"I admit I wasn't a saint back then," Michael confessed. "But the time I was with you, I was with only you. No one else, I swear." Again Michael's eyes reached out to her. But Dani only continued to stare coldly.

"Your five minutes are up."

Michael shook his head sadly. "I had hoped...," he began, but decided against finishing. "Do you mind if I call the airport before I leave? My flight is in two hours and I want to make sure it's still on time."

Dani nodded and pointed to the phone in the kitchen. It wasn't until he began dialing that she remembered the news reports. "The airport is closed," she told him from across the room. "The news said no flights in or out until the storm breaks."

Michael looked at her and a worried frown creased his face. The woman who answered on the other end repeated what Dani had said. No flights in or out until morning. After he hung up the phone, he turned and looked seriously at Dani.

"I have a problem."

"What now?" Dani sighed.

"I'm stuck here until morning and I don't have a hotel room." He looked around the living room, his eyes resting on the sofa. Dani read his thoughts.

"Oh, no. No way. You're not staying here. You can go find a hotel room." She couldn't believe he'd even think she'd let him stay.

"But the storm is really howling out there," he said, and a crack of thunder exploded as if to confirm his words.

"You got here in this storm, you can leave just as easily."

"Dani, please, be reasonable. I'll just sleep on the couch and be gone first thing in the morning. I promise you won't even know I'm here."

Dani stared at him, her expression unrelenting.

"You can't be that heartless," Michael said, exasperated.

"I don't believe you!" she spat at him. The sky outside rumbled again and lightning flashed, exposing the sheet of rain falling from the sky. Dani knew she couldn't send Miguel off in this storm, and it made her angry that she cared enough to worry about his safety. Her gaze went from the window back to Miguel, who only looked at her sheepishly. He shrugged his shoulders as if to say "What choice do I have?"

"There are blankets and sheets in the trunk by the couch," she said gruffly. "The couch opens into a bed."

Michael smiled at her. "Thank you. I promise not to keep you awake with my snoring."

Walking past him to the open platform kitchen, Dani took out a bottle of water from the refrigerator. She knew Miguel's comment was meant to be amusing, but it only irritated her. "Don't try to be funny or I might change my mind," she told him.

Michael studied her guarded expression as she stood there in the kitchen. "Don't you ever let your guard down?" he asked.

Dani slowly shook her head. "No. Not anymore," she told him firmly, and then once again walked past him and flicked off the television. "I'm going to bed," she announced. "The bathroom is in the hall. Good night."

Michael reached out and touched her shoulder to stop her. It was an innocent gesture, but Dani swirled around furiously. Her water bottle flew from her hand and onto the floor.

"Don't ever touch me!" she screamed at him.

Michael pulled back in shock. It was the same reaction she'd had at Catherine's apartment. Surely she didn't think he'd ever harm her.

"Dani," he whispered hoarsely. "Why do you hate me so much?"

Dani looked at the man who had caused her so much pain for so many years and the fury inside her finally blew.

"I'll tell you why I hate you," she hissed, shocking even herself by the venom in her voice. But she was seeing red and couldn't stop herself. She had to go on, had to let out all the pain she'd been carrying for eighteen years. "I hate you for taking away my youth. For using me, lying to me, then running away when I needed you the most."

Michael shook his head, confused. "I don't understand, Dani. I never tried to hurt you."

"You did more than hurt me, you ruined my life. Because of you, I ended up a statistic. Eighteen years old, pregnant, and single. But because I loved you so much, I thought everything would be okay. Then, when I showed up to tell you," Dani's voice cracked, "you were gone. You left without a word. Not even a goodbye."

Michael's eyes widened in surprise. "I didn't know," he whispered.

"As if it would have mattered," Dani spat.

"What did you do?" Michael had to know. Did he have a child somewhere that he never knew about?

"What else could I do? I didn't want to tell my parents. They would have been horrified. I used the money I'd been saving to buy a car and had an abortion." At this, tears filled Dani's eyes, but her voice continued icily. "But the so-called doctor was a butcher. He botched things up, and two days later I was bleeding heavily and filled with infection. My parents took me to the emergency room and my secret was out." She looked steadily at Miguel as tears streamed down her face. "You'll never know how it felt to see the pain in their faces when they found out what I'd done."

"Do you want to know why I hate you?" Dani asked Miguel, the pain of her past now replacing the anger. "Because of you, I will never have a child of my own." With that, she turned and ran out of the room and into her bedroom, slamming the door. Michael stared after her, speechless for the first time in his life.

Chapter Twelve

Miguel sat at the bar of a small, crowded saloon in Saigon. He was on a three-day pass and spent it trying to forget why he was in this country to begin with.

He ordered another drink and turned a quick glance at his friend Billy, who was sitting at a table near the door with a young Vietnamese girl. Billy was an oversized, clumsy farm boy from the Midwest who thought himself a charmer with the ladies. But he was also tough, honest, and brave, good qualities a man needed in this place and a friend needed in a buddy. Miguel and he had stuck close since being sent to the same unit in Nam.

Smiling and shaking his head at his friend, Miguel turned back to his fresh drink and took a swig. Something brushed against his leg and he looked down from the tall barstool to see a small beggar boy, one arm missing, his face grotesquely disfigured, carrying a small bag and looking up at him. Miguel just turned away from the boy and he continued on his way looking for handouts. Young children, deformed and missing limbs, were all over Saigon, one of the cruelties of this damn war. Miguel, like everyone else who had been there too long, had learned to look through them and past them since he was unable to help them all.

Once again Miguel glanced at his friend, now leaning forward, head-to-head with the girl. He noticed the beggar boy stopping only a second at Billy's table. Being brushed away by Billy, the boy headed out the door into the daylight. Through the light from the door opening, Miguel noticed that the bag the boy had been carrying lay under Billy's table and it took him only a second to realize what was in it.

"Billy, bomb!" Miguel yelled as he jumped over the bar for protection

in one smooth motion. Other military men in the bar took cover under tables and behind the bar. So engrossed in his new lady friend, Billy only looked up, confused by all the commotion before the realization of what was happening crossed his face. He pushed the girl away from the table, but before he could move an inch, the plastic, homemade bomb below him exploded. Miguel screamed his name as he watched his friend tear into pieces before his eyes.

"Billy, no!"

Dani shot up in bed at the sound of a man screaming. Not even awake yet, she instinctively jumped out of bed and ran through the darkened apartment to the open sofa bed where Miguel was sleeping.

"Billy!" he screamed again, loud and anguished, and in the moonlight through the patio doors Dani could see the horror in Miguel's face.

Quickly, she crawled into bed and held him tight, softly cooing, "Miguel, it's okay. You're home. You're safe. I'm here, Miguel. I'm here." Over and over she said this until he finally stopped struggling and grew quiet in her arms.

Dani cradled his head on her chest, rocking him back and forth like a frightened child. Still assuring him he was okay, she was there for him. She ran her fingers through his damp hair, brushing it away from his face, rocking him gently, assuring him he was home and safe. And even as he came to his senses, Michael continued to let her hold him. She was the only woman who could soothe his pain from the nightmares. It felt warm and comforting to be in her arms, so easy to allow her to soothe and comfort him.

After a time, still holding him, Dani asked Miguel, "It was the bar dream again, wasn't it?" She knew all his bad dreams, the jungle dream, the bar dream, the body bag one, each in detail from when he had told her about them years ago. She was the only one he'd ever told them to, because she had been the only one who had ever cared to listen.

Miguel nodded his head in her arms. "I should have done something," he said hoarsely. "I should have saved Billy."

"You did the best you could," Dani said softly. "No one could control who lived and who died. You have nothing to blame yourself for."

Dani sat quietly for a while longer, still holding Miguel close. She thought of his pain, of her pain, and of the pain they had caused each other. "We make a great pair, you and I," she whispered, shaking her head. And then, slowly, she lay down under the covers beside him, all the time holding him close, both finally falling asleep from exhaustion. And for the first time in years, Michael slept soundly and dreamlessly, feeling safe in Dani's arms.

* * *

Sunlight streamed through the patio doors across the sleeping bodies of Michael and Dani. He stirred slowly and carefully sat up, not wanting to disturb her sleep, and was surprised to see the clock on the opposite wall read 11:00 a.m. He hadn't slept this late on a Saturday morning in a very long time, and a smile played across his lips when he remembered the last time he had slept this late. He had woken up with the same sweet woman beside him then, only a younger version. It was like they'd never parted.

As Michael studied Dani's sleeping face, he liked what he saw. In sleep, she had the softness he remembered, not the look of bitterness she had shown him last night. He thought of last night and how she'd stroked his hair and soothed away his nightmare so tenderly. She was still the same sweet person he had known so many years ago, no matter how hard she'd tried to convince him otherwise. And she must still have some feelings for him other than hatred.

"Good morning," Dani interrupted his thoughts and looked up at him through sleepy eyes. "What are you staring at?"

"The past, the present, all rolled into one," he told her, smiling.

Dani gave him a confused look.

"I'm sorry about last night," Michael told her. "I didn't mean to wake you."

"You can't control your nightmares," she said softly, reaching up to touch the side of his face. The gesture was so innocent, yet sent shivers of remembrance within him. "Just as I can't change the past," Dani sighed. "Do they still come often?"

Michael looked down at the woman who just last night had said she hated him, now she sounded concerned, like she had long ago. "Sometimes they come often, other times I can go for weeks without one."

Dani raised herself onto one elbow and looked him squarely in the eyes. "You never went for help, did you?"

"No," he answered honestly.

She shook her head and began turning to get out of bed, but Michael caught her arm and rolled her back.

"I've missed you," he said. "I really have. You were the only one who I could really talk to, let myself go with." Gently he placed his hand in her hair and slowly drew her lips to his. Barely had they touched when Dani pulled away.

"No, Miguel. Not like this. I need to sort things out first."

Michael let her go, nodding his understanding. "Do you still hate me?" he wanted to know.

Dani got out of bed and walked the short distance to the counter that separated the kitchen from the living room before turning around. "I don't know," she answered honestly. "I've hated you for so long that I just don't know how I'm supposed to feel anymore." Pain reflected in her eyes.

Seeing her standing there, looking lost, confused, no longer the sharp-tongued adversary, Michael's heart swelled with all the feelings of the past. He then remembered what she had told him last night, and drew himself out of bed and walked up to her, clasping each of her hands in his.

"I'm so sorry," he said, staring deeply into her eyes.

"Sorry?" Dani looked confused.

"For you, for me, for the baby we both would have loved so much. I'm sorry I wasn't there. That you went through so much pain without me. I'm so, so sorry, Dani."

Dani could no longer contain her emotions. Tears enveloped her as she clung to Miguel, holding him tightly. She had waited eighteen years to hear those words, never really believing she would. And here he was, in her arms, soothing away her tears, telling her all the while how sorry he was for all he had done to hurt her.

Michael held her close, feeling her warmth through her silk pajamas. All he wanted was to hold her, to ease away the pain and hate she'd held in her heart for so long. As she shook with sobs against him, he caressed her hair and held her tight, just as she had done for him the night before. He wanted to soothe away her nightmare as she had his.

Finally, eyes red and swollen, Dani pulled away. "I'm sorry, Miguel," she said hoarsely as tears still spilled from her eyes. "I just can't seem to stop."

He smiled back at her but she could see tears in his eyes, too. He really was sorry. He'd been hurt too, she realized.

Dani grabbed some tissues from the box on the counter and finally attempted to pull herself together. As she blew her nose, Michael chuckled a bit and sat down on one of the barstools by the kitchen counter.

"What's so funny?" Dani asked while wiping her eyes.

"I was just thinking that you're the only person who still calls me Miguel," he said. "And you know what?"

"What?"

"I like it."

Dani smiled and walked over to the patio doors. "The storm's over," she said, still wiping away the last of her tears. "But it sure made a mess of everything," she noted, looking out at the fallen trees and branches everywhere in the streets and on the sidewalks. Already, there were crews of city workers out there clearing up the mess.

Michael walked over and stood beside her. "Maybe we can do some clearing up of our own," he suggested. And Dani nodded agreement as the two stood quietly together in the sunlight.

Chapter Thirteen

Later that day, cleaned up and dry-eyed, Dani and Michael sat in a corner booth of a restaurant ordering lunch. Luckily, neither Dani's car nor the one Michael had rented had been harmed by the storm. Only a few leaves and branches had fallen, no trees. Michael had decided, and Dani agreed, to stay the day and give them a chance to talk over all the questions still between them.

After the waitress had taken their order and left them with a full pot of coffee, Dani asked the question most prominent on her mind. The one question that had been eating away at her all these years.

"Why did you leave so suddenly? No warning. No word at all?"

Michael sighed. "God that seems so long ago, yet like only yesterday. My father had a massive heart attack and died. My mother called me and insisted I come home, for good. I either had to come back and take over the family business or give up the family completely. Well, my mother could be a pretty persuasive person when she wanted to. She was a real tough lady. But she had instilled family loyalty into me, and deep down, I knew I couldn't run away from my obligations any longer. Besides, I had Vanessa to consider, too." He watched as Dani nodded, absorbing it all, then he continued.

"I decided I had to make a clean sweep of everything, so I packed up what little we had and left." He reached across the table and took Dani's hand in his. "Believe me, I did think about you and how my leaving might affect you. But you were so young. I honestly believed it was better for us to make a clean break. I thought then you'd have a better chance of forgetting me, even if it meant hating me for leaving. You'd go off to school and eventually find someone else and do all the things you should be doing. Things I couldn't offer you at the time. If I had only known..." his voice trailed off.

"Would it have made a difference?"

"I don't know," he answered honestly. "I was a different person then, not very reliable, still hooked on pot and suffering the aftershock of Vietnam. I really don't know how I would have reacted. And I'm not very proud of admitting that either." Michael shook his head and released his grip on her hand, grasping his coffee mug instead. Those years had been a mess of pot and booze and women with Dani being the only bright light in it all.

"But I did straighten myself out when I got back to New York and into the business," he continued. "I really had no choice but to do so, and my mother made sure of it. Then, when I finally realized the business was a legacy I could leave to Vanessa, that's when I began to put all my energy into it. It finally made sense to me why my father and grandfather had worked so hard. It wasn't for the money, or the business itself. It was to be able to leave the next generation something better than they had known. For the first time in my life, I had a goal and a purpose that was worthwhile, and it felt good."

The waitress brought their sandwiches and left again. It was late afternoon and the restaurant was quiet. Dani stared out the large, plate-glass window beside her that viewed the busy street and tree-lined sidewalk. Everywhere there were traces of the storm, and people busy working to clean the mess up. After taking a few bites of her food, she once again turned to Miguel.

"Where is your mother now?"

"She died a couple of years after my dad. I was born late in their lives, so they were up in years." Michael stopped a moment, his eyes far away, then turned back to Dani. "You know, I really did the right thing going back. My mother was happy to see me take over and proud of the work I was doing. She also had a chance to know Vanessa. When she died, I knew she was content with the way things turned out. I can live with myself knowing that."

Dani nodded. "Yes, you did the right thing. I only wish I'd known, at the time. It would have saved me a lot of years of regret."

"I'm sorry, Dani. I know that doesn't change things, but please believe me, I'm sorry." Michael's face looked pained again, like it had earlier when he'd professed how sorry he was. "I wish I could do something, anything, to make it all better. I would give anything to do that for you."

"You have already," Dani said softly. "By telling me what happened, by being sorry for the past. That's all I could ask for. It really has helped."

Michael stared across the table at Dani for a few seconds, his pained expression turning soft, relieved, then the two finished their meal in comfortable silence. The stretch of years since their last relationship seemed to fade and the warmth of that time slowly emerged. As they ate, both were remembering the smiles, the happiness, and the love they had felt for each other.

They left the restaurant with Dani driving and she took Miguel on a tour of the city. He'd been to Minneapolis on business several times, but never had he seen its sights. They ended up wandering through the Mall of America, walking from shop to shop, level to level, and stopping for a while above the indoor amusement park to watch the people on the rides. Seeing parents with their children waiting in line for rides reminded them of the times they'd taken Vanessa to the small amusement park near his apartment, and they reminisced about the fun they'd shared there.

Sometime during their wanderings, they began holding hands like the younger couples they passed in the corridor. By the time Dani realized it, she felt so warm and comfortable with his touch that she didn't say a word, only continued holding his hand and smiling up at him occasionally. His gray eyes were bright with excitement and she loved the way they sparkled each time he looked at her.

On the third level, they passed a small jewelry store and stopped to look in the display window. Michael noticed a small, costume jewelry pin that depicted a blonde woman wearing a long, red coat, its buttons made of tiny rubies. He chuckled a little and pointed it out to Dani. "That looks like it was made for you," he said slyly.

Dani glanced at the pin and glared at him. "Don't get me started on that again," she said, her eyes teasing his.

But Michael just laughed. "I still think you need that coat," he told her.

Dani shook her head at him and continued to walk on with Michael trailing after her. They decided to go up to the fourth floor and check out Planet Hollywood to see if they might be able to get in and take a look. Luckily, because it was still afternoon, they beat the evening crowd and were able to get a table against the wall and they had drinks and a quick snack. Again, they sat in comfortable silence as they people-watched and admired the movie memorabilia surrounding them on the walls. Finally, they made their way back to the enormous parking lot and headed north to Dani's apartment.

It was early evening and Highway 169 North running through the affluent suburb of Edina was aglow with light. Dani popped in an old Eagles tape and they drove awhile listening to the lyrics they both knew so well.

"Remember the first time we heard this song?" Michael interrupted as "Lying Eyes" began playing through the speakers. "It was the very first time we went out together, alone, without Vanessa."

"I remember," Dani said as a smile of reminiscence touched her lips. "We went driving along Highway 1 and stopped at the wharf for a hot dog and fries. Then we took a walk on the beach."

Michael looked over at Dani, happy to see the memory didn't bring sorrow to her face. "It was a cool day. The wind was blowing, and you borrowed my sweatshirt to keep yourself warm." He chuckled warmly. "After you went home, I put that sweatshirt back on to feel close to you. It still had your scent."

Dani sighed. "You know, it took me a few years after you left to be able to listen to this song without crying. Crazy, huh?"

Michael reached across the automatic stick that separated their seats and placed his hand on her leg. "No. Not crazy," he told her. They rode the rest of the way back to her apartment this way, with his hand warm on her thigh.

* * *

As they walked into her apartment door, Michael hesitated a bit.

"What's the matter?" Dani asked, noticing the falter in his step.

"Well, I was just thinking that maybe you might want me to get a hotel tonight."

"You might as well stay here again," she said, seeing the pleasure spring up in his eyes. "On the couch, of course," she added.

Michael closed the door and walked into the room behind Dani, his eyebrows raised. "Oh," was all he said. He tilted his head a bit and scratched the side of his beard. Dani laughed at his reaction.

"You didn't think things had changed that much, did you?" she teased.

"Oh, no, the couch is fine," Michael said.

"Help yourself to a soda or water," Dani told him as she walked toward her bedroom. "I'm going to get out of these jeans and into some comfy sweats."

Michael walked over to the refrigerator, opened it, and took out a cola, then wandered back to the couch.

"Why don't you pick out a movie from my tapes under the television?" Dani suggested from behind the bedroom door. "I can make some popcorn in a minute."

"Okay." Michael opened the cabinet and began rummaging through the tapes. He was amused by the diverse selection she had.

"What's that smirk for?" Dani asked, heading toward the kitchen in gray sweat pants and a Minnesota Vikings sweatshirt.

"I was just admiring your collection of video tapes." He pulled out an old movie. "What is it with you women and Bogart?"

Dani gave him a wry smile as she placed a bag of popcorn in the microwave and beeped the timer. "What's wrong with Bogart? And what do you mean 'you women'?"

"Just that you and Cathy have the same tapes. What's so hot about Bogart?"

Dani shook her head at him as if he were a child who would never understand. "It's not just Bogart," she told him, walking over and placing her elbows on the back of the couch that stood between them. "It's the whole Bogie and Bacall thing. The way they look at each other. The sly smiles between them that make you think they're sharing a secret. There's just a special energy between them like no other couple ever had."

Dani sighed, her eyes dreamy. "As for Bogart, he's sexy in

his own way. He has the look of someone who is mean or angry, but when he smiles, his face opens up and his eyes brighten like a little boy. And when he smiles at Bacall," Dani sighed again and just left it at that.

Michael pulled out another tape and flashed it at Dani. "What about Stallone?" he asked.

Dani laughed. "*Rambo* is left over from an old boyfriend. I guess he forgot to take that one with him."

Michael's brows lifted. "Old boyfriend? Should I be jealous?"

"What? Did you think I'd been living like a nun all these years? There have been other men." The microwave beeped and Dani went to get the popcorn. "Why don't you put in *Key Largo*? I haven't seen that one in a long time."

"Women," Michael said good-naturedly under his breath. He took out the tape and popped it in, then sat down on the couch and hit play on the remote. Dani came back into the room with the bowl of popcorn and a bottle of spring water for herself. Watching her sit down beside him, Michael couldn't help but notice she looked good, even in sweats. She had taken her hair out of its French braid and it fell loosely around her shoulders. She looked warm and inviting, but he forced himself not to bridge the few inches that separated them.

"I love this movie," Dani said between mouthfuls of popcorn. "The little innuendoes, and the looks that pass between Bogie and Bacall. I love it almost as much as *Casablanca*."

"Yeah, you and Cathy both," Michael said, scooping up a handful of buttery popcorn and tossing it into his mouth.

Dani chuckled. "Cathy and I were both old movie freaks in college. We'd stay up late and watch the old movie channel then have to skip our morning class in order to get some sleep. When movies came out on video, we both had to have copies."

"Ah, so that's how you both ended up with the same tapes,

huh? Except Cathy doesn't have any Stallone ones."

Dani gave Michael a sideways look and threw a piece of popcorn at him, making them both laugh. They settled into a comfortable silence, watching the movie a while. After a time, Dani broke the silence.

"Why did you break it off with Cathy?"

"Me?" Michael looked confused. "I didn't break it off with Cathy. It was her idea."

Dani stared at him. "Why?"

He sat a moment, collecting his thoughts before answering. "She wanted more out of the relationship than I could offer. We had a lot of good times, but I wasn't ready to make it permanent." He sighed a little. "I haven't changed all that much, I guess."

"Do you still have feelings for her?" She had to know. After all, Cathy was her best friend and she didn't want any hard feelings between them now that she and Miguel had rekindled their friendship.

"Cathy is a great person and I'll always care about her. But she and I are just friends now, nothing more. Besides," he added, "she's seeing that accountant guy now and they seem to be hitting it off fairly well."

Dani's eyebrows rose as she looked at him. "And you're okay with that?"

"Of course. I want her to be happy."

Dani turned her attention back to the movie, but her heart was dancing a little. And it beat even faster, when a few minutes later, Michael reached past the popcorn bowl and took her hand in his. He just held it, occasionally rubbing his thumb along the side of her palm, a simple gesture of familiarity. It felt warm and sweet, like the movie they were sharing, and Dani appreciated the fact that he was letting her decide just how far things would go between them tonight.

Chapter Fourteen

When the movie ended, Dani sighed and stretched as Michael hit the off button on the control. Taking the bowl and her empty water bottle, she walked over to the kitchen and set them on the counter, flicked off the light over the stove, and headed back to stand beside the couch. Michael was still sitting in the corner of it, watching her.

For a moment their eyes connected. "Well," she finally said. "It's pretty late. I guess I'll go to bed."

Michael only looked at her, no expression reflecting his thoughts.

"Do you want me to help you get the couch ready?" she offered, uneasy as to how to end the evening.

"No. That's okay. I can do it myself."

"Okay." She walked a few steps toward the bedroom, hesitated, and then looked back. "Do you mind if I use the bathroom first? I promise I won't be long."

"That's fine. Take your time."

Dani nodded. "Okay. Well, goodnight."

"Goodnight."

She walked the rest of the way into the bedroom and closed the door behind her.

Michael watched her the entire time, his elbow leaning on the arm of the sofa with his face propped up in his hand. He heard the door to the bathroom close and the water running in the sink, and he sighed at the closed door. He lifted himself off the couch, slid over the television on its rolling cabinet, and began making up the sofa bed for the night.

Dani entered the bathroom from the door in her bedroom and softly closed the hall entrance before turning on the tap to wash the day's makeup off her face. She quickly creamed and rinsed, then stared at her reflection for a moment as she dried the last of the water drops from her skin.

She couldn't help but wonder if she was doing the right thing, and it made her angry to be so indecisive about her feelings. She always knew what she wanted, and rarely had a second thought about it. But with Miguel, it was different. In only a twenty-four hour period, she'd had a complete change of emotions for him, from hatred to caring again, from coldness to warmth. There was no doubt about it that the old feelings for him had revived as soon as the hatred had melted away. The way he'd held her hand today as they walked in the mall, and tonight during the movie, had opened her heart to him again like no other gesture could have. But how could she even think of spending the night with him in her bed after only one day?

Dani shook her head to clear her thoughts and finished her nighttime routine, rubbing lotion over her face and brushing her teeth. She tossed the towel and washcloth into the wicker hamper and opened the hallway door to let Miguel know she was done before heading into her bedroom and closing her door to the bathroom behind her.

Walking to the window, she stared out at the quiet sky that only the night before had been howling and screaming with rain and thunder. Now the stars shone brightly in the cool fall air, and she watched them a moment, again thinking about the turn of events from the night before. She closed the open window, pulled the curtains shut, and walked over to her dresser to take out a nightgown and change for bed.

From the bathroom, she could here sounds of water

running as Miguel readied for bed, and she smiled into the dresser mirror as she pulled the short, peach colored satin nightgown over her head. It was a simple slip style, loose and flowing from its thin straps that crisscrossed in back. Twirling once in front of the mirror, making the skirt rise and fall from her thighs, she wondered if Miguel would think she was sexy in this. Then she got mad at herself for even thinking it and turned down the bed, determined to go to sleep.

The bathroom door squeaked as Miguel went back out to the couch. Dani sat in her semi-dark room with only the light from the bedside lamp on, wondering if he was in bed yet, remembering how they had slept together the night before and how warm and comforting it had felt. Sitting on her bed, her back against the pillows, she tucked her legs up under her nightgown and hugged them close, thinking, and thinking some more, about Miguel and the feelings that were growing within her. Was it really possible that her feelings could change so quickly? Could she really believe him when he said that he still cared?

Thoughts of the past enveloped her, and she indulged her senses with them. The touch of his thick, silky hair through her fingers. His strong, bare arms holding her close. The tickle of his beard as he kissed the hollow of her neck. With a deep intake of breath, she allowed herself to remember it all, and as she did, she finally knew what she wanted and what was right. Dani knew that she wouldn't regret her decision, no matter what the outcome in the morning. With her resolve leading her, she quietly padded across the bedroom floor, opened the door, and took two steps into the hall with her hand extended toward Miguel.

Michael had been standing beside the couch, shirtless and barefoot, wearing only jeans, poised to turn out the light before getting into bed when he heard Dani's door open and saw her standing before him, her hand offered out to him. He didn't need to ask what it meant, he knew what she was saying to him, and although it took him by surprise, it seemed so natural to walk toward her, take her hand in his and follow her into the bedroom.

Together, hand in hand, they entered the bedroom, and Dani stopped when they reached the side of her bed and turned to face Michael. They stood that way a moment, quietly facing each other holding hands. Finally, slowly, Michael bent to place his lips on Dani's and they kissed softly, lips barely touching before he pulled away only inches from her face.

"Are you sure?" he asked huskily, his breathing making his chest rise and fall against her breasts.

"Yes," Dani said as she stared into those warm gray eyes. The same eyes she thought of as cold steel only days before.

Again, Michael lowered his head toward hers, but this time his kiss became more demanding as his hands let go of hers and slowly found their way up her arms to the bareness of her shoulders. Dani slid her arms around his neck, returning his kisses and embrace with equal intensity, their bodies fitting together perfectly as they had so many years ago.

When the kiss ended, Michael once again pulled away slightly, but this time only to look at Dani as he slowly slid the straps of her nightgown from her shoulders. As the silky gown crumpled to the floor, he took a sharp intake of breath at the sight before him. She was as beautiful as he remembered, even more so as maturity had filled out the places that youth had not yet fully developed. Slowly, he kissed her neck, trailing his lips down over her shoulders to the full, curved tips of her breasts. His hands explored each curve first before his lips followed, moving from her breasts, down across her firm stomach, and finally reaching the warm, loving spot that was waiting for him. Gently, his hands slid down her satin panties, and those, too, fell to the floor to join the nightgown at her feet.

On his knees in front of her, he kissed the very part of her that wanted him most, and a low moan escaped from Dani's lips as he explored her with his tongue, his hands caressing the back of her legs.

Yes, Dani thought, this was how she remembered it, and she tilted her head back and allowed herself the pure pleasure of his touch as her fingers ran through his silky hair. The warmth of his tongue filled her and flowed up through her entire body until she could stand it no longer and wanted to feel his full body pressed against her own.

Gently, she pulled him up and pressed her entire length against him as he continued kissing her neck, face and lips. Running her hands over his chest and stomach, she explored the tightness under her fingertips, then tugged at the upper buttons of his jeans, loosening them enough to reach her hands inside and feel his firmness. Her breasts pressed tightly against his chest while her hands explored him freely as their breathing became stronger and more intense until neither one could contain themselves and the feelings they were evoking.

Michael gently eased Dani onto the bed and quickly undid the rest of the buttons on his jeans, eased out of them, then joined her. Together they caressed and fondled, kissed, nipped, and held each other until both needed to end the torture of wanting.

As Michael slid his full length above Dani, he stopped a moment and studied her face. She smiled and brought her hands up to his face, tracing the outline of his jaw with her fingers through the silkiness of his beard. The gesture was so simple, yet it melted his heart as her fingers slowly made their way across his jawline and down his neck, her own eyes smiling up at him.

He bent his head low. "Do you have protection?" he whispered into her ear.

Dani had to clear the fog from her head a moment before she realized what he meant. She smiled and pointed to the nightstand drawer. Michael leaned over and opened it, pulling out a small blue packet from a box inside the drawer. His eyes sparkled with amusement as he looked from the packet, then back to her.

"Left over from the Stallone boyfriend?" he asked, teasingly.

Dani chuckled warmly. "Jealous?"

Michael leaned over her and softly kissed the hollow of her throat. "No. Because I'm with you now."

Dani reached up her arms. "Here," she told him, taking the packet from his hands. Quickly, she opened it and ever-so-slowly rolled it over him.

Michael reached out and ran his fingers through her hair, a moan escaping his lips as she did it. Then, finally, both joined together in the pleasant release of body and spirit.

* * *

Later, they both lay in the quiet room, curled under the cotton quilt. Michael had turned out the light on his way back from the bathroom and lay beside Dani, his left leg lying possessively over her. Strands of city lights from below filtered through the edges of the curtains, illuminating the room just enough so Michael could study Dani's face as they lay facing each other.

Dani seemed unaware of his searching eyes as she unconsciously followed the trail of the scar that ran up Miguel's leg. She knew its winding path perfectly, like a river beginning at the knee and zigzagging down to the ankle where it ended in a large expanse of scarred skin like a river flows into the wide ocean. This was his legacy of Vietnam, the scar that held together the leg that he had almost lost. It was proof that his nightmares were real, proof that would never let him forget his tour in hell.

Michael continued watching Dani's face, savoring the way her hair framed it and the smoothness of her skin in the semi-darkness. Her expression was tender and caring, reflecting the way she was touching his leg now, as she had so many times in the past. She had accepted his pain without flinching or being horrified by it, so unlike any other woman he'd known. Even though she had been so young, she'd been more woman than any other who'd passed through his life.

He reached over and brushed the hair away from her face, tracing it behind her ear, making her turn her soft eyes toward his. "What are you thinking?" he asked quietly.

She continued to trace her finger up and down his leg as she answered him. "I'm two-thousand miles away, eighteen years in the past, lying in a bed in a small apartment where I spent the happiest time of my life." Her eyes reflected her trip into the past, all hazy and misty.

"Those were happy times," he told her, running his hand down her bare arm and stopping to hold the hand that was touching his leg. Together they made the slow trip up and down the river.

"Do you really remember much about our time together, or are your memories just a haze of me and all the other women who passed through your life?" She wasn't angry or accusing, only searching for the truth.

Michael rolled over onto his back and Dani's hand trailed and stopped to rest on the inside of his thigh. She cocked her elbow and rested her head in her hand, staring down at Miguel as he studied the ceiling. But his expression was not as she had expected. His lips had a touch of a smile on them, and his eyes sparkled in the dim light.

"I remember the first time I saw you in regular clothes, not that silly green uniform you wore at work," he said. "You were heading out the diner door into the May sunshine, wearing tight bell-bottomed jeans, platform sandals, and the tiniest yellow tank top with ties going up the front. And I remember thinking how much I'd like to see it untied."

"Which you did," she commented slyly.

He turned his head a little towards her and continued. "I remember the first time I took you to the beach alone, without Vanessa. It was windy and cold and you borrowed my sweatshirt as we walked along the shoreline. All I could do was look at you with your golden hair blowing back, the sweatshirt billowing around you, and I wished I was that sweatshirt, encircling you."

"I remember the first time we made love," he continued softly. "And how sweet you looked, yet so inviting, and how scared I was that I might hurt you. How for the first time in my life, I wanted to protect someone, thought of someone else's feelings over my own. Like the way I felt tonight. That I wanted you, yet I wanted to protect you from any harm that might come your way."

Touched by what he'd said, tears stung Dani's eyes and spilled uncensored down her cheeks. Never had she known how deeply he'd felt for her. Never had she dared dream he had feelings for her at all.

"You really do remember," she whispered, and Michael reached up and brushed away a tear that rolled down her cheek.

"Yes," he said. "And I always will." Then, slowly, he pulled her into his arms as together they found the passion between them again. The passion that had never really died even in the disguise of hate. The passion that only two people who knew each other completely could share.

Chapter Fifteen

The morning sun peeked through the edges of the curtains and spread its warm long fingers across Dani's back as she lay under the quilt. She opened one eye slightly, then turned her head in the other direction, snuggling deeper under the blankets, wanting to return to the dream that had drifted through her sleep.

In her hazy, half-asleep state, she wondered if last night had been a dream. At some point during the night, she thought she'd awakened to see Miguel staring down at her, gently stroking the side of her cheek. *I love you.* The words had come softly from his lips, then he'd curled up beside her and fallen to sleep as she, too, drifted off. Had it been a dream?

Eyes still closed, she reached over toward the other side of the bed but found it empty, the spot no longer warm. The faint smell of toast drifted into the bedroom, along with coffee and another aroma she couldn't quite identify. Dani sighed and smiled, knowing immediately where Miguel had gone to, and once again drifted toward sleep.

Michael padded into the bedroom and tucked one window curtain behind the window's turnstile handle, allowing the room to fill with warm, golden rays. Standing as he had the night before, in jeans only with the top button undone, he crossed his arms over his broad chest and smiled. "Hey, wake up sleepyhead."

Dani turned her head toward him, opened her eyes, and let them adjust to the light that spilled in from the window. She saw

Miguel standing there, the sunlight outlining his body and glistening through the silky darkness of his rumpled hair. "Good morning," she said, her eyes half-closed.

"Good morning yourself. Breakfast is almost ready, so don't move out of that bed. I'm bringing it to you."

"Can I pee?"

Michael rubbed his hand through his beard as he pretended to ponder that for a moment. "Okay," he said in mock stern voice. "But then you get right back into that bed, you hear?" He turned and left the room as Dani watched him, admiring the slight ripple that appeared along the expanse of his back as he walked away.

Once he was gone, she reached over the side of the bed and retrieved the nightie that lay rumpled on the floor, then headed to the bathroom while slipping it over her head.

Looking into the mirror, she grimaced at what stared back at her and picked up her brush to try and mend the damage as best she could. After doing what she had intended, she re-entered the bedroom and smoothed the sheets and blankets into place, propped her pillows up, and crawled in under the quilt, smoothing it as she sat there, waiting.

Michael entered balancing a tray that held one large plate, a smaller plate with a pile of toast, two steaming mugs of coffee, and two glasses of orange juice.

"Here," he said, handing her the tray. "Hold on tight." He walked to the other side of the bed and, in one smooth motion, planted himself next to her, crossing his legs at the ankles, a pleased expression on his face.

Dani liked the way his eyes sparkled at her as he took the tray from her lap and placed it in the small space between them. When he smiled like that, he looked no different from the man she knew years ago. It was an incredibly youthful smile.

"Smells good," she told him as she assessed the meal. "But

only one omelet?"

"There was only enough cheese for one," he told her, handing her a fork. "Besides, it's big. I figured we could share."

Dani took her fork, cut off an end piece, and placed it in her mouth. The eggs were so fluffy they melted away along with the cheese. "Hmm, this is great," she said after savoring it thoroughly.

"Of course it's great," Michael said, putting an extra large slice into his own mouth. "I made it."

"Oh, modest aren't we?"

Michael shrugged. "When you're good, you're good."

Rolling her eyes, Dani continued eating, enjoying every mouthful and watching Miguel enjoy his own. It felt comfortable being together like this, sharing breakfast and a few stolen smiles. Dani couldn't remember ever feeling this comfortable with anyone else she'd been with. Never had there been the easy silences or carefree banter. She wondered briefly why it was like this with only Miguel.

"So," she finally said after taking a small bite of toast. "What's the game plan for today?"

"Whatever you'd like. Just so we're back here by three o'clock."

Dani cocked an eyebrow. "Why? What happens at three? You turn into a pumpkin?"

"If I keep eating like this, I probably will," Michael teased. "No. I made a plane reservation for five, so I have to get my stuff and to the airport in time to catch it."

"Oh," Dani tried to hide her disappointment and reached for her glass of juice to keep her hands busy. But Michael saw her expression drop and clasped her hand before it reached the glass.

"That doesn't mean it's the end, you know. This isn't like before, I promise. It's just that I've been away for three days and

I have to get back to the office."

"Sure, I understand. I have to be to work early tomorrow, too." Dani hesitated, her hand still held tightly in his. She wanted to believe this wasn't going to be the end but she couldn't bring herself to completely believe it. She'd known what she was doing when she started this last night, so she'd better handle it like an adult.

It was as if Michael could read her thoughts. While still holding her hand, he peeked at her downturned face, making her look up into his eyes.

"How about next weekend? You could fly over to Chicago, and I could return the hospitality." He smiled at her and it eased the tension of the moment.

Dani took her hand back and shifted a bit in the bed to get comfortable again, but her hand touched something under the covers and she pulled it out into the open. Recognizing the empty blue packet, she blushed a bit. "Seems we missed the trash can with this one," she said, staring at it.

Michael only chuckled, but Dani continued studying the crumpled packet. Finally, she looked from it to him.

"Do you worry about that?" she asked. "I mean, well, you know, about AIDS? After all those women you were with years ago. Do you ever think about it?"

"I did worry about it a few years ago when AIDS came into the open," he said honestly. "That's why I had myself tested. I'm one of the lucky ones, it came back negative." He tried to read her face but couldn't. "What about you?"

"I was worried, too, after knowing you'd been with so many others, and also after that botched abortion. I was tested. Negative."

"Well," Michael brightened a bit. "Now we know we don't have to worry about these." He took the packet from her and tossed it into the trash can beside the bed.

"Why did you, last night, if you knew you were HIV negative?" Dani asked, looking puzzled.

"Because I didn't want you to think I was taking anything for granted. I'm not, you know. Not one minute of the time we spend together. You know that, don't you?" He leaned over the tray of dirty dishes and breadcrumbs and lightly kissed her lips.

When the kiss ended, Dani studied his face a moment, leaving the question unanswered. Michael took that for a yes.

"Well, why don't you go shower and I'll do these dishes. Maybe we could go down to that lake I saw near here yesterday and feed the ducks or something."

"Sounds good to me."

But the dishes never were washed because no sooner had the water begun to run over Dani's body, then Miguel joined her. Not that she minded, because she enjoyed the company.

They spent a lazy afternoon sitting on the shore of Lake Harriet throwing breadcrumbs to the ducks and Canadian Geese that still littered the waters, fattening up for their upcoming trip south. The sun shone brightly across the water and on the sand, but the air held the crisp beginnings of fall in its breeze which made little difference to the couple as they walked the shore hand in hand.

Michael bought ice-cream cones from a bicycle vender and they enjoyed their treat while giving each other sideways glances and smiles. They felt young and carefree and happy without a problem in the world between them, and neither wanted the afternoon to end.

But the day did end as they entered through Dani's apartment door once more. Michael silently put his few belongings into his small suitcase while Dani busied herself with the few dishes left over from breakfast. The clock ticked away their time together until they could no longer put off the goodbyes that had to be said.

Dani placed the dishtowel on the counter and walked up to where Michael stood over his suitcase, not knowing what to do next.

"Do you want me to drive you to the airport?" she asked hopefully. It would give them a little more time together.

"No. I have the rented car, remember?"

"Oh, that's right." Together they stood, only inches from each other, neither touching nor speaking. Finally, Michael reached both hands up and cupped her face in them. His eyes reached out to hers, as if trying to tell her all the feelings inside him as words could not. Dani could feel the intensity of his stare, returning it, cupping her own hand over his and caressing it lightly. She wanted to believe he was feeling everything she felt. She truly wanted to. Yet, a small shadow of doubt crept up on her that this could be the last goodbye.

"I'll see you soon, Dani-girl," he said quietly, using the endearment of long ago that nearly melted her heart. "I'll call you as soon as I get to my place. Okay?"

Dani could only nod in reply, and ever so slowly, Michael drew her to him and placed a soft kiss on her lips.

"I'll call," he whispered, their lips still touching. "I promise." Then, pulling away, he picked up his bag, slung his coat over his arm, and headed to the door.

Dani watched him open the door and turn once more in the doorframe, flashing her one of those boyish smiles.

"Goodbye."

"Goodbye."

The door closed and he was gone.

Still standing in the spot where he had kissed her, Dani stared at the door for a full minute before turning slowly and aimlessly walking toward her bedroom. She didn't try looking out the window to catch a glimpse of him driving away. She no longer felt happy and carefree as she had just an hour ago. She only felt empty and alone.

But when she entered the bedroom, she was surprised to see a small, wrapped box lying on the nightstand. She approached it gingerly, then lifted it and turned it over in her hands. Finally, she unwrapped the paper and opened the lid and there, staring back at her, was the enamel art deco pin of the blonde lady in the red coat. Dani let out a small laugh that eased the tension within her as feelings of elation began to take over the ones of emptiness only moments before.

Inside the box was also a note, which she opened and read.

I still think the red coat would look great on you. Love, Miguel.

Nothing else could have brought such sheer joy to her as this small gift and note. Dani hugged the pin to her heart and twirled three times, laughing and smiling to herself before falling back onto her bed. All her doubts were cast aside, and she knew right then and there what the first thing she was going to do the minute she got to work tomorrow.

Chapter Sixteen

Michael reached Minneapolis-St. Paul International Airport without a hitch and deposited his rental car before going through the usual procedures to board his flight. Once on the commuter plane to Chicago, he settled in for the one-hour flight.

The plane was mostly filled with business men and women dressed in black, gray, or navy suits, and Michael looked out of place in his jeans and sweater. When a man in a navy suit sat beside him and looked him over once then turned his attention to his laptop computer, Michael smiled. At least he didn't have to worry about having a talker beside him, and he watched out the window as the plane took flight.

He wondered if Dani had found the surprise he'd left for her, and what her reaction had been. He would have loved to see her face when she opened it, but he had to be satisfied with hearing about it on the phone when he got home to his apartment.

He still couldn't believe how the weekend had turned around for them. Never in his wildest dreams would he have thought they'd have come this far, this fast, but he was so happy they had. Already, he was making mental notes about what they would do when she visited him next weekend, the places he would take her, and the time they'd spend alone. For the first time in years, he felt excited about this new relationship. Everything felt so right this time. No one had ever made him feel this good before. At least not for eighteen years.

Feeling excited for the first time in years, he couldn't wait to tell Vanessa. He knew she'd be happy to hear that he and Dani were together. And Cathy. How would she take it? He'd have to feel that one out first. But it didn't matter, he felt great. For the first time in years, he felt he was actually in love.

Yes, he admitted to himself, he was in love. He knew it as surely now as he had last night when he'd rolled over and looked at Dani's sleeping face. He'd gently stroked her cheek and the words had come out so effortlessly that he had even surprised himself. *I love you.* He wondered if she had heard him, and decided that he would make sure she did this weekend.

The plane landed at O'Hare International and Michael collected his bag and found his car in the short-term parking lot. The trip through the suburbs of Chicago to his apartment building was short, and he walked through the door with only one thing on his mind. He would call Dani right away and let her know he meant every word he'd said. This time was different from the past.

Dropping his bag on the entryway floor, he crossed the room while depositing his coat over the leather sofa and headed to the desk where the telephone sat. He saw the light blinking on his answering machine and smiled to himself. Maybe she'd already tried calling him. With a touch of the button he listened to the taped messages as he searched through his wallet for Dani's number.

Beep. Michael, this is Cathy. Something's come up. Please call me as soon as you get in. It's Sunday, about 1:00 p.m. Call me, please.

Whatever Cathy wanted to tell him could wait, Michael thought as he found the scrap of paper containing Dani's number.

Beep. Michael, it's Cathy again. Please, give me a call. It's important. Michael glanced at the machine as the second message played. Cathy's voice sounded strained, almost frantic. What could be so important?

Beep. Michael. Please call me. I have to talk to you.

Michael tensed at this last message. Cathy sounded nearly hysterical. "I'd better call her first," he mumbled to himself, but before he could lift the phone off its cradle, the doorbell rang, and he heard keys rattling in the door.

"Jesus, what the..." The door opened as he reached it and Cathy almost walked right into him.

"Oh, thank God," she said, as Michael caught her before she trampled him.

"Hey, kiddo. What's up? I was just going to call you back."

"Oh, Michael. I've been trying to get you all weekend. I finally gave up and decided to come look for you myself. I still had my key, so I just used it," she paused, breathless. "Oh, Michael. I'm so glad you're here."

Her face was drawn and pale as if she hadn't slept in days. Concern crept into Michael's voice as he shut the door and led her to the sofa. "What is it, Cathy? What's going on? Are you all right?"

Cathy looked up at Michael with tired eyes.

"It's not me," she said gently, but then the anxiety of the moment overwhelmed her and she blurt out at once. "Michael, it's Vanessa. She's been in a terrible accident, and she's at the hospital in Southampton. The hospital tried reaching you at work and I got the message and have been trying to get ahold of you since yesterday."

The blood drained from Michael's face and his lips turned pale. "Vanessa," he said, not quite registering the information Cathy was giving him.

"Yes, Vanessa. When I couldn't contact you, I called the hospital to find out what was going on. All they would tell me is she is in intensive care and is comatose. Since I'm not family, they wouldn't say any more about her condition. Oh, Michael," she said again, unable to continue. She placed her arms around him and hugged him close a moment before he pulled away, looking at her, puzzled.

"How? Why?"

Cathy kept a firm hold on his arms as she continued. "I talked with the police. It seems they were in a car accident Saturday night on their way home from a friend's house. The other driver swerved into their lane, and they crashed head-on. The other driver was drunk."

Michael couldn't seem to process what Cathy was saying. He could only think in single words.

"They?" he asked, confused. "Oh, God. Not Michelle, too!"

"No. Michelle is fine. She wasn't with them. She's at the Southampton house with Mrs. Carols. It was Matthew who was with her." Cathy hesitated, which only made the news harder to say. "I'm sorry, Michael. He didn't make it. He died on impact."

At this, Michael fell on the sofa behind him, clutching a fist to his lips, completely stunned. Matthew was dead. And Vanessa was in the hospital. What had Cathy said? In a coma? Oh, God, no.

Cathy sat down beside Michael and linked her arm through his. Together they sat in silence, staring at the patterns in the carpet, neither one speaking. Finally, it was Cathy who broke the silence.

"I've made plane reservations for you to Kennedy Airport and then on to East Hampton. I had to make several because I didn't know when I'd be able to contact you." She looked at her watch. "The next one leaves in an hour. If we hurry, you can catch it."

Michael only sat, still stunned by the news. Knowing she had little time to get him to where he was needed the most, Cathy persisted. "I'll pack a few things for you so you can get going.

And I'll drive you to O'Hare, it will be quicker that way." She rose to her feet but Michael caught her hand in his to stop her.

"No, Cathy," he said, suddenly coming to his senses. "I'm still packed from this weekend. I'll just take that." He motioned to the suitcase still sitting in the entryway. "Anything else I need I can get at the house."

Cathy nodded. "Good. Then let's get going. My car's out front."

But Michael still hung onto her hand and wouldn't let go. "Shouldn't I call the hospital first? Let them know I'm coming?"

"I'll do that for you as soon as I get you on that plane. I think it's more important for you to just get there."

"What about Matthew's parents?" Michael looked up at Cathy with pained eyes. He was still pale, and his eyes looked almost black against his skin.

"I'll call them, too, and let them know you're on the way." She reached her free hand out and clasped his in both of hers. "I'll come with you, if you want me to," she offered gently.

Michael was tempted to have her beside him through the long flight ahead and whatever else he'd have to face. But good sense told him where she really belonged.

"No. You'd better stay here and run things. The office will need you here, and I'll inform the New York division that you are in charge until further notice." Michael rose heavily to his feet, still clasping Cathy's hands. "Don't mention anything about the accident to anyone though. I don't want a bunch of reporters on this if I can help it."

Cathy nodded her understanding. Someone as affluent as Michael DeCara suffering a tragedy would make news. "I won't. Now, we really have to leave. Vanessa needs you."

Cathy was in complete charge all the way to O'Hare, and getting the tickets straight and Michael to the right gate on time. She filled him in on instructions of flights and a car waiting for him in East Hampton that would take him directly to the hospital. They reached the gate just as the plane was boarding, leaving little time for words of goodbye. But none were necessary, and Michael was grateful to Cathy for her devoted friendship.

He turned to hug her at the boarding gate. "Pray she'll be all right."

"I already am."

After a brief kiss on the cheek, and a look that only passes between the closest of friends, Michael boarded the plane that would take him to his daughter.

Chapter Seventeen

The two-hour flight to Kennedy International seemed endless. Michael sat in his seat, dazed, ignoring the people around him, and the attendant who kept asking if he wanted anything. *All I want is for my daughter to be all right.*

His mind wandered over the few facts that Cathy had given him. Saturday night. The car had crashed Saturday night. His daughter was being taken to the hospital, already a young widow, while he had slept on Dani's sofa. And Sunday, all day and into the night, he had enjoyed life to its fullest with Dani at his side while his own flesh and blood lay comatose, all alone in the hospital.

Guilt washed over him as a river over a waterfall. While he had been selfishly enjoying life, she had been immersed in death and pain. How could he ever shake the guilt of not being there when she needed him most?

Another thought hit him hard. Dani. He had to tell Dani. But how could he? She cared so much for Vanessa, even after all these years. No. It wasn't fair. How could he put all this pain on her after just having eased eighteen years of pain from her? He'd just wait and see how Vanessa was doing, and when she pulled out of it, he'd let Dani know. But what if Vanessa didn't make it? No, he wouldn't even allow himself to think about that possibility.

By the time the plane landed at Kennedy, it was ten-thirty at night and it was a weary, worn Michael who transferred to the small, four passenger plane that was waiting to take him to East Hampton. Twenty-five minutes later, he was in the waiting limousine and on the way to Southampton Hospital where he arrived just before midnight looking very much like a patient himself.

The time for visitors was long past but he was able to get past the receptionist at the front counter by explaining who he was. She directed him toward the ICU, down the long, florescent-lit corridor and to the left. Once there, he was again stopped by the nurse in charge. After explaining he was Michael DeCara, she led him to the main room where the intensive care patients were being monitored.

The halls were dimly lit, which gave an eerie feeling to the quiet halls. Together they passed through double doors that were marked "Hospital Personnel Only" and it was here that Michael had his first shock. Lined along the walls on both sides of him were beds with only curtains to separate them. Several were filled with patients, all unconscious or sleeping, and hooked up to machines, tubes, and IVs. Nurses in blue smocks were everywhere, keeping a constant vigil on the patients. The demanding beep of a heart monitor followed the pumping of his own heart.

The nurse touched his elbow and led him to a bed halfway down the aisle. The curtain was drawn around the three sides of the bed. "Wait here," she said quietly, before entering the curtained cubical alone. A moment later, another nurse came out with her. "Only a few minutes please," the first nurse told him softly. Then the two left him to enter the cubical alone.

Ever so slowly he stepped through the curtain opening, stopping short at the sight that greeted his eyes. He'd been to hell and back in Vietnam, but nothing he'd experienced there could have ever prepared him for the sight now before him. Here was his own flesh and blood, his beautiful little girl, hanging onto life by tubes and wires.

"Dear God," Michael said, as he slowly stepped toward the side of the bed, afraid that the slightest movement might disturb her lifelines. There were IV tubes everywhere, running into her arms and hands, one hooked up to her chest. An oxygen tube was strapped around her face, attached to her nostrils, and wires from the beeping heart monitor were streaming from her chest, out from under her hospital gown. But it wasn't the tubes and wires that disturbed him the most. A large patch of her beautiful auburn hair had been shaved from the side and back of her head, and replaced by bandages.

"What have they done to you?" he cried hoarsely, dropping to the chair that sat beside her bed as his eyes filled and blurred with tears. He swiped at them with the back of his sweater's sleeve and once again made himself look at his daughter. She seemed to be sleeping peacefully, despite the horror she was living. Carefully, he reached for her hand, gently placing his under it so as not to disturb the tube that was hooked into its back. Then, looking into her sleeping face, he said quietly, "Daddy's here honey. Everything's going to be all right." And he bent his head over her hand and let the tears flow.

* * *

Michael didn't know how long he'd sat that way until the nurse in the blue smock came and gently touched him on the shoulder. "Mr. DeCara," she whispered. "Mr. DeCara. You should go now, sir."

Michael raised his head slowly and looked into the nurse's warm, brown eyes. "No. I have to stay. Just a few minutes longer." His eyes were red-rimmed and he looked almost delirious.

The nurse kneeled down to his level and placed a hand on his shoulder. "You can't do anything for her tonight," she offered softly. "You can come back tomorrow and see her when you're rested."

When he made no effort to move, she tried again. "Please, Mr. DeCara. You won't do her any good by getting sick yourself. You need your strength for the days ahead. Please. It's late."

Michael looked down once again at Vanessa, finally realizing that the nurse was right. He slowly rose from his chair and stepped through the curtains with the nurse right behind him. He was so tired he suddenly felt a hundred years old, and his shoulders slumped as a world of heartache fell upon them.

He turned back to the nurse. "Tell me what's wrong with her," he said, trying to keep his voice controlled. "Why is she in a coma? Why is her head bandaged?" And then, pleadingly, "Will she live?"

The nurse looked at him steadily, the warmth still in her eyes. "She's been in a coma since she was brought in and the doctors had to operate to relieve the pressure that was building in her brain. That's really all I can tell you for now. Tomorrow, the doctors will be here and you can speak to them about her condition."

Seeing the desperation in his eyes she added. "She has been stable for the past twelve hours, and we might be able to transfer her into a room by tomorrow. That's a good sign."

Michael only stared at her, unable to say anything more. The nurse patted his shoulder again. "Go home, Mr. DeCara. Come back in the morning after you've slept. I promise, we'll take good care of her."

"Thank you," Michael said, and turned and walked down the aisle of beds and out through the double doors, out of the room that seemed to him to hold only death.

Chapter Eighteen

Michael awoke in his own bed in the Southampton house, not remembering how he got there in the first place. He remembered leaving the hospital and walking to the limousine still waiting for him, but his mind went numb after that. Yet, here he was. Vanessa lay in the hospital, Matthew was dead. It wasn't a bad dream. It was real.

Studying the familiar room around him did little to pacify his feelings of dread. The soft gray tones that once seemed soothing to him now looked morbid and forbidding. Gray curtains held the sunshine at bay from the large windows that flanked the four-poster bed, but he had no desire to let the flood of rays in, or to look out at the rolling ocean waves that so often soothed him.

He pulled himself up to a sitting position and ran his fingers through his hair as a great sigh escaped his lips. He was still tired, so very, very tired. Never in his life had he felt so weighted down from weariness. Yet, there was so much to do. He wanted to get to the hospital as soon as possible to check on Vanessa and talk with the doctors. But he also had to contact Matthew's parents about the funeral. That task seemed as unpleasant as the first. He'd grown to love Matthew like a son in the few short years he and Vanessa had been married. Burying him would be another tear in his soul.

He also had to call Cathy and let her know what was going on. And Dani. He should call Dani. Or should he? He pondered this as he forced himself out of bed and stared at his haggard face in the dresser mirror. Another sigh escaped him. How could he call Dani and lay all this pain on her now? He knew how she felt about Vanessa, and this would be a big blow to her. How could he do that to her after all the pain he'd caused her in the past?

No, he decided. He wouldn't drop this on her until he knew more about what was going on. Or until Vanessa's condition grew better. Then he would be able to let her know.

The very first thing he had to do was see Michelle. His face brightened a bit for the first time in twenty-four hours at the thought of his granddaughter. Yes. He'd see her and make sure she was safe and sound. She'd bring a smile back to his face and hope back to his heart. With that thought in mind, he walked across the plush gray carpet to his bathroom to clean up for the trying day ahead.

Less than thirty minutes later he encountered Mrs. Carols in the hallway on his way to the nursery. He had showered and put on clean jeans and a sweater, but his face still held the tired look of a man with pain in his heart. Mrs. Carols reached out a hand for his and held it warmly in her own.

"Oh, Mr. DeCara. I'm so glad you're home. We've all been so worried about Mrs. Chandler."

"Thank you, Mrs. Carols." Michael tried to smile at her, but it didn't reach his eyes. It seemed so hard just to smile. "I'm afraid I can't tell you much yet about her condition. It was late when I arrived last night so there was no one to talk with me about it. But I'll be going there first thing this morning."

Mrs. Carols nodded, slipping her hand from his. "Don't worry about Michelle. I'm taking good care of her, poor little thing. She's so young, she doesn't even know anything has happened. She's asked about her mother, but I haven't told her anything because that's not my place to do so. I thought it best to leave that up to you."

"I appreciate that. And thank you for taking such good care of Michelle. I'm going to need your help more than ever now."

"Anything you need, just let me know. I love that little girl like one of my own. And I'm praying her mother will come back to her."

The sincere look on the elderly woman's face both warmed and tore at Michael's heart. He wasn't use to his emotions running so rampan, and had trouble trying to control them again just now. He squeezed her arm in a friendly gesture. "I'm going in to see her right now," he offered.

Mrs. Carols nodded, understanding his need to see his granddaughter. "She's still asleep, but go right in. I won't disturb you." Then, with another reassuring smile, she went into her own room which was adjacent to Michelle's.

Michael entered the semi-dark room gingerly, afraid of waking Michelle and frightening her. Light crept in through the corners of the closed curtains, enough so that he could peek into her crib and see her peaceful sleeping face. Small red curls hung over her closed eyelids and her arms hugged a small pink rabbit she'd received for Easter that year. Just the sight of her eased Michael's tension, and his body slowly relaxed.

As he turned to leave the room, he noticed all the little details that Vanessa had done to make it the perfect nursery for Michelle. The beach mural she'd painted on the wall by the window that overlooked the ocean. The stenciled seashells that framed the wall. The glittering stars that reflected from the ceiling. All done with love by a mother for her daughter. His emotions flowing again, Michael quietly closed the bedroom door vowing to his little granddaughter as much as to himself, "I'll bring back your Mommy. I promise."

Michael arrived at the hospital a few minutes past nine o'clock and retraced the footsteps he'd taken the night before to the ICU. The hospital was a much friendlier place in the daylight, a bustle of people and activity, the halls brightly lit. He hoped the ICU room reflected this cheerier appearance because he dreaded returning to the room of last night. But when he approached the desk, he was told by the nurse in charge that Vanessa had been transferred to a private room this morning on the second floor. Relieved, thinking this was a good sign, he found the elevator and headed to room 207B.

Down the corridor and past the nurse's station, Michael found the room by himself and entered quietly through the closed door. Two men in white coats stood beside Vanessa's bed with charts. Both turned as Michael entered.

"I'm Michael DeCara, her father," he offered, walking toward them. Both men turned completely to face him, the man on the right offering his hand in greeting.

"I'm glad you have come," he said, shaking Michael's hand briefly. "I'm Dr. Bradseth, Chief of Surgery, and this is Dr. Carlson from Internal Medicine." The other man nodded, but stood quietly by as Dr. Bradseth continued talking.

"We just came in to check on Mrs. Candler's condition. Have you been briefed on it yet?"

"No. I came in late last night and the nurse wasn't able to tell me much."

Dr. Bradseth cleared his throat. "Your daughter has been through much trauma since the accident. When she arrived, she had a severe head injury and was already in a coma. After monitoring her for some time, we found there to be extensive swelling of the brain from the head injury, so we had to operate to relieve the swelling. Dr. Kantak, our specialist on brain injuries, performed the operation. So far there are no signs of swelling again, so we are hopeful the surgery was a success."

Here the doctor took a breath before continuing. "Also, one lung was punctured, which we had to operate on to repair, so that is the reason for the respirator she is attached to right now.

We hope she will be able to breathe on her own in a few days."
He gave Michael a moment to take it all in.

Michael stared past them to the sleeping form of Vanessa.
She looked a little better than she had the night before, but that
could be due to the light. She was still very pale, but fewer tubes
and wires were connected to her.

"How long will she be in the coma?"

"That, I'm afraid, we cannot answer. It will depend upon
how the rest of her body heals from the trauma it has received."

Frustrated, Michael ran his fingers through his hair. "Can
you tell me if she'll come out of it at all?"

"Again, Mr. DeCara, I sorry. We can't predict these things."
Both doctors looked at him squarely. They'd done all that was
possible and there was nothing they could say to give him any
shred of hope.

"Are you telling me...," Michael hesitated, afraid to ask the
question. "She might die?"

"I can't tell you what might happen," Dr. Bradseth said. "I
can tell you that she is off the heart machine and monitor and
her heartbeat and pulse is at a normal level, which is a good sign.
In a few days, we hope to get her off the respirator and breathing
on her own. As for the head injury, well, I'll be quite honest with
you. We aren't yet sure how much damage, if any, has been done
to the brain, and we won't know until we are able to do a CAT
scan, which we have scheduled for later this week. All we can do
is continue monitoring her progress and hope for the best."

Dr. Bradseth raised his arm and placed his hand on
Michael's shoulder, the first human gesture he had made since
Michael entered the room. "We've done all we can for her, and
we'll continue to do so. All we can do now is wait."

Michael looked into the doctor's eyes and knew he meant
what he said. They'd done as much as possible, now it was only
a matter of time. He nodded at them, then both doctors left the

room after assuring Michael they'd keep him informed.

With heavy footsteps Michael walked to the side of Vanessa's bed and fell into a chair. She continued sleeping on, as if without a care in the world. Someone had combed her long hair and it fanned out around her. Her face was freshly washed, and the tubes that had been in her left hand were now gone. He gingerly touched a tip of her curly auburn hair, then clasped her pale hand in his.

"Well baby, it's up to you now," he whispered as he laid his head on her hand and began to pray.

Chapter Nineteen

Early Tuesday morning Dani appeared at work with such a cheery attitude that her co-workers couldn't help but comment.

"Must have been some weekend," Traycee said, noting the sparkle in Dani's eyes.

"Actually, it was quite a weekend at that," Dani commented, giving Traycee a mischievous sideways glance.

Later that morning, Dani took a break and went down to the coat department to buy the red wool coat Miguel had teased her about the previous Saturday. Kelly recognized the coat immediately and was surprised to see Dani purchasing it. "You had a change of heart I see," she said as she whipped a Chance's coat bag over it.

"You could call it that," Dani replied.

When she arrived home that evening, she took the coat out of its bag and pinned the enamel brooch on the lapel, admiring the effect of the two together. She couldn't wait for Miguel to see it on her. He'd be shocked with surprise.

Although she hadn't heard from him yet, she wasn't worried. She figured he probably got home late and had some phone calls to return and it was too late to call her. She'd actually tried calling him last night to thank him for the pin, but only got his answering machine, and from the long beep at the end of the message, she could tell he had a lot of messages. She was sure he'd try to call her tonight, or at the latest, tomorrow night.

Dani placed the bag back over the coat and hung it in the

hall closet. She wouldn't wear it until she saw him again. Maybe this weekend. She could hardly wait to see his face when she stepped off the plane wearing that coat. She actually hoped the weather would be cold so she could wear it. As the hall door closed on her new purchase, she had no idea just how long it would hang there, unworn.

As the days passed, her mood became more sullen. When Wednesday had gone by without a word from him, she didn't think too much of it. By Thursday night when there was no call, she fell into a gloomy state. If he'd meant for her to come for the weekend, he'd have called by now. By Friday she was edgy at work, and Traycee noticed the change in her attitude immediately but was tactful enough not to say anything. Carl asked her if she was feeling okay to which she replied a short, terse, "I'm fine."

Friday night found Dani on her stair-step machine in front of the television paying little attention to the show while reflecting on the events of the past weekend.

He'd done it to her again, she thought, as her legs pounded up and down on the machine. And she had let him. This time she couldn't blame him for taking advantage of her. She knew what she was doing when she let him back into her bed. But did she regret it?

She pondered this one over and over as the sweat trickled down her neck and back. Although she felt she'd been used again, she couldn't really bring back the hate she'd felt years before. They had worked through that, and she did believe he was sorry. But then, why leave her hanging again?

Tired and sweating from her workout, Dani tried turning her thoughts from Miguel and showered, then had a bite to eat while she watched the news. There was still the slim chance he might call her, but she really doubted it. One thing she knew for sure, he wasn't going to show up at her door tonight as he had only a week before. She resigned herself to spending another weekend alone, in a series of lonely weekends to come.

* * *

Two weeks later Traycee was opening Dani's mail at work, as she usually did, stapling the envelopes to the letters and sorting it by matter of importance. One particular letter caught her eye.

"Dani, isn't Catherine Jamison a friend of yours?" she asked from her side of the partition.

Dani looked over the wall that divided their desks. "Yes. Why? Is there something interesting in the mail?"

"Here, take a look. Seems there has been some changes at Regal."

Dani took the offered letter and sat back down at her desk to read it over. It was from the Chicago Corporate Office of Regal Coats and was addressed to the Coat Buyer at Chance's.

"Effective immediately: Catherine Jamison, Assistant Executive Vice-President of Regal Coats, Chicago, will be taking over all duties previously held by the president of the company. President Michael DeCara has returned to the New York Office for an indefinite period of time.

Please direct all inquiries or concerns about operations to Ms. Jamison."

The letter continued on but had lost Dani's interest. She could only stare at the sentence that stated Miguel had returned to New York. So that was it. He was gone for good. He'd decided to put as much distance as possible between them. She waited for the news to hit her hard, but instead, she only felt numb.

"That's good news, right?" Traycee broke in.

"What?"

Traycee walked around the partition placing the rest of the mail in Dani's IN box. "Good news about your friend. Head of the division now. It's great for her, huh?"

"Oh, yeah. It's great." Dani tried to sound enthusiastic for her friend but it was hard, considering Cathy's promotion meant that Miguel had run away from Dani a second time.

* * *

Michael's days blurred into one another to the point that he didn't know which day was Monday or Friday, nor did he care. He spent each day, from early morning to late evening, at Vanessa's bedside, leaving only to sleep and eat, doing the latter out of necessity, not hunger.

Three days after he'd returned to New York, he attended Matthew Chandler's funeral, another sad affair. It was a quiet service attended by immediate family only. Matthew had been the youngest of four sons, and watching his mother bury her baby boy made Michael's heart ache.

Michael offered his deepest sympathies to the family, shook Mr. Chandler's hand, and hugged Mrs. Chandler, who expressed concern over Vanessa's condition and told Michael she was praying for her.

They had all agreed it was best to not bring Michelle to the funeral. At two years old, she was too young to understand what was happening, and neither family wanted her to have any memory of the sad event. When Michael left the Chandlers with a final goodbye, he hurried back to the hospital to see Vanessa to reassure himself how lucky he was that she was still, at least, alive.

But as he watched her sleeping peacefully, he realized that maybe she was the lucky one for not having to go through today. Although it would be a painful loss to her when she finally woke up, it was far better than having to walk through the motions of a funeral, hear endless condolences, and watch tear-stained faces.

Michael's days went on, hospital, home, hospital, home. He ate so many meals at the hospital cafeteria that the workers all knew him by name. The nurses who came periodically into Vanessa's room to check her pulse and IVs and record everything on her chart also became familiar with the ever-present father. They all made an effort at lifting his mood but the truth was Vanessa's condition was serious and they could never offer him even the slightest ray of hope.

He spent his time talking to his daughter about everything he could think of that might spark her interest. Someone had told him that talking about past experiences and common things sometimes triggered coma patients into consciousness. Michael talked about her past and the times they'd shared with Dani, which he knew had been happy memories for Vanessa. He talked about work, what little he kept in touch with out of necessity, hoping she might respond from the commitment she'd always had for her position at Regal. He talked about Michelle and what new word she had said that morning or new antic she'd been involved in the day before. He read to Vanessa from books by her favorite authors, even books from her childhood that he hoped might spark a memory. Daily, he massaged her legs and arms to keep the muscles limber and the blood flowing smoothly as he continued his stream of conversation. Sometimes he'd sit there for so long, he'd fall asleep holding her hand and a night nurse would wake him gently and send him home. The very next morning he could be found by her bedside once again, as if he'd never left.

All through these days and nights the doctors offered no morsel of hope. He really needed someone to talk to, to share his pain, to tell him everything was going to be okay, and his thoughts instantly returned to Dani. It took all his strength to keep himself from calling her and asking her to come and be by his side. Yet, how could he do that to her? He didn't want to add more pain to her life, so he continued on his own, waiting, talking, reading, and praying.

The results of the CAT scan showed no major damage to the brain and there was no additional swelling. If Vanessa did come out of her coma, she should have all of her functions in working order. But that didn't explain why she wasn't waking, which continued to puzzle the doctors.

They had also tried, unsuccessfully, several times to take her off the respirator, but each time her breathing became so labored that they had to put her back on it. Dr. Bradseth ordered x-rays to recheck the condition of her lungs. It was important that they get her breathing on her own, he explained to Michael. Michael didn't understand why but had to believe that the doctors were doing all that they could for his little girl.

The nurses took good care of Vanessa, and Michael was thankful for their tender touch. Her hair was always clean and combed, her nightgown changed and fresh smelling. The bandage on her head had become only a small patch, and the hair around it began to grow back like the soft fuzz on a fresh peach. The nurses had lovingly dubbed her Sleeping Beauty, and whenever one came into the room, she'd ask Michael how the princess was doing. He took it in good humor, and began calling her that himself.

One night, after an especially long day, Michael sat next to Vanessa in his usual place, holding her hand, frustrated that he hadn't yet managed to get her to open her eyes. A male nurse, unfamiliar to Michael, came in to check on her IV and pulse rate, giving Michael a friendly smile.

"So, how is our Sleeping Beauty doing?" he asked, but Michael only threw him a suspicious, sideways glance. The male nurse looked more like a football player to Michael with his closely cropped hair and thick build, and Michael resented his familiar attitude with his daughter.

But the nurse seemed unaware of Michael's suspicious look and gently took Vanessa's pulse and adjusted the IV to make sure the drip was perfect. As he recorded the information on the chart, he looked up to see Michael staring at him hostilely.

The nurse smiled at him again, showing less than perfect teeth. The smile revealed lines around his eyes that gave away his true age, much older than Michael had first thought. The nurse had to be close to Michael's own age, which still did little to endear him to Michael.

"Well," the nurse offered, "her vitals are still steady. Maybe we'll see the princess smile sometime soon."

Michael made no response as the nurse hung the chart back on the foot of the bed and turned to leave the room, then turned back and faced Michael again.

"You know," he said, gently. "I've been told that if you keep up a steady stream of conversation, or read to a coma patient, that it sometimes helps bring them around." It was an innocent piece of advice, but it outraged Michael, who stood suddenly with his feet planted apart and fists clenched.

"I have been talking to her," he said, starting in a slow, angry voice that grew louder as he continued. "I've been talking to her, and reading to her for days and days and it's not working. She just lies there, asleep, not responding or caring or even listening. So, who the hell are you to come in here and tell me I should..." Michael stopped mid-sentence and slumped his shoulders, a deep sigh escaping his lips.

"I'm sorry," he said, quietly.

The nurse nodded, his face calm as if he were used to these kinds of outbursts. "It's okay. I understand." He turned and left, leaving behind a torn, confused father grieving for his daughter.

Mid-October came to Long Island in all its fall glory, bringing with it tourists from all over the country to bask in the colors and admire the rich gardens so famous in the Hamptons.

But Michael saw none of this as he made his way back and forth from his home to the hospital. He spent time on work that he couldn't ignore in his home office, having papers and files sent by FAX, or to his home computer. He didn't want to go into New York City for even a moment in case Vanessa's condition changed.

The only joy in his life during this time were his visits with Michelle in the mornings, and sometimes in the afternoons when he'd force himself away from the hospital to give the young child the much needed time she deserved. Michelle didn't understand where her parents were, or why they weren't around anymore. Michael did the best he could explaining to her the circumstances without trying to scare her. But how did you tell a little girl that her father was never coming home and her mother might not either? He kept waiting and hoping that Vanessa's condition would turn around and he could then tell Michelle that Mommy would be home soon.

But life doesn't always work out as one hopes, and Vanessa's x-rays came back showing more damage to her lungs, necessitating another operation. So, two days later, Michael sat for hours waiting for Vanessa to come out of the operating room and recovery, praying that this might help bring her back to him.

And even though the doctors said the operation was a success, and even after Vanessa no longer needed a respirator to breath for her, she continued to sleep on as Michael sat beside her bed, waiting.

Chapter Twenty

The choppers flew in low through the mist and smoke of artillery as the men below hurried to place bodies of the dead and wounded into them to be taken to the nearest medical unit. Miguel DeCara helped the medics load the men from his unit. There had been heavy casualties all day from grenades and gunfire, and it seemed they would never be done with the gruesome work of body counting.

Gunfire continued all around them as the men filled one chopper after another with casualties. After placing a man who had lost his arm into the chopper, Miguel crouched and headed toward the next wounded man when one medic, carrying a dead soldier, called after him. "Hey, this one lost his dog tags. Come see if you can identify him."

Grudgingly, Miguel turned back to the noise and wind of the chopper blades to perform a task he had no heart for. He hoped it was a stranger he didn't know or else he'd see that face for the rest of his life in his nightmares. As he approached the body, slung in the makeshift hammock between the two medics' arms, he couldn't see the face at first because the helmet had slid over it. Coughing from the smoke that the whirling blades of the chopper only made worse, he watched as the medic moved away the helmet so he could get a closer look. But it wasn't the dead eyes of a stranger that looked back at him. As the helmet was lifted, a shock of red hair tumbled out and the lifeless emerald eyes of Vanessa stared back at him.

Anguished screams could be heard up and down the second floor corridors of Southampton Hospital. Kevin Lindstrom, the floor's night nurse, ran into room 207B where the screams were coming from and stopped for only a second to see Michael

DeCara thrashing beside his daughter's bed screaming "No!" His eyes open but glassy and unseeing.

Kevin quickly grabbed him bear-hug style from behind to prevent any harm to Vanessa, and pulled him away from the bed, all the while talking in a calm, even tone. "It's okay DeCara, you're okay. Calm down. You're in the hospital and everything is okay." He continued saying this over and over, all the while holding Michael tightly, until finally Michael's eyes began to focus and he slumped in Kevin's grasp.

Kevin led him toward the door when Michael suddenly turned back to Vanessa. He had to make sure she was still breathing, still alive. When he saw that she was, he let Kevin gently lead him from the room, past the staring faces of the other nurses, and to a bench down the hallway.

"Stay here a minute," Kevin told him. "I'll get you some coffee." He was gone for only a minute and returned with two paper cups steaming with vending machine coffee.

After handing one cup to Michael, Kevin sat opposite him on another bench. The hallways were dimly lit as they were every night to allow patients enough darkness to sleep. But it gave off an eerie, quiet, almost deathly feeling to the hallways and rooms when all was still and dim.

Kevin sat staring at the man across from him for a few moments, then broke the silence. "Some nightmare, huh?"

Michael looked up, still a bit dazed and glassy-eyed, and nodded his head.

"How long were you in Nam?"

Startled, Michael stared at the large man in front of him, finally recognizing him as the male nurse he'd blown up at before. He wrinkled his brow. "How'd you know I was in Nam?"

Kevin's face softened, but no smile appeared. "I've been around enough vets to know the look. I was in for two tours myself. I worked the 254th MDHA Unit west of Da Nang as a

Corpsman in '68 'til '70."

Nodding his head, Michael stared into his cup of coffee. "I was at the Da Nang Fire Base in '70. But I didn't finish my tour. I was wounded and sent home after 10 months."

"Ah, one of the lucky ones, huh?"

"Yeah," Michael grunted. "Lucky."

Silence surrounded the two men again as both resurrected memories in their minds. Once again, Kevin broke the silence. "Do the nightmares come often?"

"They come off and on. When I'm under a lot of stress, they come more often." Michael ran his hand through his hair and took a sip of coffee. "With all that's going on these days, it's no wonder the nightmares are so steady."

"Do you belong to a vet group, or see anyone about the nightmares? Most vets find it's easier talking about it with someone else who understands."

Michael stared hard at the man before him, wondering why he would care enough to ask. He seemed the most unlikely candidate for playing guardian angel to wayward vets. But as he studied Kevin's face, he realized he was being sincere. Michael had let Kevin's coarse appearance color his view of this large man. But he really did look concerned.

"I never believed anything would help," he answered honestly.

"Well, the nightmares will never go away completely but most guys find they lessen if they get some of the tension out by talking about them." He hesitated a moment, letting his words sink in, then continued. "We have a group of vets who get together here every Tuesday night at six. We meet in one of the conference rooms on this floor, room 225C. There are no doctors or psychologists there, just a bunch of guys talking about what's going on inside their heads. You're invited to come and join us, if you'd like."

Michael couldn't imagine himself sitting in a room full of men rehashing his past. "I don't know..." he began.

"Just think about it," Kevin interrupted. He stood and tossed his empty cup in the garbage can beside him. "I'd better get back to work. You should go home. It's getting late and you look shot."

"Yeah, I guess I am." Michael stood, tossing his own cup. "Thanks for the coffee," he offered.

"No problem," Kevin told him, then turned back down the hall to tend to the patients in his wing.

Later, lying in bed in his dark room, Michael couldn't get to sleep. His dream of Vanessa in the body bag had disturbed him so thoroughly that he just couldn't get it out of his mind. Nightmares of Nam had been coming steadily over the past two months, chipping away at what little energy and sanity he had left.

He thought of what Kevin had said, but had trouble picturing himself spilling his guts to a room full of strangers. Aside from always believing he could cope on his own, he also felt that he really didn't fit in with the typical idea of a troubled vet. After all, he'd been lucky enough to come out of the war in relatively one piece. He had never experienced violent rages like so many others he'd known or heard about. And he'd had a business empire just handed to him. Who was he to walk into a room full of people and ask for help?

Sure, there was that time in his life when he had needed pot and a string of women to keep him going, but he had turned that all around years ago. He was living the perfect life, wasn't he?

But the truth was he knew he needed help to cope with everything going on in his life right now or else he might go berserk like so many other vets like himself. Men living ordinary lives who just suddenly snap one day.

"Dani, I need you so much," he whispered into the silent

room. She was the only one who'd ever understood him, and she had been the first one to suggest he get help.

"If not for you," she'd told him gently, "then for Vanessa."

Michael pondered this for some time in the black stillness. It was too late to help himself for Vanessa's sake, but there was still Michelle to think about. He couldn't go cracking up on her when the rest of her world was falling apart.

Finally, he fell asleep with his decision made. He would do what needed to be done, no matter what, for Michelle.

The next morning Michael awoke with a quiet resolve. He stayed home to have breakfast with Michelle and met her downstairs in the breakfast dining room. His cook, Marianna, was so pleased to see him there that she whipped up every breakfast dish he loved, and he enjoyed every bite with Michelle's giggly presence to lift his spirits.

Then, before leaving for the hospital, he entered his home office to make a phone call that was long overdue.

It was ten in the morning, New York time, so it would be eight in Minneapolis. As he dialed Dani's number, he silently prayed he'd catch her before she left for work, and before he lost his nerve.

Dani's voice sounded rushed when she picked up the receiver. "Hello."

"Hello, Dani."

There was silence on the other end for one long minute. "Miguel?"

"Yes. How have you been?" He felt so awkward. He didn't know what to say.

"Well, I..." Dani stopped and silence swelled in the distance between them.

"I know this phone call is long overdue," Michael finally said. "I'm sorry I didn't call you sooner. But so much has happened..." he trailed off at a loss for words.

Dani finally found her voice. "It's okay, Miguel. There's no need to be sorry. I knew what I was getting into that weekend, and I did so with my eyes wide open. We made no promises and there were no expectations." She paused a moment and sighed. "Maybe everything worked out for the best after all."

Dani's words were not angry or hateful. But the tone of her voice, with the sad, quiet resignation in it, tore at Michael's heart. "I've hurt you again, haven't I Dani?" he asked. "It seems all I do is hurt you."

"It really doesn't matter now, Miguel," Dani's voice cracked over the line. "We resolved a few things that weekend, and I no longer carry the hate I felt for you all those years. Maybe that's where we should leave it."

"But Dani I..." he wanted to tell her why he'd left, the reason for all the pain and hurt. But she didn't give him a chance.

"It's late, and I really have to get to work," Dani told him.

"Can I call you again? Another time when we can really talk?" Michael sounded desperate, but Dani didn't hear it in his voice.

"I don't think that's a good idea, Miguel. I really have to go. I'm sorry. Goodbye."

The receiver clicked on the other end of the line leaving Michael to stare at the silent phone for several seconds before replacing the receiver into the cradle.

He didn't need to see her face to understand how she felt. Her voice had told him everything. He'd loved her and left her again without an explanation. He'd hurt her once too often, and she couldn't bear to be hurt again.

Michael rose from his desk and stood in front of the windows. The drapes were drawn open, allowing the fall sunshine to stream into the room. He watched the waves break against the shore, as the wind began whipping up outside. He'd stood at these windows many times, yet the time he remembered best was when Dani had stood there with him. Then, everything was fine. Vanessa and Matthew were full of life, he was busy with his business, and contact was finally being made with Dani.

How could it all fall apart so quickly? Now, here he stood, all alone. He was completely drained, physically, mentally, and emotionally. It felt as if everyone he'd ever loved or cared about was lost to him. Never in his life, no matter what the pain, had he felt this lonely, this desolate.

Michael went to the hospital as usual and tried to keep up some form of conversation with Vanessa, but it all seemed so useless. He held her hand, brushed his fingers through her hair, and wished hard to be able to see those emerald green eyes sparkle up at him again. But she just laid there, breathing, but making no effort to rejoin him and ease his pain.

Late afternoon approached and he kissed her cheek goodbye. "I'll see you tomorrow, honey. I love you." He walked out of her room and went into the men's room down the hall. Splashing cold water on his face and wiping it with a rough paper towel, he ran his fingers through his hair and assessed his appearance. Several streaks of gray had taken over where dark hair had once been. Even his beard had strands of gray that hadn't been there only weeks before. His skin had paled from lack of sun, and his eyes had lost that sparkly mischief that had once made him so appealing to women. For a man who had once taken such care of his appearance, he looked like a wreck.

"Well, I certainly look the part of a down and out vet," he told his reflection, then left the bathroom and headed down the hall.

His footsteps were heavy with despair, mimicking the feelings of loneliness and depression that had enveloped him. Never had he felt this low, this isolated, this desperate. Going to this meeting was like grasping for the last straw.

It was 6:05 p.m. when he entered through the door to room

225C, and all the men in the circle before him looked up. The room was similar to the hospital rooms, except larger. There was a row of windows on the far wall that spilled the last rays of the day's sunlight through vertical blinds. The men had formed a circle of chairs in the center of the room, one man sat in a wheelchair. As they all looked up in Michael's direction, he saw Kevin in the center of the group and he rose from his chair and greeted Michael.

"Mr. DeCara. I'm so glad you came," he said, offering his hand in greeting and patting Michael's back with the other.

"Please, just call me Michael," he offered nervously.

"Okay. Come join us, Michael." Kevin led him to a chair between the man in the wheelchair and another man of husky build. Then Kevin sat back down opposite of Michael.

"Guys, this is Michael," Kevin told the group of men. "He served at the Fire Base in Da Nang in '70."

All the men nodded and a couple of them said hello. Michael was surprised Kevin remembered where and when he'd served in Vietnam. There was much more to this male nurse than he had given him credit for in the beginning.

As he surveyed the group around him, he was surprised by the differences in each person. The man in the wheelchair beside him had lost both legs at the knees. His hair and beard, so much like Michael's, were black, and he had a worn, black cap atop his head. His clothing, T-shirt and jeans, was also black. If he had not been in a wheelchair, one would think he'd climb aboard a Harley and speed off.

The man on his left was quite the opposite. He was husky and blonde, dressed in clean jeans and a flannel shirt. He had a mid-western look about him that reminded Michael a little of Billy back in Nam.

Kevin asked each man to introduce himself, starting with the man in the wheelchair. To Michael's surprise, they did so by telling where and when they served in Nam.

"I'm Joe Pilanski, 1st Battalion, 7th Marines, Da Nang, 1968," the man said with a heavy Jersey accent.

"John Perry, 25th Infantry, Cu Chi, 1967 and '69," offered the man next to Joe. His voice was small like his build, and he looked down at the floor as he talked.

"Kevin Lindstrom, 254th MDHA Unit, '68 and '70," Kevin boomed out in his clear voice.

"Dr. Allen Cox, 13th Evac Hospital, 1969," said the tall, thin, silver-haired man beside Kevin. Dressed neatly in a green Ralph Lauren polo shirt and tan slacks he certainly looked like a doctor off duty.

"Wayne Garrison," said the last man in the circle, the one to Michael's left. "Helicopter Pilot, Tan Son Nhut Airport, 1969 and '71." His voice was definitely Midwestern in accent, and he offered both a wide smile and a handshake to Michael.

Michael nodded to each man as they introduced themselves, then sat uncomfortably when the introductions were done. What was he supposed to do now, he wondered.

But Kevin took care of the silence. "Joe was talking about his trip back to Vietnam last year," he explained for Michael's benefit. "Go ahead with your story, Joe."

"I was just saying how calm and quiet it all is there now. Not the mad, chaotic place we remember. Driving up Highway One or floating down the Saigon River is pure joy now. No smoke or noise or smell. Just a peaceful calm."

Dr. Cox nodded in agreement. "The country there was always beautiful but when we were there, it was a menacing beauty. You never knew when you'd step into a booby trap or on a mine. But now you can enjoy the beauty without the fear, and see the people as they really are, not as the enemy. It can do wonders for the mind, going back."

"You ever been back to Nam?" Joe asked Michael bluntly.

"No, I haven't. I guess I never thought about it before. When I think of Nam, I think of horror. I can't even imagine wanting to go there again."

"It changes everything, man," Joe told him. "The way you think, the way you feel. Hell, I even went back to the very spot I lost my legs. It was a positive thing for me."

Michael had to ask. "How did you lose your legs?"

Joe gave a short laugh as if it were a joke. "Why, I heard the 'click' man. Stepped on a mine and *POW*, it blew them right off." He spread his arms wide when he said this. Michael paled involuntarily.

"What do we have here?" Joe asked, sarcastically. "A queasy vet?"

"No," Michael said quietly, staring directly at Joe. "I was just thinking how lucky I am. You see, I heard the 'click', too." He bent forward and rolled up the left leg of his trousers, exposing the jagged scar from his ankle to his knee as all the men watched. "But it only blew my leg apart. I was lucky that the doctors there could save it."

All the men in the room, including the outspoken Joe, sat silently, nodding their understanding. They had all faced death and lived to tell about it. As Michael studied the faces that surrounded him, he felt for the first time since returning from Vietnam that he had finally come home.

Chapter Twenty-One

The phone call from Miguel unnerved Dani so much that it showed in her work that entire week. She was short with everyone around her, couldn't seem to concentrate on even the simplest tasks, and forgot to return calls and keep appointments. After the weekly Friday afternoon buyers' meeting in Trindell's office, he asked Dani to stay a moment longer.

Perched on a front corner of his desk, Trindell spoke gently to Dani. "I know you've been piled up with work ever since taking over coats for Janette. Maybe it's been too much to handle at one time. If you think you need a few days off, we could arrange it," he offered.

"I'm fine," Dani protested. "This is the busiest time of the year. How can I take time off?" The holidays were fast approaching, and there were store sales and promotions to take care of along with lining up the buying trips for the spring collections. Dani knew if Trindell was offering her time off now, she must really seem like a wreck.

"Well, it's only a suggestion," Carl told her. "Everyone has a breaking point, and I don't want you to reach yours, that's all."

"I'm really okay," she told him, trying to sound calm. "But, you're right. I have been busy. I hope Janette makes her decision soon."

The rest of that day, Dani made an effort at being calm and organized. She was angry at herself for letting Miguel upset her so much that it showed in her work. And yet, it seemed ever since the weekend she'd spent with him, work just wasn't as important to her as it had been. After re-examining her past and her hatred of him, and then finally letting it go, she began to think of all the other things life offered that she wasn't experiencing. Love, marriage, and a family. Was it just her age, or was it meeting Miguel again that had brought on these new emotions and desires?

"Damn you, Miguel!" Dani blurted out that evening as she hung her coat in the closet and spied the red one she'd bought just for him. "Damn you for making me feel alive again, then leaving me!" She had another long weekend to look forward to, alone. Maybe it was time that changed.

Winter spilled across Minnesota two days before Thanksgiving Day, giving the bare trees and brown grass new life with its sparkling white blanket. Dani's parents came to her apartment for the holiday, knowing it was a busy time for Dani to get away because of Friday being the busiest shopping day of the year. It also gave Dani's mom a chance to do some holiday shopping of her own in the city.

They enjoyed a peaceful turkey dinner on Thanksgiving Day, and the next day joined the throngs of shoppers hitting the malls. Dani's father joined them in their shopping excursion and the three came back to her apartment loaded with packages and stories of crazy shoppers.

Dani had given her parents her room and taken the sofa bed for herself. That evening, as her mother helped her make up the sofa bed for the night, her father softly snoring in the other room, her mother probed just a little into Dani's personal life.

"Anyone special in your life these days, honey?"

Dani smiled, not the least bit put off by the question. Her mother kept hoping that someday she would find that someone special who would make her happy. She knew her mom meant well by it.

"No Mom. Not really." Tucking a corner of the sheet under the mattress, she added, "But I was invited to go to the company Christmas party with the manager of the Men's Department. I've known him for years. He seems nice."

In truth, Mark Phillips had been asking Dani out for the past two years, but each time she'd declined. He was good looking and personable, but she didn't feel a spark. But this time, when he asked, she'd said yes, surprising both him and herself.

"So, are you going with him?" her mother wanted to know.

"I said yes."

Joan smiled. "I'm sure you'll have a wonderful time."

When they were done, Dani sat on the freshly made bed and looked up into her mother's brown eyes. Both her parents had brown hair and eyes, quite the opposite of Dani's light coloring. Her mother always said Dani got her blue eyes from her side, a great-uncle Dani had never met. But the shape of her face and tilt of her nose were reflected in the older woman's face. Dani had her mother's looks, and her father's serious disposition. Both of her parents had easy temperaments, but her father was always the serious one of the two.

"Mom," Dani said, hesitantly. "How did you know when you met Dad that he was the one for you?"

Joan chuckled, and sat down on the bed opposite Dani. "I didn't at first. Actually, I was dating your father's best friend when I met him. We used to all go around together in a big group to parties and picnics and things like that. Your father was in his second year of college and I had just graduated high school. I always thought he was too serious, so I never really paid much attention to him."

"So, what happened?"

"Well, one night we all went to the beach for a bonfire and the guys decided it would be funny to throw the girls in the water. Your father thought they were being ridiculous and had no part in it. When they picked me up and dropped me in the ice cold water, it was your father who came and helped me out. I stood there in ankle deep water, shivering, and he gave me his sweater to keep warm. I remember looking down and seeing his brand new penny loafers immersed in the water, knowing they would be ruined. And when I looked up at him again, well…" Joan looked down shyly. "He just kissed me."

Dani looked at her mother, amazed. It was hard enough picturing her parents as young and silly, let alone standing in the ocean kissing. "Is that what did it?"

"It wasn't so much the kiss as the way I felt when he kissed me. It felt so warm, so right. I just knew he was the one for me."

Joan patted Dani's hand. "Do you think this man you're going to the party with is the right one?"

"I don't really know, Mom," Dani replied as she stared down at the blue tufts of fuzz on the thermal blanket.

"Well, you'll know it when it happens, honey," her mother assured her.

Dani ran her hand over the blanket, remembering the night she and Miguel had held each other in this very bed. Being with him had felt just the way her mother described. Warm and right. Yes, she knew just what her mother was talking about. Both times she had felt it, and both times she had lost it.

Chapter Twenty-Two

Thanksgiving Day came and went for Michael as if it were just another day. Vanessa held on, and Michael did, too, each day sitting beside her bed, talking, holding her hand, praying. The doctors kept telling him that there was no reason they could detect for her not coming out of the coma. So he waited.

Some things had changed for him though. He attended the weekly vet meetings, and felt better each time he went. By sharing stories with them, and listening to the other vets, he felt like some of his demons were being peeled away from his soul, one layer at a time. It was like a bad sunburn finally peeling away to reveal new skin. And it all looked, and felt, so fresh again.

Each week, Michael became more comfortable around the men and opened up a little at a time. He talked about his nightmares, his endless wait for Vanessa to wake up, and his past when he had jumped jobs and been hooked on pot. At one meeting, the subject of how being a Vietnam Vet affects family and friends came up. Wayne Garrison surprised them all by admitting the reason he had to leave his hometown in Oklahoma, a reason that struck a chord with Michael.

"When I got back home, I had trouble concentrating on anything for long periods of time," he said in his southern drawl. "I couldn't keep a job more than six months at a time, and all my friends from high school acted like they didn't know me. I felt like such a loser. I was twenty-two and most of the women my age didn't want anything to do with a Vietnam Vet. I started dating teenaged girls, one after another, like I couldn't get enough. I never thought about whether I was hurting any of them by dumping them as quickly as taking them on. I just needed them. Their youth and their innocence. I really needed that."

Wayne sighed and ran a thick hand through his short hair before continuing. "Anyway, I ended up with a girl who was younger than she said, only fourteen. Even though she had consented to being with me, well, her parents found out and threatened to press charges against me for rape. My parents had had enough of me at that point and told me to just get out of there and don't come back 'til I was normal again." He gave a short laugh. "Normal. I'll never be normal again. But I did straighten out my act and have been very careful since moving here."

Michael stared at the man who had just bared his soul, and said quietly. "I know what you mean. I went through the same thing with women, jumping from one woman to another. It was like I was trying to lose myself in them in order to forget about the hell Vietnam had been."

Wayne nodded his head in agreement. "Sometimes, I wonder how many of them I hurt. Not physically, but emotionally. I feel really bad that I did that to them."

"Vietnam hurt the people around us like it hurt us," Kevin added. "The way we act, and the things we do to others are all by-products of our war experience. In many ways, they are as much victims of the war as we are."

Michael thought of Dani and the pain he had caused her. He knew Kevin was right. She was as much a casualty as any of them.

At another meeting, Michael talked about his constant nightmare of the day Billy was killed. Until that night, John, who had been at Cu Chi and been one of the many men known as a "tunnel rat" because they would squeeze into the tunnels and search out the enemy, had been quiet and withdrawn. But his small black eyes darted up in interest as he listened to Michael's description of Billy's death.

"That happened to me, too," John said in a hushed voice. Then his eyes dropped again to the floor as if he were sorry for having said anything.

"You mean you saw a friend die the same way?" Kevin asked gently, trying to coax John on.

"Yes," he said, still studying the carpet. "Except we were in a tunnel at the time," he stopped again.

Michael knew that John never spoke about his experiences and this was the beginning of a breakthrough for him. So he tried to keep him talking.

"What happened?" he asked, quietly.

Feeling some connection with Michael, John locked eyes with him as he spoke. "We'd been clearing out this one tunnel of Viet Cong for a couple of weeks, and we thought we had everything and everyone out of it. Three of us went down to check things out, you know, to make sure none had moved back in. They were always moving back in, right under our noses. We'd clear out one tunnel and before we knew it, they were back in there." John's voice was running faster, and sounded strained. He took a shaky sip of his coffee, then continued.

"Anyway, my buddy, Steve, was ahead of me, and the other guy was bringing up the rear. Steve was one of those reckless types. We'd gone through boot camp together and were in the same unit for two tours. He started getting way ahead of us, and I kept telling him to slow down. The tunnel was cramped, we had to crawl on our bellies to get through. Steve got to an open area large enough to stand up in, and that's when it happened. The damn Cong had come back all right. They'd booby-trapped the tunnel and two grenades went off under Steve, spewing pieces of him everywhere."

John dropped his head, and Kevin, who was sitting beside him, laid a hand on his shoulder. "That must have been tough on you, man," he offered.

Head down, John continued. "Sometimes, I wake up in a cold sweat, screaming, trying to pick pieces of Steve off of me. But I can't make them go away...they just won't go away..." he trailed off, his body trembling.

Kevin kept a firm hold of his shoulder. "That's what we're here for, man," he told him. "To try and make some of that go away."

Michael caught Kevin's eyes with his and knew that Kevin was silently thanking him. It was because Michael shared his story that John finally opened up. A warm feeling spread through Michael at the knowledge that not only was he getting help, he was giving it, too.

* * *

December came, bringing the winter chill to Southampton and quiet days at the beach residence since most of the summer residents were gone. Michael stayed on to be near Vanessa. Although he spent the majority of his time with her, he had begun going into New York City to his office two days a week to ease back into work. It was a busy time, with the spring showings only a month away, and he couldn't ignore his responsibilities any longer.

His New York City days were good for him, and they gave him something new to talk to Vanessa about. He rambled on about what was going on at the office, the latest gossip, and what the new styles looked like for spring. He hoped that talking about work would spark some interest in Vanessa. He talked as she slept on.

One crisp morning two weeks into December, Michael came downstairs, feeling lighthearted and positive. He'd been at work the prior day, and he planned on going in to see Vanessa today. He was also looking forward to the vet meeting that night.

But first, he decided he had to get a Christmas tree for the living room. He'd buy the biggest one he could find and tomorrow he and Michelle would decorate it together. It was time to cheer the house up and create a happy environment for Michelle. He thought he might even get a small tree and decorate it for Vanessa's hospital room.

The phone invaded his thoughts, and he picked up the one on the entryway table.

"Hello."

"May I speak with Mr. DeCara please?"

"Speaking."

The woman's voice on the other end hesitated a moment. "Mr. DeCara, I'm sorry to bother you, but I'm calling for Dr. Bradseth from Southampton Hospital."

Michael clenched the receiver. "What's happened?"

"I'm sorry, Mr. DeCara, but there's been a change in your daughter's condition and Dr. Bradseth would like you to come here as soon as possible."

"Tell me what happened."

"I don't know myself," she told him. "The doctor only told me to have you come to the hospital immediately."

Michael took a deep breath to control his emotions. "I'll be there right away."

He left the house without a word to anyone and was at the hospital within minutes. All the way there, he kept telling himself that a change in her condition could be something positive, too. Maybe she had awoken and the news was good. But the closer he came to her room, he realized that wasn't the case.

Walking into room 207B was like a bad flashback from the

first night he'd seen her in ICU. Once again, Vanessa was hooked up to a respirator, IV tubes were strung into her from all directions, and a heart monitor filled the room with its constant, grating sound. Dr. Bradseth stood at the end of Vanessa's bed, quietly conferring with a nurse, and both looked up as Michael entered.

"Mr. DeCara, thank you for coming," the doctor greeted him in his usual serious tone. The nurse slipped quietly from the room as Michael continued staring at the pale, thin form lying in the hospital bed. When had Vanessa become so thin, he wondered, confused by all that was going on before him. Had she been that way before and he hadn't noticed?

The doctor brought his attention back to him. "Mr. DeCara, I'm afraid your daughter has had a relapse. The damage to her internal organs must have been more extensive than we realized, and the length of her coma has weakened her strength to fight back. She experienced a massive heart attack this morning. We are still evaluating the extent of the damage that it caused her, and I must warn you, it doesn't look very good at this point."

The doctor's low-key, droning voice only confused Michael more. All his words seemed to run together. The only ones most prominent in his mind were relapse and heart attack. But he couldn't have heard right. Only old people had heart attacks, not young, strong women.

"I don't understand," Michael finally managed to say. "She was fine the other day. How could all this happen?" He searched the doctor's face for answers, but all he got was the same, monotone voice replying.

"Like I said, Mr. DeCara. Her body was run down from the coma, and there must have been more damage than we first realized to the internal organs..."

"Yes, yes, yes." Michael interrupted, irritated now at this calm man before him. "I know all that. But how could this happen? She was supposed to get better, not worse." The heart monitor continued its grating beeping sound, which pounded in Michael's ears. "And what is all this equipment for? Why does she need that damn thing?" Michael angrily pointed toward the heart monitor.

Dr. Bradseth remained calm and controlled from twenty years experience with similar heart-wrenching experiences. It was never easy, every loss was a tragedy. But he continued explaining as best he could to the emotional father before him.

"Your daughter's vital organs were damaged during the accident, and the heart attack she experienced this morning only made her condition worse. Right now, she is on complete life support."

Michael stood dumbfounded as the doctor continued. "We've done a scan on the brain to see exactly what the extent of the damage has been. The technicians are still reading the x-rays now, and we should know more about her condition in the next hour or so."

"And then what?" Michael asked, quietly. The words 'life support' had knocked all the fight out of him.

"Let's just take this one step at a time," Dr. Bradseth suggested, trying to put off the biggest blow.

Michael looked him squarely in the eyes. "I need to know, Doctor. Please."

Dr. Bradseth sighed. "Depending on the results, you will have to decide whether or not to keep her on life support."

Michael's eyes widened as he took in a sharp breath. Dr. Bradseth placed his hand on Michael's shoulder. "Let's wait for the results. One hour at a time, okay?" Dr. Bradseth promised to come back as soon as he knew, then he left the room with silent footsteps.

Walking past Vanessa's bed, Michael stood and stared out the window of her room. The day was frigid, and ice encrusted the edges of the glass, frozen in odd-lined shapes. Beyond, on the street, people were rushing to and fro, cars were passing through the quiet intersection, and employees were busy in the shops beyond. Outside, life was going on while he stood in a room where death seemed imminent.

He turned from the activity outside and sat heavily in the chair he'd sat in for countless hours. The heart monitor continued its noise, sometimes at a slow steady beat, sometimes erratic, as he studied the small form that no longer resembled his daughter.

There were dark circles under her once sparkling eyes, her skin was sallow, no longer porcelain, and even the light freckles that she used to hate on the bridge of her nose were discolored. Her hair, once thick, and a shiny auburn color, now looked a dull brown. And the arms that extended over the blankets looked more like twigs covered in parchment.

As he listened to her erratic breathing, despite the respirator, he wondered when she had begun wasting away and why he hadn't noticed it before this. Had he wanted her to come out of the coma so badly that he had been blind to her growing frailty?

He could now understand what the doctor had been trying to tell him. Her body was much too frail to withstand even the slightest disruption, let alone a massive heart attack. Slowly, as he continued staring at Vanessa, he silently prepared himself for the worst.

An hour later, when the doctor returned, Michael stood stoically and nodded as he was told the diagnosis. There was severe damage to Vanessa's brain. She was considered brain-dead, and her body could not survive without the life support system.

"I'm sorry, Mr. DeCara," Dr. Bradseth told him, trying his best to be kind. "But there is no way that your daughter will come out of this."

Michael stared at the doctor from his chair, never letting go of Vanessa's cold, frail hand. "So, what do I do now?"

"The only humane thing you can do is take her off of life support and let her go naturally," Bradseth answered him honestly. "But the decision as to when you are ready to do that is up to you. Sometimes it takes families a while to get used to the idea. It's a hard thing to do, no matter what, I know."

As Michael remained silent, Dr. Bradseth probed him a bit. "Is there anyone else we can call for you? Her mother, maybe? Another relative? It might help to have someone here with you."

Michael shook his head. "There's only me and Vanessa. We're all that's left."

"We have counselors on staff who are experienced in helping families facing this type of crisis. Would you like me to send someone up here to be with you?"

Again, Michael shook his head. "I'd like to be alone for a while, if you don't mind."

"Of course." Dr. Bradseth headed for the door, then turned to face him again. "Take all the time you need. Let us know if there's anything we can do, and when you've made your decision." With that, he walked out the door, closing it softly behind him.

* * *

Time ticked away with every beat of Vanessa's heart monitor, every labored breath from her body. Michael stared blindly down at her, thinking, remembering, wishing.

When he'd told the doctor that there was only he and Vanessa left, it wasn't completely true. There was Michelle. Sweet, innocent, two-year-old Michelle, who would suffer the most from the decision he was about to make. Now he had to become both mother and father to her, to make up for her great loss. How could he do it alone? How could he do it at all when all he wanted right now was to lie down and die beside his beautiful daughter? She was the only good thing that ever came from his life.

Why had God done this to him? Why had he let her live on all these months only to take her away from him?

Her labored breathing told him he couldn't let her continue suffering this way. Each breath, each heartbeat, seemed to shake her entire body. He had seen too much suffering in his lifetime to allow it to happen to Vanessa. So, finally, after what seemed like an eternity, he walked to the door of her room with heavy footsteps and asked the nurse on duty to please contact Dr. Bradseth. He had made his decision.

Chapter Twenty-Three

It took Vanessa's body six hours after being taken off all life support systems to finally find peace in eternal sleep. Michael sat with her the entire time, holding her hand, with little else to do but dwell on the past. He had watched Vanessa enter this world, all pink and wrinkled with a swatch of damp, orange hair on her head. Now he watched her leave, gasping painfully for air, as the baby had once gasped her first breath of life. He saw her take her last breath.

The doctor had warned him she might live up to three days after being taken off the machines, but it took only six hours. He was fortunate, one nurse told him in an effort to ease his sorrow, that she had gone quickly and quietly. Yeah, fortunate, he thought.

As he walked out of room 207B for the final time, the night nurse standing in the doorway patted him on the back. "You can call us in the morning about the arrangements," she told him, brushing away her own tears for losing their princess. "Try to get some rest, okay?"

Dry-eyed, Michael nodded at her, and headed down the hall with no direction in mind. Unconsciously, he walked to conference room 225C and stepped inside, letting the door close softly behind him.

The vet meeting was over for the night, but Kevin was still there, rearranging the chairs and picking up the paper cups from the meeting. He watched Michael walk into the room and straight past him to the window beyond, as if he were invisible.

Michael stared out the window at a tall oak tree illuminated by floodlights. The sturdy tree was all but bare except for a few die-hard leaves hanging onto its branches. He watched as one curled, brown leaf broke free of its grasp in the gentle breeze and fall slowly to the ground, finally released of its hold.

"She's gone," he said aloud.

"I know." Kevin came up behind Michael and laid his hand on his shoulder. "I'm sorry, man."

For the first time that day, Michael broke into heart-wrenching sobs over the loss of his beloved daughter. His whole body shook as he stood in front of the frozen window, the other man's hand steadfast on his shoulder offering what little solace he could.

"Why?" Michael managed to choke out. "Why let her live all these months and then take her away? What was the purpose? It's so cruel!"

Kevin's large hand squeezed Michael's shoulder, then loosened again. "Sometimes it's hard to understand the reason why these things happen. Look at how many of us are still questioning the reason for Nam. But there's always a reason, and it will show itself sooner or later."

Michael shook his head slowly and managed to calm down a bit. He turned and looked up at the husky man before him, feeling better from the few words he'd offered. Kevin was big and rough around the edges to look at, but he had a way of handling people under stress like no man Michael had ever met. His calm blue eyes always seemed to be saying, *I understand. I'm listening.*

Michael bore his soul. "Vanessa was my reason for living, the only reason I cared about anything. Now what do I live for?"

Kevin's brow creased as he stared hard at Michael. "For yourself, man," he said without hesitation. "For all the things you haven't done yet. For all the things that you are. For you." His face softened. "And if that's not enough, there's a little girl at home who's going to need you more than ever now, remember?"

Michael stared at the carpet and nodded his head. Of course. How could he be so selfish to forget about Michelle? Poor little Michelle, who had lost both her parents, who must now rely on him for everything.

"Come on, I'll drive you home," Kevin said, placing his hand on Michael's back and leading him from the room. "You can pick up your car later. You have a lot ahead of you tomorrow."

And the next day and the next day... Michael thought as he let Kevin lead him out the door and down the hallway.

* * *

Vanessa DeCara-Chandler was buried in the family plot beside her husband, grandparents, and great-grandparents, in a small ceremony of guests. Only a few close friends and colleagues had been invited, along with the Chandlers, whose presence both warmed and saddened Michael all at once. Catherine also came out for the funeral and to spend a few days at the house in Southampton with Michael and Michelle to help out.

Michael walked in a trance the days preceding and after the funeral, allowing Cathy to run the house for him, and grateful for her being there. The hardest thing he had done, besides burying his only daughter, was telling Michelle that Mommy would never come home again.

"She's an angel in heaven now," he explained softly to the two-year-old child.

"Mommy and Daddy are angels?" the little girl questioned.

"Yes, sweetie. They're together now."

She smiled up at her beloved grandfather. "Then they're

happy," she told him. He was amazed at how easily she understood and accepted this fact of life. He wished he could understand so readily.

A few days after the funeral, Cathy took it upon herself to buy a Christmas tree and the three of them decorated it in silence. Michelle enjoyed the twinkling lights and colored glass balls, bubbling with anticipation over Santa's upcoming visit. But Michael only went through the motions, not noticing or seeming to care.

Cathy and Mrs. Carols decorated the rest of the house in the hope of lifting his spirits, but to no avail. That evening, after Michelle had been put to bed, Cathy switched on the gas in the living room fireplace and sat with Michael on the sofa, staring into it.

"Christmas is only a week away," Cathy said, breaking the silence between them. "Would you like me to go shopping for Michelle? I'd love doing it for you."

Michael looked blankly at Cathy. He looked so tired and run down.

"I'd appreciate that," he told her, returning his stare into the fire. "You've done so much already. I don't know how I'll ever be able to thank you."

Cathy laid her hand on his leg. "I'm here for you, Michael. For whatever you need," she told him.

He looked up at her again, this time as if he was finally seeing her. Laying his own hand over hers, he said, "You're spoiling me. You'd better stop before I get used to it."

"I'll stay as long as you need me, Michael. As long as it takes."

Michael smiled for the first time in days, warmed by the sweet concern in Cathy's eyes. "And you know I'd keep you here for as long as I could," he told her, still squeezing her hand. "But you have a life that you need to get back to. And someone waiting for you," he added.

"Right now, what's important are you and Michelle. Everything else can wait."

Michael lifted her hand up to his lips and kissed it ever so gently. "No sweetheart, it can't wait. You need to get back to your life, your job, and your man." Seeing concern crease her face he added. "Don't worry about me, Cathy. I'm a survivor. I survived Vietnam, I survived drugs, and I survived the last three months of hell. I'll keep moving on and coping like I always have."

Cathy looked up past him to the table in the hallway stacked high with sympathy cards that Michael had, so far, refused to open. She sighed.

"Will you keep attending the vet meetings at the hospital every week?"

"Yes, ma'am," he promised. "That's the one good thing that's come out of all this. I wouldn't miss them."

Cathy nodded her approval. "Okay. I'll stay long enough to help you with Christmas, then I'll head back home."

Michael seemed satisfied with this and continued holding her hand as they both were left with their own thoughts while staring into the red-blue flames. Cathy hoped and prayed Michael would be able to accept his loss and move on with his life, while Michael wished he had someone like Cathy to help him cope with the years ahead.

* * *

Michael did cope, one day at a time, sometimes taking it an hour at a time. He made it through Christmas Day with as much joy as he could muster for Michelle, yet all the time thinking how sad it was that Vanessa and Matthew weren't there to share Christmas with their daughter.

As promised to Cathy, he continued going to the vet meetings at the hospital, where Kevin always greeted him with a warm handshake. The two had become close friends since the night Vanessa died, sometimes even staying late past the meetings to talk about how things were going for Michael as he struggled through.

He also appreciated the time spent with the other vets, and the stories they shared about life during and after Vietnam. He didn't even mind Joe, who could be abrasive, and who always said what he thought, no matter who he pissed off. Joe really set Michael off at one meeting when he told him that what he needed was a woman in his life.

Michael had been talking about his recurring nightmares of late, and the stress of worrying about Michelle's future when Joe threw that one at him.

"What do I need a woman in my life for?" Michael retorted to Joe's casual observation. "I don't need any more complications right now."

"Complications?" Joe snorted. "A good woman isn't a complication. Hell, I don't know what I'd do without my old lady. She keeps me on the straight and narrow and always tells me like it is."

Michael narrowed his eyes at the man in the wheelchair beside him. Dressed in his usual black T-shirt and jeans, his hair looking like he just got out of bed, he couldn't imagine any woman putting up with him. He was pretty haughty for a man with no legs in a wheelchair.

"I think what Joe is saying is it's always good to have someone you can trust to stand beside you," Kevin offered, trying to smooth things over. "You know, like the buddy system they use in the service. Someone to always back you up when you need him."

Michael thought of Billy and Vanessa. "Almost everyone I

ever cared about is dead," he said, quietly. "That makes me one hell of a buddy, doesn't it?"

Kevin and the others remained silent at this, but Joe wouldn't let it go. "Oh, come on man, there must be someone out there who you're close to. A hunk like you, and rich, too. Can't tell me you have no one."

Michael shot him an evil look. "Yeah, there was someone, once," he replied, thinking of Dani. "But I hurt her, too. Like everyone else who comes in contact with me, I drove her away."

"We vets tend to do that a lot," Kevin interjected. "We're so afraid of getting close to people that we push them away. When all along, what we need are more people around us, not less."

Michael and the others nodded at this, each one understanding what Kevin was saying.

Joe continued shaking his head at Michael. "You need a woman, man," he continued under his breath. "You really need someone."

Michael rolled his eyes at the man beside him, but deep down he understood what Joe was saying. He really did need someone beside him right now. And the only person his thoughts kept returning to was Dani.

Chapter Twenty-Four

The crisp winter breeze nipped at Dani's face as she stood on the deck of her parents' house, staring across the frozen lake. The light dusting of snow that had fallen earlier that day swirled around her feet, but she felt warm and snug in her thick parka and snow boots.

It was Christmas Eve day and Dani had driven up to spend the holiday with her parents. Like most of the retirees on the lake, her parents had a winter place down south but they never closed up the cabin until after Christmas so the three of them could spend it together.

Dani sighed at the thought of having missed both summer and fall here at the cabin. She loved coming up here to the peaceful quiet, fishing with her father, and berry picking with her mother. She loved hiking through the woods in the fall, when the leaves were golden and orange and the pines and cedar trees smelled fresh in the cool, wet mornings. There was no better place to relax and reflect.

But she had been so busy with work, she'd missed it this year. And then that business with Miguel on Labor Day weekend. She would have spent the weekend here if it hadn't been for him. Maybe she would have been better off, too.

"Hey there little girl. What are you doing out here? You'll freeze." Dani's father, Jim, interrupted her thoughts as he came out onto the porch with a wide smile and linked his arm through Dani's.

She returned his smile. "I was just thinking of all the time I missed up here this year," she told him. "It seems all I do is work lately."

"Well, work is important," he said, staring off into the same frozen distance she was.

Dani looked over at him. "But it's not everything, right Dad?" she asked, reading his thoughts.

He only cocked his silver head and raised his eyebrows in question. "I think your mom needs help cracking walnuts for the stuffing," was all he said. "Let's go see if we can snitch a few in the process."

She smiled at her dad as she followed him in. The aroma inside was glorious, from the pies her mother had baked earlier and the cinnamon bread that was now rising in the oven. The decorated pine tree in the corner also added to that perfect Christmas scent. Dani loved her parents' cabin. It was warm and inviting, the furniture familiar and comfortable. To her it was home.

Later, as Dani and her mother sat cracking walnuts for tomorrow's stuffing. and her father watched the news in the living room, Joan turned the conversation to Dani's Christmas party.

"Did you have a good time with your friend?"

"It was okay," Dani said, searching for the right words. Her date with Mark had been fun, but not exciting. He'd been very polite and hadn't even tried to kiss her at the end of the evening. And, she'd been relieved.

"Are you seeing him again?" her mom prodded.

"He asked me to go to a New Year's Eve party with him," Dani answered. To her mother's upraised eyebrows she replied, "I said yes."

"Oh, good. I'm so happy you're getting out, honey. I hate to think of you always working and having no fun." Dani only smiled at her mother's concern.

That evening at Christmas Eve church service, Dani's thoughts wandered over the past year. She wondered where Miguel was right now, and what he was doing. Was he with Vanessa and her family? Would he be watching Michelle open her presents Christmas morning with those chubby hands and delightful squeals? She tried hard to push the thoughts away, but they lingered on.

Chapter Twenty-Five

January placed its icy fingers over Minnesota as life went on for Dani and the rest of the workers at Chance's Department Store. As the weather made its daily changes, so did change occur to the people it touched.

Dani had rung in the New Year with Mark at his friend's party, but when he placed a kiss on her lips to celebrate the strike of midnight, and later at the door of her apartment, Dani felt nothing inside. No spark, no interest, nothing. Not like the warmth and burning desire she'd felt from Miguel's kisses. And although it angered her for thinking it, she felt she might never find anyone else who heightened her senses the way Miguel had. With that weighing heavily on her mind, she declined any further invitations from Mark, and fell back into her lonely weekends.

At work, change prevailed. Janette finally made her decision not to come back to work. By this time, it didn't surprise anyone at Chance's, least of all Dani. Carl offered the job to Dani, but she declined, offering instead the advice to promote Traycee to it. No one else in the department wanted to switch, and Traycee had been working on the accounts over the past months and was familiar with them.

"I'm confident Traycee has the drive and desire to do a good job," she told Trindell. After some consideration, he agreed, as long as Dani promised to help her over the rough spots.

Dani knew Traycee was a good choice. Her opinion of the young woman had changed greatly over the past months, a complete turnaround, like so many other things going on around her. Dani agreed to help and was satisfied so far with her decision. Traycee's youth and enthusiasm was what a job like that needed. And her good fashion sense showed through with each order.

Sitting at her desk one bleak, January morning, Dani pondered over price reductions for upcoming clearance sales. The phone on her desk buzzed, and she picked it up. "This is Dani."

"Well hello 'this is Dani'. This is your friend, Cathy. Remember me?" The voice on the other end was cheerful and laughing, warming Dani's heart.

"Cathy, it's so great to hear from you. How have you been?"

"Okay. Well, actually, wonderful as of this minute. I have some surprising news to tell you."

"Well, tell me," Dani urged her. "Don't make me guess."

Cathy practically squealed. "I'm getting married! Can you believe it? Me?"

"Oh, Cathy, that's wonderful." Dani hesitated a moment. "To your accountant friend?"

"That's right," Cathy confirmed. "Me and the accountant, living happily ever after. Can you believe it? He surprised me with a ring on New Year's Eve."

"I'm really happy for you, Cathy," Dani told her.

"Don't make any plans for July. That's when we're having the ceremony, and I plan on you being my maid of honor."

"You know I will," Dani said. She sat a moment letting the news sink in. Then she remembered about Cathy's promotion.

"I guess congratulations are in order twice for you," Dani said. "I heard about your promotion to head of the Chicago division. Sorry I never called about it, but I am really happy for you."

"Oh, that's okay. Thanks." Cathy's tone became serious. "It would have been exciting except for the circumstances. It was all so sad about Vanessa."

Dani's heart pounded. "Vanessa? What happened to Vanessa?"

"Oh, I thought you knew," Cathy said, sounding surprised. "But of course, you wouldn't know. I'm sorry. Everything was kept pretty quiet."

"What happened?" Dani persisted.

Cathy sighed. "Vanessa and Matthew were in a car accident last fall. Matthew died instantly, but Vanessa was in the hospital in a coma for three months. She died right before Christmas."

"Oh, my God," Dani said, her heart breaking. "What about Michelle? Was she with them?" She silently prayed not.

"No, she wasn't. She's doing okay. She's still young enough, she seems to handle everything fine, which is more than I can say about Michael. He sat by Vanessa's side the entire time. He was there when she died. It was all so heartbreaking."

"Oh, poor Miguel," Dani whispered. "Vanessa was everything to him," she said a little louder. "How is he doing now?" She had visions of him giving everything up. He loved Vanessa so much. She had been his entire life for as long as Dani remembered.

"He's coping. He knows he has to for Michelle's sake. He started going to meetings with other Vietnam Vets while Vanessa was still in the hospital and that has helped him a lot. But he's still very..." she hesitated, searching for the right word, "withdrawn. Like, he's just moving through life, but not really there. It's all so sad."

Dani slumped in her chair, overwhelmed by the information Cathy had just relayed to her. In her mind, she could picture Vanessa as a little redheaded girl running ahead of her on the California beach, jumping waves, and full of life. Now, that same little girl, the beautiful woman she had become, was gone forever.

"Dani, are you okay?" Cathy's voice echoed concern over the line. "I know you were close to Vanessa once. I'm sorry I had to be the one to tell you all this. Dani...?"

"I'm okay," Dani answered quietly. "It's just such a shock." She was quiet another moment, then asked. "When did the accident happen?"

"Labor Day weekend," Cathy replied. "That's why Michael left here and went to New York. He's been there ever since."

Dani lost all focus on the conversation after that. When she finally hung up the phone, she sat quietly at her desk. So that was why he left. It had nothing to do with her, it was because of what had happened to Vanessa. And all this time she had been selfishly thinking of only herself.

"Are you okay?" Traycee came around to the front of Dani's desk, concerned by Dani's sudden pallor. "Dani?"

Dani looked up slowly into her co-worker's questioning eyes. "No, actually I'm not okay." She stood slowly, every movement feeling dreamlike. "Will you take my calls for the rest of the day? I think I need to go home."

"Sure, I'll be glad to. Anything else I can do for you?"

Dani shook her head. "No. I just need to go home." She stood and took her coat from the rack, slipping it on, leaving her desk as it was, not even bothering to close the notebook she'd been working in. "Thanks, Traycee."

"Sure thing, Dani. Take care of yourself. Okay?"

Dani nodded as she walked past the row of desks to the elevator.

While driving home, Dani's thoughts were only of Miguel. Why had he chosen to go through all this alone when he knew she would have dropped everything to be there with him? Had what they'd shared that weekend meant nothing? Then she remembered that he had tried to call her. When was it? Last month? The month before? He had tried to reach out to her, and she had pushed him away.

By the time she reached her apartment, Dani knew what she had to do. She had to let Miguel know how sorry she was, for everything. But she couldn't call him. Not after all this time. So she sat quietly at her kitchen table and tried to put into words everything she was feeling as best she could, addressing the letter to Miguel DeCara.

Chapter Twenty-Six

"My old lady and I are planning another trip to Nam next year," Joe told the vet group one Thursday evening in February. "We plan on staying there two or three months. There's a vet there I know who has helped open an orphanage, and we plan to help out there awhile."

"Now that Washington has opened up diplomatic relations with Vietnam," Dr. Cox broke in, "It will make traveling there much easier."

Joe snorted. "I have mixed feelings on that one," he said. "But anyway, I was thinking that if any of you might want to go too, we could maybe arrange a group travel trip. It cuts down on the cost." He looked pointedly at Michael, who, up to that point, had only been listening to the conversation that evening, and not participating. "What about you, DeCara. You think you might be interested in going back?"

Michael looked at the legless man dressed eternally in black to his left. His tone implied more of a challenge than a question.

"I haven't really thought about it," Michael told him. "I don't understand the point of going back. I'd like to forget all about Nam, not add to the memories."

"Going back there is a way of facing the demons instead of running away from them," Kevin offered. "It helps you see Vietnam as the country that it is, not as the war we remember."

"Yeah, I've been back once and I wouldn't mind going again," Wayne Garrison added. "I went to the spot that my plane was shot down, even found some small pieces of wreckage still there. It helped me put into perspective what really happened, instead of believing the nightmares I kept having."

"It's sort of like the feeling you get when you visit The Wall," Wayne added. "You see the name of a buddy who was killed and you can finally say to yourself 'Yeah, it was real and my friends didn't die for nothing.' The effect is kind of...calming. A relief."

"You have been to The Wall, haven't you?" Joe challenged Michael, referring to the Vietnam Veterans Memorial Wall in Washington, DC. Holding in his anger at Joe's relentless probing, Michael shook his head no.

"God, man," Joe spouted, shaking his head in disbelief. "You been hiding under a rock or something? No wonder you can't shake those nightmares."

Michael's eyes narrowed at Joe. "What's the point of re-living pain? What good will it do to go somewhere that I know will tear me apart?" he asked, his voice filled with anger.

Kevin interjected again. "Tears help wash away the pain. I'm sure you can relate that to having gone through all the cards and letters after Vanessa's death. It hurts to read them, but it helps ease the grief."

Michael lowered his eyes to the floor, his anger abated. It had been two months since Vanessa's death and he hadn't yet touched the stack of sympathy cards that sat on the hall table. Just like Vietnam, he wanted to forget that part of his life ever happened. Yet, the harder he pushed it away, the stronger the memories came.

"Think about the trip to Nam," Joe said quietly to Michael. "And go to The Wall. I'm sure there's a friend or two there that have been waiting for you."

* * *

As the weekend settled in, Michael couldn't shake Joe's words from his thoughts. As much as he disliked the man's coarse behavior, Michael had to admit that his observations were usually correct. How many times had he felt guilty for not visiting Billy's name at The Wall? Had anyone ever made the pilgrimage to see it? Yet, he didn't want to face the reflecting black stone of names alone. Who could he possibly go to such a heart wrenching place with?

Sitting in front of the living room fireplace that crackled warmth against the mid-February chill outdoors, Michael's gaze turned to the stack of cards and letters on the table in the hall beyond. He was all alone with nowhere to go and nothing to do. Michelle was upstairs, taking a nap, the weather was too cold to do anything outside, and he didn't even have any work to finish on his desk. There were no more excuses.

Slowly, he stood and walked to the pile bidding to him. He picked up the stack and went down the hall to his office, placing the cards on his desk. After staring another full minute at them, he finally walked around the desk, sat, and began opening the cards one at a time.

The late afternoon sun tried at intervals to spill into the room between clouds that were blocking its way. Michael paid no attention to its efforts as he opened one card after another. It was hard. Friends, acquaintances, and business associates all telling him how sorry they were for his loss. Some recounted a memorable incident that they would never forget, while others only scrawled a name under a pre-printed verse. Michael's own memory was jolted several times from the writings in the letters and tears spilled from his eyes as he remembered.

A quarter of the way through the pile he stopped, wondering how many more he could endure for the day. But as he stared past the cards and out the window to the gray ocean beyond, he realized that reading the cards was helping him. They reminded him of people and events that he had forgotten, and of all the people who had been touched by his daughter's short life. Kevin was right. Pain was helping to heal the hurt.

As he contemplated going through more cards, one envelope in front of him caught his eye. It was addressed to Miguel DeCara. No one called him Miguel anymore, except Dani. His heart pounded. Quickly, he opened the envelope and read the script on the enclosed card.

Dear Miguel,

I am so sorry about the loss of your beloved Vanessa. I have just heard, and the shock is still strong. Of all the people who know you, I might be the only one who understands just how much you loved your daughter and how much you will miss her.

I wish I could say or do something that would ease your grief, but I know that there aren't enough words to do so. All I can do is let you know that I will always remember the smiling face of the beautiful, redheaded girl as she jumped waves on the California beaches, and the beauty of the woman she had become. She will be forever in my heart.

Take care of that lovely daughter she has left behind. I know that you will give her all the love and care she needs, as you did her mother.

My heart is with you.

Dani

Staring at the card in front of him, Michael read and re-read it several times until it finally sank in. Dani. She had written to him to try to ease his pain, just as she had always eased his pain from the nightmares that haunted him. Once again, she was there for him. He wondered how long her letter had been waiting for him and looked at the postmark on the envelope. January 15th. The card had been sitting here over a month and he hadn't even known it. She had reached out to him again, like that night months ago when she had given him her outstretched hand and led him into her bedroom.

Did he dare reach out to her? Would she give him one last chance?

Reverently, he pulled his wallet from his back pocket and slipped out the piece of paper that held her phone number. Giving himself no time to think, no time to reconsider, he dialed the number.

The phone rang twice before her familiar voice touched the line. "Hello."

"Hello, Dani."

"Miguel. How are you doing?" she asked, softly.

"Better, now that I'm talking to you."

There was silence on the other end, so Michael kept on talking. "I just opened the letter you sent me about Vanessa. Thank you for writing it. For caring enough to write it. It really has helped."

"I'm so sorry, Miguel. I only wish...," her voice faltered. "I wish I had been able to share more in her life," she finished softly.

The catch in her voice made his insides twist into knots. "Dani, I was wondering, well, I mean," he stumbled over his words like a nervous teenager. "Would you come out and see me? Your summer buying trips must be coming up, and, well, I thought if you were going to be out here sometime soon, maybe you could take a few extra days off and spend some time here at the house."

"Oh, Miguel, I, I don't..."

"You'll be out here anyway, won't you? The summer coat showing is the first week of March," he persisted.

"I'm not in charge of coats anymore."

"Oh. But you'll be coming out for your other departments, won't you?"

"Well, yes, but...,"

"Please Dani. Please," he interrupted. "Just a couple of days. That's all I'm asking." He sounded desperate, but he didn't care. He suddenly realized that he needed to see her, even if it was the last time. "Please. I really need to see you."

The line was silent for several moments as if Dani were wrestling with her thoughts. Finally, she answered. "Okay. I'll let you know when I'll be able to come."

"Thank you, Dani," he said, relieved.

"But Miguel," she continued. "Please don't expect too much from me. Okay?"

"Okay," he agreed before saying goodbye and replacing the receiver. "Don't worry, Dani," he said quietly to himself. "This time I'll be the one to do all the giving."

Chapter Twenty-Seven

The office was silent except for the hum of the florescent lights above and the laptop computer sitting on Dani's desk. It was a little past seven in the evening on a Monday night, and she was the only one left in the office, except for Carl Trindell, who was sitting in his office with his door slightly ajar.

Tomorrow, she and Traycee were headed to New York City for their last summer buying trip of the season. Dani was only responsible for the sportswear and jewelry showings this time, but would help Traycee with any ordering questions she might have after the coat shows.

Dani looked at the laptop one more time to assure herself she was familiar with the new ordering procedures for Chance's. Instead of filling out endless paperwork, they were going to send information electronically to Chance's via computer so orders and invoices could be sent immediately.

As she stared at the screen, her mind went instead to thoughts of Miguel and the two days she planned to spend with him at his Southampton home. She had talked with him for only a few moments on the phone to let him know when she was coming, and all he said was that he had a couple of things planned that he hoped she would enjoy doing.

What sort of 'things' do you do with a man you once loved, then hated, then fell back in love with, only to be put off by him again? What exactly did he want from her and what did she have left to give?

"All ready for your trip tomorrow?" Trindell's voice made Dani's head snap up and she placed a hand over her heart.

"Carl, you scared me."

"Sorry," he said and sat down on the corner of Dani's desk, something she had never seen him do before. Dressed in simple gray slacks, a white shirt, and sensible black leather shoes, his shirt sleeves rolled up to the elbows and his tie loosened, he looked like a man on the tail end of another era, another time. The fatherly concern that creased his face reminded her of Robert Young in *Father Knows Best*.

"Got that thing all figured out?" he asked, pointing to the new laptop computer on her desk.

"Oh, yes, no problem. Just making sure I have everything in order."

"I'm not worried about that," Carl said, taking his glasses off and rubbing his eyes. "You always do. That computer will come in handy on this trip," Carl continued. "Especially since you'll be taking some vacation time while you're there."

Dani tipped her head in question. "Is that a problem, Carl? Because if it is..."

"No, no, not a problem at all," he interrupted her. "I'm glad you are taking some time off. You really need it after all the work you've had these past months. I think the time will do you good. You've been very preoccupied these past few weeks. Besides," he stood up and rubbed the back of his neck. "This contraption will get all the orders to us so you won't have to worry about rushing back."

Dani only nodded, not sure what to say. She knew Carl was trying to get at something, but being a man of few words, she realized it was hard for him. He paced a couple of steps and then turned back to her.

"We've worked together a long time, haven't we Dani?" he asked, quietly.

"Fifteen years," she offered.

"Longer than most people stay in one place in the retail business."

Dani nodded again, remembering the many changes that had occurred in the office staff over the years, especially the most recent with Janette and Traycee.

"You know, Dani," Trindell trailed on. "I've seen a great many people come and go through the years, and some I don't even remember. But you're someone I'm really going to miss when the time comes for you to leave."

She looked up at him in stunned silence. Finally, she found her voice.

"What makes you think I'm ever leaving?"

Trindell smiled in that knowing, fatherly way. "Nothing. I just wanted you to know that. Well, you have a good trip to New York and enjoy your time off." He lingered only a second, then headed back to his office as Dani watched him go, a confused expression on her face.

Chapter Twenty-Eight

The trip to New York City was uneventful for Dani. To her, it was just another buying trip in another large city. Before she knew it, Friday arrived and all the orders had been placed and sent off to Chance's via computer. Traycee was on the airplane heading home, and by early afternoon, Dani was riding the train through Long Island toward Southampton.

Miguel had offered to pick her up at her hotel but she insisted on taking the train instead, afraid of the two-hour car ride alone with him. She had her suitcase on the floor beside her and her coat bag, containing the red wool coat, lying over the back of the seat next to her. She'd brought the coat on a whim, but hadn't yet worn it and didn't know if she would. The March climate in New York was warmer than that of Minneapolis, but heavy coats were still necessary some days.

As the train entered the Southampton station, Dani's heart pounded in anticipation. What would she say when she saw him again? Was there anything left to say?

Picking up her suitcase and coat bag, she stepped out the double doors of the train and let her eyes scan the station. In only moments, she found a pair of gray eyes looking back at her.

"Hello, Dani," Michael said as he walked up to her with long strides and placed a light kiss on her cheek. "I'm so glad you came."

Dani was relieved that her hands were full of luggage because his casual welcome, especially the gentle kiss, unnerved her. How could the slight brush of his beard against her cheek cause so much turmoil inside her? All she could muster was a simple, "Hello, Miguel."

"Here, let me take those for you," he offered, relieving her of both suitcase and coat bag. "I have the car just outside. Follow me."

Dani did just that, moving as if in a trance. He led her outside the station to a black, four-door sedan, first unlocking her door then rounding to the back to place her things in the trunk. No limousine, no driver. For some reason, this surprised her.

She studied him a moment as he loaded her luggage. He was dressed simply in blue jeans, sneakers, and a moss-green sweater. He didn't look at all like the rich coat mogul he had become, he looked like the Miguel she remembered from long ago.

Looking up at her, poised to slam the trunk in place, he questioned her puzzled look. "Something wrong?"

"I guess I expected a limousine," she said before thinking, then turned slightly pink from her own words.

The trunk slammed as Michael chuckled. "That's only for business," he said. Unlocking his own door, he looked over the roof at her. "Are you disappointed?"

Dani shook her head. "No. Not at all." Then they both slipped into the car and he took off.

Once they were out of the station traffic, Michael slid a glance in her direction. "You look good," he told her.

"Thanks."

"Did you have a successful buying trip?"

Dani fingered the armrest beside her. "Yes, it went well. Traycee, she's our new coat buyer, she found some great buys at your showing."

"Oh, that's good," he replied as he watched his rear-view mirror before turning into the left lane. "I hear the show was a great hit this year. We had a larger amount of orders than usual."

She looked up at him, surprised. "Weren't you there on Thursday?"

"No," he said, shaking his head. "I always stay here on Thursdays. That's my meeting night. Besides, that's what all my employees are there for. And I trust my management's judgment."

"Oh," was all Dani could manage. Still looking up, she studied him closely. His hair and beard had gained some gray strands since the last time she'd seen him and his face looked a bit thinner than before. But he still looked handsome, and the sparkle was still in his eyes when he glanced over and caught her staring at him. She snapped her attention back to the road ahead.

"Guess what I found the other day?" he asked, but didn't wait for her to answer. Reaching down between the seats, he picked up a cassette tape and popped it into the player. "Hotel California" by The Eagles began strumming through the car speakers.

"I didn't even know I still had this," he told her, smiling like a child at his discovery. "When I found it, I immediately thought of you."

The song embraced Dani like a comfortable sweater, bringing back the warmth and love of their California days. Only the good memories swept through her mind, the beaches, the sunsets, and little Vanessa. If his motive for playing this music had been to put her in a nostalgic mood, his plan had worked.

Brimming with past emotions, she reached out a hand and placed it lightly on his arm. "I'm really sorry about Vanessa," she told him, knowing it had to be said before anything else could be.

"I know," he whispered back, then looked over at her with an attempt at a smile. His gray eyes were warm, the pain still evident in them, and the light strokes of time that appeared around them only added to their charm. Looking into them that brief moment gave Dani the sudden urge to draw him into her arms and kiss his pain away. Instead, she dropped her hand from his arm, and her eyes back to the road in front of her.

When they reached the house, he parked right outside the front door then once again made the trip to the trunk to retrieve Dani's luggage. She followed him through one of the large doors into the grand entryway, and once again marveled at the home's beauty. The white marble below her feet gleamed to perfection, while thick Abusson rugs with patterns in black, white, and green lay strategically placed, adding warmth. The oak stair railing shimmered as it curved up to the top of the grand staircase. To her left, the afternoon sun spilled in through the white French doors that dominated the ocean side of the living room. An oversized fireplace with marble and oak trim stood invitingly in front of the overstuffed brown leather sofa, even without the glow of a fire within.

"I'll take you up to your room," Michael offered, bringing her attention back to him. "Then you can change into some play clothes and get comfortable."

Dani looked down at her navy, wool pantsuit, silk blouse, and heels. "Play clothes?" she questioned, one eyebrow raised.

"Sorry," he chuckled. "I guess I've been with Michelle too long. I just meant something more comfortable than work clothes."

"Ah." She nodded her head and followed him up the curved staircase.

They took a left at the top of the staircase and passed several doors before he stopped in front of the last one at the end and set the suitcase down to open the door.

"I hope you like this room. It's the cheeriest one in the house."

And it was. She stepped into the largest bedroom she'd ever

seen in her life, done up in white wicker furniture, yellow walls, and white lace curtains over the tall expanse of windows and French doors facing the ocean. The bed was dressed in a very old yet lovely star quilt made of yellow and calico print, and several throw pillows were strewn across the head of the bed. Lace doilies, yellow calico print pillows, and tablecloths adorned every chair and table in the room, each a different print, yet each blending beautifully to bring the room to life. Dani loved it immediately.

"There's a small bathroom through that door," Michael offered, pointing to the right. "And the French doors open out to a balcony outside."

She looked toward the doors, then back at Miguel. "It's beautiful. I love it."

He smiled his endearing smile. "I thought you would. It seemed like the perfect room for you."

For a moment, as Miguel stared at her, Dani thought he might take her in his arms, their pull feeling as strong as the midnight tide. But instead, after a moment too long had past, he backed his way to the door, stuffing his hands in his pockets.

"I'll wait for you downstairs. Michelle should be up from her nap. I thought we could go for a walk on the beach."

Dani nodded her assent, smiling at his sudden shyness and the way he was backing away from her nervously. It struck her as funny how this man who usually seemed so in control, with his sharp wit and flair for teasing, could suddenly behave so differently.

Once he left, Dani dressed quickly in a cream cashmere sweater and jeans, slipped on a pair of brown loafers, and headed to the bathroom to pull her hair back. The bathroom was small, but lovely, done in lemon yellow with a white pedestal sink, brass fixtures with a large, gilt-framed mirror over it. The shower stall was also white with brass fixtures, and boasted a yellow striped shower curtain. Expertly, Dani pulled her hair back in a French braid, banded the end, then headed out of the room and back the way she'd come just minutes before.

Michael and Michelle both looked up from their seated position on one of the rugs as Dani descended the staircase. There was a Pomeranian puppy prancing between them, almost dancing with excitement from the attention it was receiving. The puppy's glossy red coat paralleled that of the spiraled tendrils that touched the shoulders of the little girl sitting beside Michael. They both smiled up at her, making her heart pitch for a single moment as she felt transported in time to the same man with another little girl at his side.

Michael stood up, slinging a giggling Michelle up into his arms as the puppy bounced happily at his feet.

"Wow, you're fast," he exclaimed to Dani. Then shifting his attention back to Michelle, he said, "Honey, this is the lady I was telling you about. You met her last summer. Her name is Dani."

The little girl smiled as Dani stepped up to her. Touching her arm gently, Dani said, "My, you've grown a lot since the last time I saw you. And your hair's much longer, too." She gently touched one silky tendril, unable to resist it.

"I'm three now," Michelle announced proudly, her emerald eyes sparkling with the same mischief as Michael's did. Her 'three' came out 'tree', which brought a warm chuckle from Dani.

"Well, that explains why you're so big," she told her.

"See my puppy?" Michelle asked Dani. "Her name is Fruff."

"I think Fluff," Michael corrected Michelle teasingly as he set her back on the floor, "is trying to trip Grandpa."

Dani kneeled on the floor beside Michelle and ran her fingers through the puppy's thick fur. "Fluff is beautiful. She has red hair just like you."

Michelle giggled. "That's what Gampa says, too."

"Well, Grandpa is right," Dani replied, looking up into Miguel's sparkling gray eyes. The warmth and tenderness he felt for the little girl beside her was displayed openly in them, and when he looked at Dani, that same loving look stayed, making her heart melt.

"Okay you two. How about a walk on the beach?" Michael suggested. "It's cool out, but the sun feels good. And I think that little puppy could use a good run."

Michelle nodded yes vigorously, and Michael offered a hand to Dani and pulled her up from her place on the floor. As their hands touched, their eyes did also, and a spark was felt between them.

"I'll have to go up and get my coat," Dani said, hastily retrieving her hand from his and busying it to smooth out her jeans.

"Don't bother. We have plenty in the hall closet." He walked the few paces to the door in the entryway and opened it to reveal several coats hanging neatly on padded hangers. He handed Michelle a small, puffy blue one with pink trim and she quickly slid herself into it and began trying to zip it herself.

Turning back to the closet, he studied it a moment, his hand brushing first upon a green jacket, then a purple one, before moving on to another blue one and pulling it out. "Do you mind wearing one of mine?" he asked Dani, handing her the coat. "It might be a bit big."

Dani guessed that the others in the closet had belonged to Vanessa and Miguel didn't have the heart to see them on anyone else. She nodded slightly. "It will be fine," she assured him. He looked relieved and picked out a black jacket for himself and slipped it on.

"Hey squirt, let me help you with that." Michael bent down on one knee and helped a frustrated Michelle zip her coat, then tapped one finger on her little freckled nose before saying, "All ready? Let's go!"

The late afternoon sun felt warm on their backs as the three of them made their way slowly down the strip of beach. Michelle ran ahead with the puppy, which continually tangled itself around the little girl's feet. From time to time, Michelle would trip in the sand, catch herself, and giggle, then continue on as the puppy did its little dance.

Michael and Dani kept a slow, steady pace behind her, enjoying her laughter and the puppy's antics. Despite the chill in the breeze, Dani felt snug in Miguel's jacket. Occasionally, a faint scent of his cologne would tease her senses as it drifted up to her from the jacket. She inhaled it fondly, wanting to remember every scent, every scene, and every step of this moment. At times, it seemed much like the past, the days before the pain and the hate. She just let herself imagine it was so, not wanting to spoil the moment with reality.

After a time, Michael called to Michelle to turn back toward the house and he and Dani stopped to let the little girl catch up to them and run ahead before the two continued their trek in her tiny footsteps. Both were silent, neither knowing what to say. And yet, there was a comfortable feel to their silence, as only people who have been together for years can share.

When they reached the house, Michael allowed Michelle a few more moments on the sand while he and Dani took a seat on the steps of the veranda. They sat, watching the ocean waves ease their way up on the shore, the tide steadily coming in closer as evening approached.

Wordlessly, Michael turned from the view in front of him to look at the woman beside him. Dani's cheeks were pink from the cool air, and a few strands of golden hair had escaped from her braid to blow gently around her face. It took great effort not to reach out and gently brush one of those silky strands back with his fingers.

"I'm glad you came," he said, quietly, breaking the silence at last. "Thank you, Dani. I know it took a lot for you to come here."

Dani turned to face Miguel. "I was afraid of coming at first," she admitted. "But now I'm glad I did."

"Afraid?" Michael creased his brow. "Why?"

She glanced over at Michelle, running carelessly in the sand with Fluff, then turned her gaze back at Miguel. "Because it gets harder and harder every time we say goodbye."

Michael was about to reply when Michelle came bounding up beside him, breathless and flushed from her play. She whispered something into his ear that made his face break out into a full smile.

"Michelle is wondering if you would like to go to a movie tonight," he said to Dani as Michelle waited eagerly for her answer.

Dani's brows rose. "A movie?" she asked playfully. "And what movie does Michelle want to see?"

"The latest Disney cartoon, of course," Miguel replied for Michelle. "She's only seen it three times, but she was worried you might have missed it. Have you seen it yet?"

Dani laughed. "A Disney cartoon? I haven't been to a kid's movie since…" she stopped, remembering that the last time had been to see *The Jungle Book* cartoon with him and Vanessa. "Well, let's just say it's been a long time."

"Ah ha! Michelle, you were right. I guess it's our duty to take her to see it now." Michelle nodded her little head eagerly, her eyes bright at the prospect of seeing the movie again. Michael turned from her and asked Dani quietly, "Do you mind?"

"Mind?" She pretended to be insulted. "Any movie Michelle recommends must be good. Besides," she added for him only. "I think it will be a lot of fun."

Michael brought his hands together in one loud clap. "Then it's settled. To the movies we go. But first," he said, looking straight at Michelle. "We have to get the sand out of our shoes and have a bite to eat."

And together they did just that, just as any family might do, making Dani feel a little bit closer to Miguel and Michelle, and a little bit closer to the heartache she knew she would feel when she'd have to say goodbye.

Chapter Twenty-Nine

The three ate a quick meal of soup and sandwiches in the cozy family dining room at the rear of the house by the kitchen. The cheerful little room was really meant as a breakfast nook, with its white lace curtains dressing up windows that overlooked the beach and ocean and charming white table and chairs with blue and white striped cushions. There was also a formal dining room off this room, Michael explained, but they preferred the little one instead. "Sometimes the house just seems too big," was how he put it.

After eating, they were off with Michael at the wheel of his car to the little, old fashioned theater in Southampton. So used to the mega-theaters of Minneapolis, Dani was charmed by this old-time theater with its enormous lobby, snack bar, and balcony seating. The seats were large and padded in red velveteen, matching the carpet and wallpaper, and the screen was larger than any she'd seen in years.

They chose seats in the very middle and Michelle plopped herself between Michael and Dani, insisting on holding the extra-large bucket of popcorn in her lap so everyone could reach it. Dani chuckled at Michelle's little feet, unable to reach the floor, swinging back and forth, and her big eyes barely able to see over the large bucket on her lap. Over Michelle's head, Dani caught Miguel's eyes, and they both shared a secret smile at the sight of her.

Dani enjoyed every minute of the movie, it was heartwarming and upbeat, and the music was catchy. Of course, she contributed part of what she was feeling to the company she was with. At intervals, Michelle would tug Dani's arm and whisper to her what was going to happen next, and Michelle also sang along quietly to every song. Dani was amazed at the little girl's memory. A couple of times, Dani and Miguel both reached into the popcorn bucket at the same time, bumping hands, then exchanged looks over Michelle's head. It felt so right sitting here together that Dani wished the movie would never end.

The popcorn disappeared and the movie ended, its theme song playing as the credits rolled on screen. The house lights brightened as Michael, Michelle, and Dani stood, stretched, and put their coats on to leave.

"That was a great movie, Michelle," Dani told her as she helped zip the little girl's jacket. "Thanks so much for taking me."

"Maybe we could see it again." Michelle told her, making Dani laugh out loud.

"Maybe so," Dani replied.

"Let's see, that would make it five times then," Michael interjected. "And just wait until the video comes out." He rolled his eyes good-naturedly as the three of them left the theater and headed back to the house.

The drive was quiet, and Michelle began nodding her little head in the back seat, tired from her long day. By the time they reached the house, she was sound asleep, so Michael carefully lifted her from her car seat and carried her inside.

Dani followed them upstairs, carrying the little rag doll that had been sitting in the seat with Michelle. They took a right at the top of the stairs and entered the nursery, just a short walk down the hall. Mrs. Carols had heard them come in and appeared at the door that separated her room from Michelle's, but Michael quietly told her he'd put Michelle to bed so she went back into her own room and silently closed the door.

Dani studied the room around her in awe as Miguel expertly changed Michelle into pajamas and tucked her into bed. The beauty and details of the room with its seascape mural and stenciled seashells, white bedroom furniture, and toy furniture with brightly printed cushions overflowing with dolls and stuffed animals, all showed how much love and attention had gone into this room for this little girl. Dani didn't miss the gentle way Miguel prepared his granddaughter for bed, how lovingly he stroked her hair, and then placed a kiss on her cheek. The sight of him with Michelle reminded her why she had fallen in love with him eighteen years ago, and it touched her heart watching him now.

Michael stepped back from the bed and flicked off the nightstand light. The night light on the opposite wall shone softly, making the stars on the ceiling twinkle from its glow. Remembering the doll, Dani stepped up to the bed and laid it carefully beside Michelle's sleeping form, taking in every detail of her quiet face framed with silky red tendrils. Finally, she tore herself away, and she and Miguel headed to the door together, but as they reached it, he turned for one last look at his granddaughter.

Standing there, together, in the dark nursery watching the sleeping form, hearing the steady breathing of sleep, Dani couldn't help but think how right this felt. How perfect to be putting a little girl to bed with this man beside her. But the moment ended and they slipped out into the hallway and walked slowly toward the stairs.

"It's still early," Michael said. "We could go downstairs for a while."

Dani nodded yes and the two walked down the grand staircase in silence. The living room was aglow with only one lamp by the main couch, the rest left in deep shadows despite the full moon that played through the glass doors at the far end.

Although the room was large, the set-up of several cozy sitting areas made it seem comfortable. But it was the sofa in front of the fireplace that usually drew the most attention, and that was where they stopped now.

"I'll start a fire," Michael offered.

"You don't have to go to all that trouble," she objected.

Michael bent down toward the fireplace. "No trouble at all," he said as he turned a brass knob protruding from the stone. In a flash, the fire was lit.

"The easiest fire in the world," he chuckled. "Gas."

Dani shook her head as she sat down on the thick cushions of the sofa. "Not exactly what I'd expect in a mansion," she teased.

"It was my Dad's idea," he told her as he walked over to the stereo cabinet and turned the radio on low. Dani recognized the song as one from the seventies but couldn't remember the name of it. "He hated starting real fires so he changed all the fireplaces in the house to gas."

He walked back to the sofa and stood beside it. The soft lighting melted years from his face, and standing there with an uncertain expression reminded Dani of how he'd looked years ago.

"All the fireplaces? Just how many does this house have?" Dani asked.

"Well, let's see," he tipped his head and scratched his beard a moment in that well-known gesture Dani remembered so well. "There's one in the main dining room, one here, one in the largest guest bedroom, and there's one in my bedroom, too. I'll have to show it to you sometime." The words came out innocently, but when Dani raised an eyebrow at him, he became nervous again and shifted his feet.

"Would you like a drink, or a soda or water or something?" he asked, quickly. "Or, if you're hungry, I could get you something."

Dani shook her head slowly, a small smile playing on her lips. "I don't want anything," she told him quietly. Then, surprising them both, she asked, "Why are you so nervous, Miguel?"

Michael plopped down on the sofa beside her and let out a relieved sigh. "I'm afraid if I say the wrong thing, you'll leave," he told her honestly.

She turned to face him, placing her hand over his. "Why did you ask me to come here? It wasn't to see a movie and stuff myself with popcorn." He smiled at this. "You had a reason, I'm sure."

Michael turned his hand in hers and entwined her fingers with his. Just her touch calmed him. It was warm and familiar, like all his memories of her.

"You know me too well," he said, as his thumb rubbed gently over her own.

"I've known you too long not to," she teased him.

"Yeah, but you know what? I like that. I like the fact that you know me so well. I like that we have a past together, that we share the same memories. I like the familiarity of it all." He stopped a moment, collecting his thoughts as the music played softly in the background.

"You know, I thought about you so often as I sat at Vanessa's bedside, waiting. Whenever things got tense, you were the only person I could think of that I wanted to talk to. But then I'd tell myself that it wasn't fair to drag you into it. I'd hurt you so much already. How could I ask you to come and share this pain, too?" His grip on her hand tightened a little and she could almost feel his pain. She wanted to tell him she would have come if only he'd called, but then she remembered that he had called, once, and she had rejected him. Guilt kept her silent.

"I was at my worst when I learned about the vet meetings that were being held at the hospital. I decided to go, or else go crazy. And you know what? It really helped. Talking with the other vets who have been through what I have has helped me a lot. The nightmares come less often, and they even helped me face Vanessa's death."

"Cathy told me you were going to those. I was really happy to hear it," Dani told him.

"You were right, as usual," he said, smiling. "Years ago you told me to get help, but I was too pig-headed to do it. Actually, remembering what you told me years ago helped me decide to go after all."

Dani looked him straight in the eye. "It has nothing to do with me," she told him firmly. "It was you. You alone. Only you deserve the credit."

Michael looked at her a moment. "You know, that's exactly what Kevin told me when Vanessa died. I felt as if my only reason for living had been for Vanessa. I had put my own life aside to build a life for her. And when she was gone," he stopped a moment. Dani could see the pain still etched in his face and her heart ached for him.

"Well," he continued, "he told me I had to start living for myself. For all the things I had been and for all the things ahead of me. I've thought about that a lot over the months, especially the part about making a future."

Michael stopped again and Dani found herself staring into the depths of his gray eyes. What she saw in them startled her. There was a time when she thought of those eyes as cold steel, menacing and calculating. Yet, the warmth and tenderness he was feeling at that very moment shined through to her. Was he thinking of a future with her? And if he asked, how would she answer?

Michael spoke again, breaking her thoughts. "But first, I have to work on some of my past, before I can plan a solid future," he told her quietly. "There are some things I'd like to do to begin facing my Vietnam past. I'm even considering a trip back there to see it as it is today."

Dani's eyes opened wide. "Really?" she asked, amazed at this revelation. "I can't even imagine what that would be like for you," she said, honestly.

"I know. I can't either. But that's a long time from now. The first place I want to go to is a lot closer to home. The other vets tell me that a visit to The Wall helped them face the past. So, I was thinking, if you don't mind, oh hell!" He slammed his fist on his knee, angry at himself for being so afraid to ask. He sounded like a teenager asking her to go to the prom. "Will you go with me to The Wall tomorrow?"

Dani knew what he meant by The Wall without having to ask and she realized just how important a visit there would be. "Of course I'll go with you," she told him gently. "I'm so happy that you want to take me with you."

He breathed a sigh of relief. "Thank you, Dani," he said softly. "I was afraid to go alone, and you were the only person I thought of that I could go with. You always seem to understand that part of my life better than anyone else."

Dani smiled up at him. She felt proud that he asked her to be a part of this important step toward his healing.

"Well, it's getting late. I'll walk upstairs with you," he offered.

She watched him turn off the gas for the fireplace, then the stereo and lamps, and then together they made their way up the staircase, side by side. When they got to her room, they paused a moment, staring at each other.

"Can you be ready to leave by nine?" he asked her.

"I'll be ready."

He reached up his hand and gently touched the side of her face. Instinctively, she lifted her hand and placed it over his.

"Thanks for listening to me rattle on down there," he told her.

She smiled back at him in answer.

Then, with a soft brush of his lips against hers, he said goodnight and walked across the hall to his own room. As Dani turned the knob on her door, she allowed herself one last look in his direction and saw him looking at her, too, and for the briefest second, she wished he'd come back to her. But he only smiled, then disappeared into his own room as she did the same.

Chapter Thirty

Dani awoke early the next morning, showered in her yellow bathroom, and chose a pair of gray slacks and a matching gray cashmere sweater to wear. She tied a flowered silk scarf loosely around her neck to add a splash of color and left her hair down.

She knew it would be cold today, even though the sun was trying to stretch its rays through the floating clouds, so she reached into the closet to get her short, black wool coat. But when her hand brushed up against the bag containing the red coat, she stopped and reconsidered a moment. She had brought the coat on a whim, not even knowing if she'd have the nerve to wear it. Would it be appropriate to wear it on such a serious day as today? After a moment's hesitation, she opened the bag and took out the coat. Slinging it over her arm, she walked briskly out the door before she could change her mind. She knew seeing the coat on her would make Miguel happy, and he needed a boost like that today.

Dani made her way down the stairs and as soon as she reached the bottom, she saw Miguel walking down the hall from the breakfast room.

"Good morning," he said, smiling at her. He was wearing a green jacquard sweater and khaki slacks, looking casual and comfortable, except for his somber eyes. "You look great, as usual. Would you like something to eat before we go?"

Dani shook her head. "No thanks. I'm not very hungry right now."

"Okay. Well, we might as well get going then."

Dani slipped on her coat as Michael reached into the hall closet for his own. When he turned around, his dark eyes brightened in surprise.

"You bought the coat," he said, noting the enamel pin on the lapel, too, but not mentioning it. "It looks great on you, just like I said it did." He looked thoroughly pleased that she had worn it, which made Dani happy that she had.

After slipping on his own black trench coat, they made their way out the door and into his car parked right outside.

They took the 9:45 a.m. plane out of East Hampton Airport to New York City, then the 11:00 a.m. shuttle plane into Washington National Airport. They found a cab right outside the airport terminal.

"Where to?" the cab driver asked as Dani and Michael slid into the back seat.

"The Wall," Michael answered quietly.

The driver knew exactly were he meant. He'd driven hundreds of vets to The Wall in his ten years as a cab driver. He also knew enough to leave the couple in back alone with their own thoughts during the drive.

Their trip so far had been a quiet one as both reflected on their own thoughts and feelings. Now, in the cab as they neared Constitution Avenue, Michael reached for Dani's hand and held it tight. From his firm grasp, she could feel his tension. She wished there was something she could say to help calm him, but maybe just holding her hand was all he needed.

The driver dropped them off on 23rd Street near the Lincoln Memorial, just a short walk to The Wall. Michael paid him then turned to Dani, and arm in arm they made their way up the Mall toward the black stone that beckoned them.

From a distance, The Wall looked little more than a black barrier, but the closer they came, the more impressive it became.

As the couple neared The Wall, they both stopped and stared in awe at the sight before them. The tall, glossy black granite reflected everything around it, from the clouds that cluttered the sky to the Reflecting Pool that lay beyond it. It was almost as if The Wall could look deep into the heart and soul of every visitor and reflect what was within.

After a moment of silent appreciation they continued on their way until their feet touched the stone walkway that made its journey along The Wall. They made their way down the walk, checking the directories as they passed to find the slab that contained Billy's name. Michael knew the exact date he had died, the month, day, and year, even the hour. That was something one never forgets when he sees his best friend blown to pieces before his eyes. Especially when that drama is played out over and over again in his nightmares.

Dani marveled with silent reverence at the over fifty-eight thousand names of the missing or dead etched into The Wall. As they walked together, hand in hand, she noticed the many flags, POW*MIA banners, and flowers that lined the small strip of grass along the base of the wall. Simple reminders that friends, relatives, and even strangers remembered these lost lives.

Dani knew the instant Michael found the right spot for he stopped and became tense, his hand growing cold in hers. Slowly, they both scanned the strip of Wall before them in search of one solitary name among the many. It was Michael who found the name first, and his eyes locked onto it like a magnet to steel.

He slipped his hand from Dani's and walked slowly to The Wall, raising his fingertips to touch the name before him. *William J. Berry.* "Billy," he whispered, and as his fingers met the cold stone it was as if he was transported back in time. He could see it all before him in the deep reflection of the black granite. The rice fields with the dense jungle beyond, artillery fire ablaze in the background, the choppers whirling overhead, and the intense smell of smoke all around. Then Billy, in fatigues, flak jacket, and helmet, his gun slung casually over his shoulder, walking up to him, telling him it was okay, the wait was worth it, he was finally here. Michael bowed his head, his fingers still adhered to the stone, his shoulders shaking as tears spilled from his eyes.

Dani watched Michael through her own tears, wanting so much to ease the intense pain she saw enveloping him. Seeing Billy's name on The Wall made everything so real, even for her. Although she had never doubted his existence or Michael's stories, seeing the name etched in stone brought the reality of Vietnam down hard.

Crossing the gap between them, Dani slipped her arms around his waist and laid her head gently against his back as her own tears spilled on the smooth black fabric of his coat.

They stood this way for several minutes, oblivious to all that went on around them. Once, Dani opened her eyes and her gaze rested upon a man in uniform down the length of The Wall. He stood at attention, saluting a name before him. More tears spilled down her cheeks at the sight of him, and at that same instant, she hugged Michael tighter, silently thanking God for allowing him to come home, and for not being a name etched beside the others.

* * *

After a time, they broke away from The Wall, and, arm in arm, searched for other names Michael remembered. There was the man from the poster in his home office who was missing in action, and another who was killed only days after arriving in Nam. But they weren't really men, Michael reminded her, just boys.

"Henry was only eighteen when he died," Michael said quietly as they stood in front of the name of the boy who had lasted only three days. "Eighteen. We were all so young."

As they continued down the length of wall, he began talking more, easing the original tension they had both felt upon arriving. He told her a couple of funny stories about him and Billy, making her laugh at the thought of them. She couldn't imagine Michael being that young and silly, but liked the idea of it.

By the time they had made their way completely around The Wall, Michael had shared many positive stories about the war with her. Remembering some of the good things he and his platoon had done, like the time they found the two lost children and helped them find a family member, or the time they came upon a village right after the Viet Cong had burned it down and found an unconscious mother and her baby there and called in a chopper to take them to a medical unit. These good memories helped to counteract the painful ones. He'd forgotten them, until now, and had only dwelled on the nightmares. It was then that he began to understand why the other vets said a visit here was important. The Wall helped you remember the whole story, not just the horror.

And walking beside him, listening to everything he was telling her, Dani felt closer to him than she had ever felt before. A comfortable closeness she wanted to hold in her heart forever.

After one final glance at The Wall, Michael offered to show Dani some of the other sights. His mood had lightened greatly, and he was ready to continue on. They visited the Washington Monument and rode the elevator to the top to view the city below. From there, they walked up 15th Street to Pennsylvania Avenue to view the White House. The afternoon sky had cleared by then and the sun shone brightly on the President's home and its surrounding gardens, giving the couple an impressive view.

They ate a late lunch at an Italian restaurant before making their way back to the Lincoln Memorial. Dani was impressed by all she saw, this being her first time in the Capital. Michael said he'd been here once when he was a child, before Vietnam, before The Wall, but he enjoyed looking at the historical monuments again.

The sun was making its way west as the couple walked down the steps of the Lincoln Memorial and headed back to Constitution Avenue. They caught sight of The Wall again, and Michael stopped.

"Do you want to go back again, before we leave?" Dani asked, gently.

Michael slowly shook his head. "No. I'm sure I'll be back for another visit again." He turned to her and smiled warmly. "We'd better get back and catch the last commuter plane before we miss it."

Dani nodded, and they made their way, arm in arm, back up the street to hail a cab.

Chapter Thirty-One

The sun had set and the moon shone brightly over the gentle ocean waves as Michael and Dani stepped into the entryway of his home. It was late and everyone was asleep, and there was only a small light on in the entryway when they stepped in. Michael hung up his coat and Dani took hers off and slung it over her arm. He turned the light off, and they made their way up the broad staircase bathed in moonlight.

When they reached the door of Dani's room, they stopped a moment, staring at each other in silence. It had been an incredible day for both of them, their emotions and adrenaline running strong. Neither knew exactly how to end such a day.

"Are you tired?" Michael asked her.

"Not really," she answered, not wanting the day to end.

"We could go in my room and talk a while," he suggested.

Dani looked across the moonlit hall to his door, then back at him.

"I promise, I'll behave," he told her, noting her hesitation.

Dani smiled. "Okay. For a few minutes, I guess."

They entered his room and he hurried to turn on a bedside lamp, then walked over to the fireplace that was across from his bed and turned the knob.

"Instant fire again," he said, teasingly.

Dani walked over to the small sofa in front of the fireplace and laid her coat over its back. She assessed the room a moment, silently approving of the tones of gray and the massive sized furniture. The room suited him perfectly, she thought. It looked...regal. A short laugh escaped her when that word came to mind.

"What's so funny?"

"I was just thinking how well this room suits you and the word 'regal' came to mind. Quite appropriate, don't you think?"

Michael smiled. "Regal room, Regal Coats. Yeah, it seems to fit."

They both sat down on the sofa, facing each other.

"I used to like this room," he told her. "But lately I think it's sort of morbid with all this dark gray and dark furniture."

"No, Michael. It's perfect for you. It's tasteful and unassuming, like you."

Michael tilted his head and stared at her in amazement. "You just called me Michael, not Miguel."

"I did?" Dani thought about it a moment. All day she had been thinking of him as Michael, not Miguel. For the first time ever, she was thinking of him as he was now, not as he was years ago. "That's funny," she said. "Michael seems to fit you better now."

"Maybe you've just heard it so often from everyone else that you're used to it," he suggested.

Dani shook her head. "No, I don't think so. The way I think of you has changed. I've seen so much change in you over the past two days that it just seems right to call you Michael."

He smiled at her and his eyes sparkled in the firelight. "You know what? I'm going to miss you calling me Miguel. I was getting used to it again."

"Well," she gave him a sideways glance. "Maybe I'll call you that when I'm mad at you, so you won't miss it so much."

They both laughed then, feeling carefree for the first time that day. The deep color of the room seemed to wrap around them in warmth and closeness, like a thick wool blanket feels as you huddle beside a campfire. Michael took Dani's hand in both of his, changing his expression back to the serious look of earlier.

"Thank you for coming with me today," he said sincerely. "I would never have survived today without you being there."

"Thank you for taking me. I'm glad I could share today with you. It was very special for me."

"You were there for me when I needed you the most. You always were."

Dani lowered her head, not wanting to meet his eyes. "Not always," she said, quietly. "I should have been with you a few months ago, and Vanessa."

Michael placed his hand under her chin and drew her eyes up to meet his. Their blue depths were warm and moist. "That wasn't your fault," he told her firmly. "It was my fault for not telling you."

"But you did try to tell me, and I wouldn't listen," her voice cracked. "I blew you off when you needed me the most." Two tears trickled down her face. "I wish I could have seen her, one last time."

"Oh, Dani." Michael pulled her close, hugging her tight as he spoke into her hair. "It's not your fault. I hurt you so much in the past, I don't blame you for running from me. You're here now, that's what's important. You're here." He held her close for a long time, feeling the silkiness of her hair brushing against his cheek, smelling her sweetness, not wanting to ever let her go.

And she let him hold her, feeling safe and warm in his arms. When they broke apart, she searched his dark eyes with her own, and their lips met in such passion it surprised them both, but neither tried to break away. They kissed each other hard for a long time, and it was Michael who finally came to his senses and pulled away.

"Oh, Dani," he said, breathing hard, running his fingers through his thick hair. "I'm sorry. I promised I wouldn't do this.

But it's so hard not to touch you." He cupped his hands around her face. "I love you so much," he whispered. "You're the only one I think about, the only one I want. I was such a fool to let you go the first time. I need you so much."

He kissed her again, unable to control the emotions he felt for her, but she didn't care. She wanted him to hold her, to kiss her, to make love to her. She wanted him next to her, if not forever, then for tonight. So when he pulled away a second time, she shook her head, placed her hand behind his neck, and pulled him to her.

They kissed that way for several minutes as the passion within them grew stronger. Michael pulled back slightly, taking both her hands in his, and they stood together before the firelight. Slowly, he untied the silk scarf from around her neck and slid it off, dropping it on the couch. The sweater came next, as he slipped it over her head, letting it fall to join the scarf.

He pulled her to him and held her tight, moving his hands up and down the soft skin of her back, feeling the silkiness of her satin bra push against his sweater. The firelight gave her skin and hair a soft golden hue, the color of wheat on an autumn day, as he held her close, wanting to feel her, smell her, experience her with all his senses.

Shivers of excitement ran through Dani at his touch. She ran her hands up the back of his sweater, eager to feel him, too. His muscles flexed at her touch, and a soft moan escaped his lips. Would it always feel this way with him, she wondered, as her excitement grew stronger with each caress. It never mattered how many years or months passed between them, his very touch erupted burning desire and passion within her. And she pulled him even closer, wishing it could be this way forever.

Finally, no longer able to control the desire that was ablaze between them, Michael led Dani to his bed, pulled back the covers with one swift movement, and together they shed their clothes and joined in a sweet release of passion.

"I love you," Michael whispered again to her when their passion was spent and they held each other close.

"I love you, too," Dani told him. And together they drifted off to sleep, comforted in each other's arms.

Chapter Thirty-Two

The sun was barely making its way up into the sky when Dani slowly awoke, confused at first, then smiling as she remembered where she was. She turned carefully, not wanting to wake Michael, and watched him sleep, a peaceful expression on his face. She wanted so much to touch the silky strands of dark hair that had fallen over his forehead, but refrained herself so as not to wake him. She satisfied herself instead with just watching him sleep as she replayed yesterday and last night in her mind.

He'd said he loved her. Not just once, but many times. And that he was a fool for leaving her the first time. How many times over those first few years after he'd left had she wished he'd come back and say those very words to her? Even when she had hated him, at times she thought she'd take him back if only he'd come back and tell her those exact words.

And now here she lay, years later, beside the only man she ever truly loved, ever really wanted. Yes, she loved him. She had told him so last night. She realized that even through her hate for him, she had still loved him. The hatred had been a way of holding onto his memory and not letting him go. But now that was all over, and she was here. What now?

He had loved her before, and left her. Would that happen again? Could she live through that pain a third time? Did she even want to?

Michael stirred in his sleep and Dani tensed until she saw he hadn't awakened. Even tousled in sleep, he looked handsome and inviting. It made it hard for Dani to think about anything else except losing herself in his arms again.

But she had to make herself think of more than that this time. She needed to be alone with her thoughts to sort out all that had happened between them.

Quietly, she slipped from his bed, slipped her coat over herself, and picked up the clothes that lay scattered on the floor. Then she crept from his room and across the hall into her own room. Slipping the coat off and some sweats on, she crawled under the comforter on the bed and lay staring at the ceiling above.

Alone, in the solitude of her own bed, she was better able to see the truth of last night. Yesterday had been such an emotional day for Michael and for her, it was no surprise that the evening ended in each other's arms. But in the cold light of the morning, would he still feel for her what he did last night? And for how long?

After much thought, Dani realized what she had to do. Although she didn't regret spending the night in his arms, and in her heart she knew that she loved him, she couldn't, or wouldn't, expect Michael to hold true to his words. He'd been under too much emotional strain at the time. He only needed someone to help him through. So, before she would wait for him to tell her, she thought it best to get on with her life first. It would be painful leaving him, but it would be less so if she did it before any promises were made and broken.

As the day broke into sunshine, Dani slipped out of bed, showered, dressed simply in a white silk sweater, navy slacks, and flats, and packed her bag to leave.

She was just stepping out into the hallway, suitcase in hand, coat bag slung over her arm, when Michael stepped out of his own room and saw her.

A big smiled appeared on his face as their eyes met, his

sparkling with mischief. He had showered and was wearing jeans and a cream shirt with a casual tan wool blazer over it. The scent of his trademark cologne drifted to her, making the thought of leaving him harder, melting her heart, but not her resolve.

"You sneaked out on me," he teased as he came near and placed a light kiss on her lips. He looked fresh and spirited and young, so different from the solemn man of yesterday. As if last night had revitalized his soul. But when he noticed the suitcase in Dani's hand and the bag over her arm, his face dropped.

"Are you leaving?"

"Yes, Michael. It's time I went back."

His brow creased as he studied her face, trying to read her thoughts. This was the last thing he'd expected. "Can't you stay just a couple more days?"

Dani shook her head, trying to look anywhere except into Michael's eyes. "No, I really have to leave. I made a reservation on the ten o'clock commuter flight to New York City from East Hampton."

Michael stared at her, trying to understand, the smile long gone from his face. In a quiet voice, he said, "I see. So this time, you leave me. Is that it?"

"No, Michael. It's just better for me to leave now before…" she hesitated.

"Before what?"

Dani sighed. "It's just time to go back to my life. To reality. Okay?"

Michael drew closer to her and placed his hands on her arms. She dropped her suitcase and let the bag fall to the floor.

"To reality?" he asked. "This is reality, Dani. You and me. Here. Right now."

"No, Michael, it isn't. This is all fun and nice right now, but we both know it won't last. It never does."

"And last night?" he asked, still confused by what was

happening. "Didn't that mean anything?"

Dani finally looked at him, her eyes sad. "Last night was beautiful, like it always is when we're together. But yesterday was such an emotional day for you. For me, too. We were caught up in the emotions of the moment. It was inevitable we ended up together."

Michael pulled her closer. "No, Dani. This isn't like the other times. When I told you I loved you last night, I meant it. And I mean it now. I love you, Dani." He dropped his lips to hers and kissed her hard, pulling her close so she was pressed against him. Unable to reign in her own emotions, she responded, opening her lips to his, savoring his taste, his touch. But when Michael pulled away, all he saw was sadness in her eyes.

"What can I do to convince you?" he whispered hoarsely. Then, suddenly, his eyes lit up and a small smile fell on his lips. "I know," he said, grabbing her hand and pulling her down the hallway to the back stairway.

"Michael, what are you doing? Wait," Dani protested. But her words fell on deaf ears as he led her down the stairway, across the hall, and into his office downstairs. It was the same thing he'd done almost a year ago at the party. Dani wasn't sure what he was up to.

When they entered the office, he let go of her hand and walked quickly to his desk, opened the top drawer, and lifted something out of it. Dani stood in the morning sunlight that drifted through the windows, watching him as he circled the desk and came back to her. The portrait of Vanessa smiled down on them from above.

"I meant it when I said I love you, Dani," he repeated. "I knew I still loved you since that first night last September. But I didn't know what to do about it then. I've had a lot of time to think about it over the past few months, and I know now what I want." He handed her a small, black velvet box.

Dani looked from the box back to him, confused. "What is it?"

"Open it," he said, that mischievous look in his eyes again.

She slowly opened the box and gasped when she saw what was inside. Against the black velvet lay a brilliant cut diamond solitaire ring in a sparkling gold setting.

"I remembered a long time ago when you and I passed a jewelry store on the wharf. You pointed to a ring just like this one and said if you ever got married, you'd want a ring like this. Simple but elegant, you'd said. Here," he pulled the ring from its case and slid it on her finger. It fit perfectly.

Dani looked down at the ring as it sparkled in the sunlight, then back up at Michael, shock and surprise registered on her face.

"Dani," Michael said, softly, clasping her hands in his. "I know I can't make up for all the pain I've caused you, or for all the lost years between us. But I want to spend the rest of my life trying to make you happy. I want to share my life with you, my work with you, and everything I have. I want to share Michelle's childhood with you. Dani, will you marry me?"

The room seemed to enfold them as Dani searched the gray depths of his eyes, trying to absorb what he was saying. Marry him? Did he really mean it? She could hardly believe it, yet he looked at her so intently, his eyes so sincere, she knew he was serious.

"Oh, Michael," was all she could say. She stared down at the ring, then back up at him. "I don't know." She was at a loss for words.

"Just say yes," he told her, smiling down at her.

Dani dropped her eyes, unable to look at him and that smile that always reached her soul. Here she was, standing with the only man she had ever truly loved, being asked to share his life forever after eighteen years of waiting, yet, she was unable to answer. It should be so easy, she thought, so simple, but it wasn't.

"I can't," she said finally, her head still bowed so he couldn't see the tears that were forming in her eyes.

"Why not?" Michael asked, then a thought occurred to him. "Don't you love me, Dani? Is that it? No, I can't believe that. Not after last night. You love me, too. Don't you?" He placed a hand under her chin and brought her eyes up to meet his. "Dani?"

Tears spilled as she answered him. "Yes, Michael. I love you. I've loved you since I was eighteen, and even through all those years that I thought I hated you, somewhere deep inside, I loved you. I never stopped loving you."

"Then what's the problem?" He smiled again, happy to hear she did love him. "We're together now, and we can stay that way forever."

Dani turned her head away and pulled her hands from his grasp. "No, Michael, it's not that easy. It's too soon. So much has happened. I need some time to think."

"Too soon?" Michael gave a short laugh. "Dani, we've been waiting eighteen years for this moment. Why make the wait any longer? We still love each other after all these years, and we've survived the pain. Who deserves happiness more than we do, together?"

She turned to face him. Her voice wasn't angry, only sad. "And if you decide in a week, or a month, or a year from now that it isn't right? What then? There have never been any guarantees between us before, what makes now any different?"

Michael bridged the gap between them and pulled her into his arms. "I'm sorry I hurt you before, Dani. But I promise you, I won't hurt you again. After all I've been through, I've changed. You have to believe me. I'm not the same man I was years ago, even months ago. Even you've seen that. You said so yesterday."

Yes, he had changed, Dani thought as she let him hold her

close. But enough to make a lifetime commitment? Enough to know that it was her he wanted to share that life with? Or was she expecting too much to want a hundred percent guarantee? Everything was happening too fast. She needed some time to clear her head.

Pulling away from his embrace, Dani slipped the ring from her finger and gently placed it into Michael's hand.

"I'm sorry," she told him, her blue eyes reflecting her sorrow. "I need time to think. It's all too much right now."

He stood quietly for a moment, staring at the ring in his hand. The ring he had picked out just for her, when he thought they could live happily ever after just like a fairy tale.

"At least wear the ring a while," he said. "Until you decide."

But Dani shook her head. "It wouldn't be fair to you. Wearing it would be like a silent promise I'm not sure I can keep."

Michael walked back to the desk and slipped the ring back into its velvet case. But he wasn't going to give up so easily. He believed they belonged together and he was determined to make her understand that. But he didn't want to press her further, he'd give her the time she needed.

Slipping the ring case into the pocket of his blazer, he turned back to her. "Promise me you'll think about it. You won't go home and pretend this never happened and let the miles between us separate us. Because you know I'll be calling you day and night, reminding you I'm here and waiting for an answer." His tone was half-teasing, but she believed that he really would.

"I promise," she said.

Michael looked at the clock and sighed. "Then I guess I'd better take you to the airport or you'll miss your plane." He walked across the room and stood looking at her a moment, then walked past her and she followed him out into the hallway.

"I'll go up and get your things," he offered, heading up the back stairs. "Why don't you wait for me in the entryway?" He was gone before she could answer.

She made her way down the oak paneled hallway, out into the sunny entryway. As she caught sight of the foot of the grand stairway, she saw Michelle and Mrs. Carols heading up the stairs from breakfast.

Michelle saw her, too, and pulled away from her nanny, running down the steps and up to Dani. "Hi, Dani," she blurted out, coming to a halt at her feet. She was wearing soft green bib overalls that enhanced her emerald green eyes, and her mass of red curls were tied back with a big green bow. Dani wanted to pick her up and squeeze her tight.

"Hi, sweetheart," Dani said, dropping to her knees to face her eye to eye. "Did you have a good breakfast?"

Michelle vigorously shook her head up and down. "We had pancakes today. Do you like pancakes?"

Dani smiled. "I love pancakes," she told her.

"Are you and Gampa ready to go walking again? I can get Fruff and we can go."

Dani looked tenderly at the little girl in front of her. She looked so much like Vanessa, it hurt. More than anything, she'd love to be a part of this little girl's life. Yet, was it enough just to want it?

Michelle shifted her feet, anxiously waiting for a reply.

"I'm sorry, honey," Dani finally told her. "I'm leaving today. Your Grandpa is getting my suitcase now." It hurt her to see Michelle's face drop, but in an instant it lit up again.

"Will you come back?" she asked innocently.

"I'll try," was all Dani could tell her.

"Good," Michelle said with a finality that made it sound as if Dani had said yes. She looked up at Mrs. Carols then back to Dani and lowered her voice as if in some sort of conspiracy. "It makes Gampa happy when you're here."

"Did your Grandpa tell you that?" Dani whispered back, surprised by the little girl's words.

"Nope, I just know." Then, with the spontaneity only a child has, she wrapped her arms around Dani's neck in a big hug.

Dani held her tight for several moments, enjoying the feel of her affection. Then Michelle drew back and headed over to Mrs. Carols again. "Goodbye," she said, waving her small hand.

"Goodbye sweetheart. Take good care of Grandpa, okay?"

Michelle giggled and Mrs. Carols nodded at Dani and said goodbye. Then the two headed up the stairs, hand in hand. Dani's heart ached as she wished it was her walking up with the little girl instead.

Slowly, she stood up again and was smoothing her slacks when Michael came up behind her.

"Ready?" he asked, setting down her suitcase and bag and handing over her coat and purse.

Dani put a hand to her chest. "You scared me," she told him. "I thought you were coming down the front stairs."

"Sorry. I came down the back way to see if I could catch Michelle. But she had already left the breakfast table."

"She just went up with Mrs. Carols. I said goodbye to her."

"Oh." He acted nonchalant, but the truth was he had been standing in the shadows of the hallway the entire time, watching them. He figured it couldn't hurt to have Michelle pull a few heart strings, too.

"Well, we'd better go," he said. He helped Dani slip into her black wool coat. She hadn't wanted to wear the red coat again, unable to bear wearing it when she said goodbye.

Picking up Dani's suitcase and bag again, Michael headed out the door with Dani trailing behind. She took one last longing look up the staircase and then headed out the door into the March sunlight.

The drive to the airport was a quiet one. Both sat in

thoughtful silence, he trying to think of ways to talk her into staying, she telling herself all the reasons why she should leave.

Behind her lay the dream of a husband and family, something she had yearned for over the years. Ahead of her loomed a job she no longer found stimulating or exciting, an empty apartment, and a life full of lonely weekends. Beside her sat a man who had professed his love for her and asked her to share his life with him. The same man who she'd loved so wildly in her youth, who she still found deeply exciting yet comfortable and easy to be with. Would she ever again find another man she could feel this passionate about? If she chose to stay, would it be for love, or out of desperation that this was her last chance for happiness?

When they arrived at the airport and parked, Dani looked over at Michael and he at her, and for several seconds they only stared at each other. She knew then, looking into those warm, gray eyes, that if she chose to stay, it would be for the love she felt for him, and for no other reason.

Their gaze broke and Michael stepped out of the car and carried her bags into the terminal for her. Together they checked her in and checked her bags. The woman behind the counter told her that the plane was leaving in ten minutes and they were already boarding. They walked side-by-side to the boarding gate, neither touching, then turned and faced each other one last time.

"I love you, Dani," Michael said, placing his hands on the smooth wool arms of her coat. "I'll be waiting here for you, whenever, whatever, you decide." He placed a light kiss on her cheek, then let her go.

Indecision filled her eyes. She glanced at the gate she was about to walk through, then back at the man she was about to leave. She took a short breath.

"Goodbye, Michael," she whispered, then turned and walked with determined steps toward the line of passengers waiting to board the plane.

With each step, her heart ached. As she looked at the plane outside the window, her steps became slower. She was doing the right thing, she told herself. She needed time to think. She was doing the right thing.

As she waited in line, staring at the plane that would take her away from Michael, the sad ending scene from one of her favorite old movies came to life in her mind. It was the famous final scene of *Casablanca*, as Rick and Ilsa stood facing each other, deciding their fate in the few seconds they had left. What was it Rick had said? *"If that plane leaves the ground and you're not with him, you'll regret it. Maybe not today, maybe not tomorrow, but soon, and for the rest of your life."*

Dani glanced back to where Michael was standing, then ahead to the plane once more, finally knowing what she had to do. But unlike Ilsa, she didn't get on that plane. She turned and ran back to the man she loved and wanted to spend the rest of her life with. With no regrets.

When Michael saw Dani running back in his direction, his expression turned from shocked surprise to a wide, open smile of delight. As she reached his arms, he lifted her up and pulled her to him, kissing her long and hard on the lips, unaware and uncaring of the stares from the people around them.

Pulling away from their embrace, he looked at Dani with that boyish look his eyes sometimes held that she loved so much. "Does this mean yes?" he asked hopefully.

"Yes, Michael. The answer is yes!"

"Yes!" he cheered for all to hear, then he fished out the ring still in his pocket, pulled it out of the case, and slipped it onto Dani's finger in one smooth motion. They kissed again, as people passed them and smiled at the happy ending they were witnessing.

Dani looked down at the ring on her finger, then back at the man she'd just agreed to spend the rest of her life with. Nothing had ever felt so right, so perfect.

"I guess this means I'm going to be a grandma," she said, her eyes teasing his.

He tilted his head back and laughed. A happy, content laugh. "And a beautiful grandma you'll make," he said. Then they turned and walked slowly, arm in arm, out of the airport and toward the life ahead of them.

Chapter Thirty-Three

The soft sound of the waves lapping against the beach was the only music present as Dani and Michael exchanged marriage vows on the outside veranda of his Southampton home. It was late afternoon in the middle of June as the bride and groom stood, facing each other before the minister, exchanging words of love and commitment with only their closest friends and relatives present.

Dani's parents were there, with little Michelle standing between them, already attached to the beautiful redheaded girl that was becoming a part of their family. Beside Dani stood Cathy, smiling in appreciation at the love she saw between her two dearest friends. Kevin stood on the other side of Michael, looking a bit uncomfortable in his gray suit and tie, but proud to be a part of Michael's important day.

Dani faced Michael as wisps of wind touched the hem of her tea-length, cream satin skirt and the pearl buttons of her fitted lace bodice sparkled in the sunlight like her eyes sparkled now as they met his. They were a beautiful couple. Michael looked regal in his dark gray suit and Dani stunning in her cream dress, her hair pulled back in a French knot, holding a bouquet of white and yellow roses. The entire ceremony was simple yet elegant, like the couple now vowing their everlasting love.

Dani hadn't left Michael's side since the day at the airport when she made the decision to stay. She'd had her things packed and sent to her from her apartment and from her desk at

Chance's. Carl Trindell was sad to hear she was leaving, but understood completely and even told her she would always have a job waiting for her if need be.

She'd spoken to Janette, too, who had congratulated her warmly on her upcoming marriage and also let her in on the news that she was expecting her second child in December. Motherhood suited Janette well, she was thriving and happy, and once again Dani marveled at the great turnaround in Janette's life, and now in her own.

Dani fit easily into Michael's life as if she'd always been a part of it. She'd already begun going to the Regal offices with him, learning the ropes at his side, and had been accepted warmly by the other employees. They all respected Michael and enjoyed being a part of his company and were happy to see he had finally found someone to share his life with. And Dani had a great sense of business, so they appreciated her input and knowledge.

During the week Dani, Michael, Michelle, and Mrs. Carols stayed at the Manhattan apartment so the two could commute to the office. But by Thursdays, they all returned to the Southampton house for the weekend so Michael could continue attending his vet group meetings. He was progressing well, and his nightmares were coming less and less. He'd begun talking about going on a trip to Vietnam in the next year or so, maybe even with some of the other vets from the group. Dani knew this was a big step for him, but a positive one, and encouraged him to do it. He wanted her to go with him, and she was very willing, even eager, to visit the place from his past.

And with every passing day Dani fell more and more in love with Michelle. Sometimes she didn't even go to the office with Michael so she could stay with Michelle and take her to the park or shopping. She was even considering staying home from the office altogether, at least for the next couple of years, to spend time with the energetic redhead. Now that Dani had a child to love and care for, she didn't want to miss a single moment of her childhood. Michael was thrilled with the idea when Dani mentioned it to him.

"Work will always be there for you," he'd told her. "But Michelle will grow up fast." He encouraged her to do what felt right for her.

Just as the vows they now finished exchanging felt right, too. After the couple exchanged rings and made the final kiss to seal their promises, there were happy smiles and hugs all around from friends and family.

"Well, you beat me to the altar," Cathy teased Dani as she hugged her tight. "But remember, you have to be in Chicago next month for my wedding."

"I wouldn't miss it for anything," Dani told her, happy they both had found someone to spend their lives with.

Kevin turned to Michael and slapped him good-naturedly on the back. "Congratulations," he told him. "You've really found someone special, man. I'm happy for you."

Michael clasped the large man before him in a giant hug. "Thank you, Kevin," he said as he stepped back. "I couldn't have made it this far without your help."

"You did it all yourself," Kevin told him quietly. "I was just on the sidelines, cheering you on."

Dani's parents came up to hug the couple and congratulate them with Michelle clinging to her new great-grandfather's arm.

"Just explain one thing to me," Joan asked, after hugging both Dani and Michael in turn. "How did I manage to skip being a grandmother and go directly to great-grandma?" Everyone laughed at this, knowing that both of Dani's parents were already enjoying their new role with Michelle.

The group turned then and went into the house where a delicious buffet and wedding cake were waiting in the grand dining room. Dani was about to enter the house when she noticed Michael was not with the party ahead, and turned to see him standing at the railing, looking out over the ocean and sky beyond.

The sun was just making its way west, and streaks of red and orange lit up the summer sky. Dani walked up behind him and put her arms around his waist.

"Having second thoughts already?" she teased him.

Michael smiled and slowly shook his head. "No," he said, still staring at the expanse of water before him. "I was thinking about Vanessa and wishing she could be with us right now. I think she'd be happy for us."

Dani stepped up beside Michael at the railing, leaving one arm draped around his waist as he placed his own around hers. Still looking up at the sky, its color so much like Vanessa's own hair, she said quietly. "I think she is with us now. And she approves."

Michael faced her then, this woman who always seemed to understand him completely, this woman he had almost lost and then found again. They'd come full circle, he and she, and they had the rest of their lives to share all the love he was feeling right now. He bent his head to kiss her, but was pushed away suddenly by a little girl with only one thing on her mind.

"Time for cake, Gampa!" Michelle insisted, planting herself firmly between them.

Michael tilted his head back and laughed heartily, then lifted Michelle up into his arms as Dani watched the two with pure love in her eyes.

"Come on, Grandma," Michael said, putting his free arm around Dani as Michelle balanced in his other. "Let's go have some cake." The three entered the house together in each other's arms as the family they had become.

Epilogue

Today

Dani stood outdoors on the veranda staring out at the beach and ocean, her thoughts lost in the water's depths. It was late afternoon, and she had just bid farewell to the last of the guests who had attended the funeral reception. She sighed heavily, relieved that the day was almost over and she could finally breathe. She had appreciated all the friends, colleagues, and neighbors who had stopped by to share their condolences, but after a time, she had felt worn down and exhausted. Now, it was finally over.

The big house was quiet. The caterers had already cleared away any stray dishes or glasses left behind by guests, packed up their van, and driven away. Martha, their housekeeper and cook, had also left for the day after checking in on Dani one last time and sharing a hug. Now, the only ones left in the house were Dani, Michelle, and Alex, and an abundance of silence.

"Grandmom," Michelle said, coming up behind Dani. Dani turned to see her granddaughter look at her with worried eyes. "Are you okay?" Michelle asked.

Dani reached out her arms and Michelle fell into them, the two hugging each other tightly. "It's been a long day, hasn't it baby girl?" Dani asked, still clinging to Michelle. She felt Michelle nod into her shoulder as the two women found comfort in each other's arms. Finally, Michelle drew back to look at her grandmother. "You look tired," she said, quietly.

Dani nodded. "I am," she admitted. When Michelle showed her worry with a frown between her green eyes, Dani patted her shoulder to reassure her. "I'll be fine," she said. "A good night's sleep and all this fresh air will help me feel better."

Michelle nodded. "Alex and I are going for a walk on the beach to clear our heads," she said. "Do you want to join us?"

Across the room, Dani saw Alex standing uncomfortably, not quite sure if he should be interrupting this family moment. Dani smiled. He was a nice boy, good looking and considerate of Michelle's feelings. Michael had liked him and hoped the two would stay together after college. Dani liked him, too. She knew he would be a great comfort to Michelle emotionally, and a shoulder to lean on when she returned to college after this.

"You two go ahead," Dani finally said. "Enjoy a peaceful walk. I think I'll just stay here awhile longer." After another long hug, Michelle went to join Alex and the two left the room holding hands.

Once again alone, Dani sat down in a chair on the veranda and watched as the young couple came into view. Hand in hand, Michelle and Alex walked slowly along the water's edge as the breeze lifted Michelle's auburn hair from her shoulders. For one brief second, Dani could almost believe it was the Michelle's mother, Vanessa, walking down the beach with her red hair whipping up in the breeze. Dani gazed up into the clear, blue sky scattered with white, puffy clouds. "You're finally together again," Dani said aloud. Michael and his daughter, Vanessa, would finally be united after years of being separated too soon. This thought comforted Dani. "I know you both will continue to look after Michelle, too," she said.

Sitting there alone, Dani thought back through all the years she and Michael had shared. Even though they had only spent eighteen years together, they had loved and shared more than most people do in a lifetime. Michael had promised to love her forever, and he had. He'd given her everything that had been missing in her life, and so much more. Love, a home, and a beautiful child to raise and care for. All the things she thought she'd never have, he had given her. They had traveled together, worked together, and raised Michelle together. It was the perfect life, one she would have never imagined she'd have until Michael and she were together at last.

But then, three years ago, the cancer diagnosis had changed their lives forever, and after fighting harder than he'd ever had in his life, cancer had taken Michael away. Now, at only fifty-five years old, Dani was alone again with huge responsibilities ahead of her.

Dani stood and walked through the open French doors into the living room, stopping at the many family photos that decorated the fireplace mantle. There were photos of Michelle's parents, Vanessa and Matthew, on their wedding day, and another of the couple with a chubby baby Michelle in their arms, smiling. There were old photos of Michael's parents and one of Dani's parents, and several of Michael, Dani, and Michelle throughout the years.

Michael had been there for Dani when each of her parents had died in turn, first her father several years ago and then her mother more recently. He had given Dani support when she had decided to stay home and be a full-time caregiver to Michelle, and had welcomed her back to Regal Coats when she'd decided it was time to work again. They had been lovers, parents to Michelle, and partners in everything they did, and had made many memories along the way. And before cancer took Michael's final breath, he'd asked Dani to promise to continue running the family business and watch over Michelle until she could, at last, be the next generation of DeCaras to run Regal

Coats. It was an easy promise for Dani to make.

Dani slowly made her way to the grand staircase and began climbing the steps up to her bedroom. Michael had kept all his promises to her, and now it was time for her to keep her promises also. She had years ahead of her, years to continue the family business, watch Michelle blossom into a woman, become a wife and a mother, and eventually take over Regal Coats. Dani was up to the challenge, because Michael had loved her so completely while alive, she knew she could live off that love for years to come.

As Dani reached her bedroom door and stepped inside, she smiled to herself as she looked around the room. The décor had changed from the first time she saw this room but the feelings of warmth and love would always remain the same. She knew she could go on because, of all the many things Michael had given her, the greatest gifts had been the memories of their life together, an extraordinary life filled with love, happiness, and wonder. It was these beautiful memories that would keep her focused and content until the day she was finally able to be by his side once more, her first love and her last love, the man she had loved forever.

###

About the Author

Deanna Lynn Sletten is a bestselling and award-winning author. She writes women's fiction and romance novels that dig deeply into the lives of the characters, giving the reader an in-depth look into their hearts and souls. She has also written one middle-grade novel that takes you on the adventure of a lifetime.

Deanna's women's fiction novel, **Widow, Virgin, Whore,** made the top 100 bestselling books on both Amazon and Barnes & Noble in 2014. Her romance novel, **Memories,** was a semifinalist in The Kindle Book Review's Best Indie Books of 2012. Her novel, **Sara's Promise,** was a semifinalist in The Kindle Book Review's Best Indie Books of 2013 and a finalist in the 2013 National Indie Excellence Book Awards.

Deanna is married and has two grown children. When not writing, she enjoys walking the wooded trails around her northern Minnesota home with her beautiful Australian Shepherd or relaxing in the boat on the lake in the summer.

Deanna loves hearing from her readers. Connect with her on:

Her blog: www.deannalynnsletten.com
Twitter: @DeannaLSletten
Facebook: www.facebook.com/DeannaLynnSletten
Goodreads: www.goodreads.com/dsletten

If you enjoyed **Memories,** you might also enjoy these novels
by Deanna Lynn Sletten

Destination Wedding
(Romance)

Sara's Promise
(Romance)

Finding Libbie
(Women's Fiction)

Maggie's Turn
(Women's Fiction)

Summer of the Loon
(Women's Fiction)

Widow, Virgin Whore ~ A Novel
(Women's Fiction/Family Drama)

Please enjoy the following excerpt from Deanna's novel

Widow, Virgin, Whore

Chapter One

"Well, what do you think?" Katherine Samuals spun in a complete circle, arms raised, her voice echoing in the empty room.

"I love it," Denise Richards replied, watching her friend complete her circle. "But this is going to take a lot of work. Are you sure you're up to it?"

Katherine slowly viewed the room around her, pleased with what she saw. The work didn't bother her. It would be like a fresh start, a new challenge. The house she lived in now held too many memories; this would be an ideal way to begin making new ones.

"I've always wanted a Victorian house like this to fix up and live in," she said, beaming. "I don't care how much work it is. All it really needs is some paint and a new finish on these floors." Her heels clicked on the oak floorboards as she walked across the room to the bay window that viewed Puget Sound. "Any amount of work is worth this view. It's beautiful, don't you think?"

From the center of the room Denise smiled, delighted at her friend's enthusiasm. It had been a long time since she'd seen Katherine this excited.

"Yes, it is. And this house will be beautiful when it's fixed up."

Katherine turned and faced Denise. "The only question

now is whether you want to live here, too? You can have your choice of any of the four bedrooms upstairs. I don't care which room I have and Chris isn't choosy either, he likes them all. The only room I want is the upstairs turret room. It's going to make a great office." Katherine stopped speaking, eager to hear her friend's reply. Her ability to afford this house rested upon whether Denise wanted to share the expenses with her. "Well, what do you think?" she asked hopefully, holding her breath in anticipation.

Denise gave her friend a small smile. "I would love living here. This beats an apartment any day. But are you sure we can stand each other, living together twenty-four hours a day?" she teased.

Katherine let out a relieved sigh, walking over and placing her arm around her friend's shoulders. They made a striking pair together, Katherine tall and lean, her rich brown hair falling straight to her shoulders, her classic features warmed by sparkling brown eyes; and Denise, slightly shorter and shapelier, her auburn hair long and thick, her blue eyes bright within her olive complexion. So different, yet both beautiful in their own way that men always took notice when they were together. "We've been putting up with each other since the sixth grade. I don't think living in the same house together will change anything." They both laughed and Katherine pivoted on her heel once more, excited that Denise had agreed to move in.

"I can't wait to get started," she said, breathlessly. "I want to paint Chris' room before school starts, and refinish the floors, and paint the kitchen cupboards, and..."

"There is one thing, Kathy," Denise interrupted, hesitantly. "I was wondering, what are you thinking of doing with the apartment over the garage?"

Katherine shrugged her shoulders. "I don't know. I haven't really thought about that yet. Why? Did you want that room for yourself?"

Denise shook her head. "No, no. I'll be happy with one of the bedrooms upstairs." She hesitated again, biting her lip. "Actually, I was thinking of Darla."

"Your sister?" Katherine scrunched her nose in distaste.

Denise nodded. "She has to change apartments again. She can't afford the one she's in now, and, well, when she heard you might be buying this big house she asked if I'd talk you into letting her rent from you."

The spark in Katherine's brown eyes dulled at the mention of Darla. "There's no way your sister and I can live under the same roof. She hates me, and I'm not that thrilled with her, either."

"She doesn't really hate you, she's mean to everyone. Even me," Denise said matter-of-factly.

"It's more than that. She's crazy! And raunchy, and rude, and mouthy, and trashy. For Pete's sake, Denise, she has orange hair and wears silver platform shoes!" Katherine shook her head. "No. There's no way I could live with her. One of us would end up dead!" She waived her hand in the air as if fanning away an undesirable smell and turned toward the window again.

Denise knew from the onset this wouldn't be easy. Taking a deep breath, she pressed on. "That's why I thought the apartment over the garage would work. It has its own bathroom and entrance from the outside, so it won't seem like she's actually living with us. We'd have to share the kitchen, but since she doesn't cook we won't see her in there much either." Seeing Katherine square off her shoulders, unyielding, Denise dealt another reason from her deck of arguments. "And it would mean more rent money to help pay for the house," she added softly.

Katherine pondered this as she slowly studied the house she so desperately wanted to own. She loved the sunken living room where they now stood that stretched out into the dining room before ending at the swinging oak door leading into the kitchen.

She stared at the louvered doors that closed off the pass-through from kitchen to dining room that she already planned to paint white and add round ceramic knobs to. The kitchen was small, but serviceable, with enough space to add a table and chairs where they could sit for breakfast every morning. She turned to view the foyer that held the beginning of the oak staircase leading up to the bedrooms above. She could picture an umbrella stand by the door, a parson's bench by the staircase, a blue woven rug on the entryway floor. And the view. She completed her circle and stepped closer to the window showcasing the view of the beach, and bay beyond. The house sat high above Puget Sound, the planked front porch overlooking the water and tread worn wooden steps that led down to the beach. A place to set white wicker chairs with striped cushions and perhaps hang a wooden swing. Yes, she wanted to own it all, despite its need of stain and paint and good old-fashioned elbow grease. And extra rent money could help make it all happen.

Sitting on the bare window seat she faced her friend, still not completely sold on the idea of including Darla in the plan. "But she brings home anything in pants. And sleeps with it!" She visibly shuddered at the thought of all the men Darla had had. It totally disgusted her.

Denise lowered her eyes to the floor, her burgundy wire-framed glasses catching the sunlight and glinting in Katherine's eyes for a split second. She played her trump card. "You're right. It was a crazy idea. Actually, I was only thinking of Chelsea when I suggested it."

The mention of Chelsea touched a raw nerve in Katherine. She was a sweet, twelve-year-old girl, the same age as her own son, who didn't deserve a mother like Darla. Chelsea had lived in as many apartments in the town of Seattle as the number of men her mother had had, and that number was intolerable. If anyone deserved a decent home, it was Chelsea.

Denise eyed Katherine and could see her resolve dwindle from the slump of her shoulders. Her own timid nature was no match against Kathy's strong will, but after twenty-four years of friendship she knew how to appeal to Kathy's heart. She ventured forward. "Chelsea's been a latch-key kid since Kindergarten. I thought, since you work at home most of the time, it might be a nice change for her to come home where someone is waiting for her. And she and Chris get along so well. They're practically like brother and sister. It would give her a real sense of family. I think she needs that."

Katherine stared down at her shoes on the bare, wooden floor and thought this over. Outside, a single gull bellowed as it made its way over the house to the beach below. The faint smell of salt air drifted in through the open front door. She inhaled deeply, wanting to experience the scents and sounds of beach life fully. The serenity of water lapping upon the shore was something she craved after a year of hectic and heartbreaking decisions. And she knew deep in her heart that this was the place where she could find the sense of peace she craved. Sharing it with family and friends might also be exactly what she needed.

With renewed vision, Katherine stood. "You're right. Chelsea deserves some sort of family life and we're the ones who can give her that." She gave Denise a faint smile as she crossed the distance between them. "We'll give it a try."

Denise reached up and hugged her long-time friend. "Thanks, Kathy. It will work out. I'm sure of it."

Katherine nodded, but her face tightened. She wagged a finger at Denise. "But if Darla does one thing to annoy me, she's out! Deal?"

"Deal. But we get to keep Chelsea, right?"

"Absolutely!" They hugged again. Denise was relieved at the outcome, and Katherine was already forming a plan in her mind to include Chelsea, and of course, Darla, into the household.

Chelsea and Chris would start Middle School in September together, perhaps making the transition in schools easier, she reasoned. Yes, it just might work.

Feeling lighthearted again, Katherine and Denise headed toward the front door where the real estate woman was waiting for an answer. "Let's go buy a house," Katherine said, and the two friends headed out the door with arms linked.

Two weeks later Katherine was up to her armpits in paint, stain, varnish, and wallpaper. She was able to begin work on the house immediately after signing the papers, so she took off a week from her job at the King County Journal and flung herself into fixing up her dream home.

The first thing she did was recruit Chris' and Chelsea's services in painting their bedrooms. Chelsea was not only thrilled with the prospect of living with her favorite aunts and Chris, but also being able to decorate a room of her own. "I've never lived in a house before," the excited teen told Katherine, her blue eyes sparkling. She had her aunt's thick auburn hair and deep blue eyes laced with dark, full lashes and brows. She was often mistaken as Denise's daughter. The only feature that resembled her mother was her high, prominent cheek bones. She was going to be a beauty, there was no doubt. But like her aunt, she chose not to flaunt it as her mother did.

The kids picked out the colors and fabrics for their rooms. Chelsea chose to paint hers in a rose and cream stripe with a thin, pink floral boarder edging the top of the walls and pink floral curtains for her window. Chris decided on a sea mist green for the walls and wanted to boarder the room with white shelving to place his seashell and rock collections on. His room would reflect him, a no-nonsense kind of kid, neat, orderly, with a place for everything. His appearance reflected this too, his sandy blond hair neat but not fussy, his clothing clean but not overly stylish.

At age twelve he was tall and already in the lanky stage of his teen years. But he wasn't at all clumsy; he was very athletic and participated in several sports.

Katherine helped both kids get started with paint rollers and brushes, then began her own work downstairs. She hired a man to sand down the living room, dining room, and entryway floors, then refinished them herself before painting the walls off-white. She hung lace curtains in the bay window and added a thick blue and white striped cushion to the seat, next turning her attention to wallpapering the tiny bathroom upstairs. Her goal was to make the place livable before moving in and then worry about any major fix-ups afterward.

Denise came in the evenings to lend a hand. Unlike Katherine, she couldn't take time off from her job at the Community Hospital near downtown Seattle where she worked as the records clerk in the Pediatric/Maternity Ward. Policy required six weeks notice for vacation time, so she had to be content with helping out on nights and weekends.

Katherine insisted Denise take the master bedroom with the small bay window that overlooked Puget Sound. She had a great view from the turret room that she was going to use as an office so the bedroom on the side of the house was fine for her needs. After much protest, Denise gave in and set out to decorate her room to her own style much as the kids had done. Everyone's tastes blended to combine rooms that complemented without clashing. The cream wallpaper with soft pink sprig roses that Katherine placed in the upstairs hallway was the perfect link between the rooms, the oak molding being the common thread that joined them all together. Looking at the rooms, one would think from their common tastes that they had all come from the same family. That was until Darla finally made her appearance.

It was the second weekend since they had begun work on the house. The day was warm and dry, so Katherine recruited the kids to paint the front porch dove gray while Denise supervised and painted the front door white. Katherine was in the kitchen scrubbing the tile countertops when Darla entered through the back door in all her tight pant, silver shoe glory.

"Oh my God, a Victorian house!" she stated aloud, a cigarette dangling from the corner of her glossy red mouth. "I should have known you'd own a tight-ass house." She leveled her gaze on Katherine waiting for a reaction.

Katherine squared her shoulders and turned to face that gaze. "If you don't like it, you don't have to stay."

"What?" Darla gave mock surprise, raising a splayed hand to her abundant breasts. "And miss out on this experiment of sisterly love and friendship? Why, I wouldn't dream of leaving." She took off her sunglasses and placed them on top of her too-stiff, orange hair. "Now, where am I supposed to park my ass?"

All the way to hell, Katherine wanted to say, but instead she pointed up the stairway on the opposite side of the kitchen. "Your room is up there. You can also get to it from the outside; the stairway is on the other side of the garage."

"Much obliged, Miss Kate," Darla said mockingly, making Katherine bristle. She hated being called Kate or Katie, and Darla knew it.

Darla turned and stepped out the door, hollering, "Okay, boys. It's the stairs by the garage. You be careful with my stuff, ya hear?"

"Okay, boys?" Katherine mouthed, and looked out the kitchen window in time to see Darla sashay on three-inch heels over to two men standing on the back of a U-Haul Truck. "Oh, great, she brought her Johns along." She watched long enough to see them unload a leopard chaise lounge before turning her back to the window and raising her eyes to heaven. "What did I get myself into?"

Made in the USA
Columbia, SC
06 August 2021